PRAISE FOR SARAH PINBOROUGH!

THE RECKONING

"...[A] gripping tale of supernatural suspense... fans of Bentley Little, Richard Laymon and Dean Koontz will be pleased."

—*Publishers Weekly*

"[A] great story complete with solid characters and an interesting premise."

—The Horror Channel

THE HIDDEN

"Quite unique… Ms. Pinborough does an amazing job. …A great read."

—The Horror Channel

"Original and gripping."

—Horror Web

ITS PREY

The rasping moan pulled my attention back to the man, his bloodshot eyes meeting mine and reflecting my own terror. His jaw worked silently before he finally got the words out, his body pushed forward on the edge of the sofa in an almost impossible position.

"Help me…"

I was about to move forward, God help me I was, when from behind him, from where slick sucking sounds drifted toward me, one milky translucent leg, thin and sharply jointed, came over his side, wrapping around him like a lover, and I froze. I stared at the shiny footless limb in disgust as another crept over the man, and then another until four held his limp body in place, one at his shoulders, then his waist, his knees and his feet. *What was it? And what was it doing to him?*

Looking over his shoulder, I could make out the smooth curved edges of the creature's body pulsing behind him, like some awful pale insect.

"Help me…pleeasse."

The desperate, dying man croaked out the words, a dribble of blood escaping from his thin, anguished lips, and I couldn't imagine his agony. I couldn't see past my own fear, as the legs contracted tighter around him, pulling the prey closer, and the awful round body rose up slightly as if to investigate the distraction, its milky white surface shining like mother of pearl, as for a moment the sucking stopped.

"Pleaasee…"

BREEDING GROUND

SARAH PINBOROUGH

LEISURE BOOKS NEW YORK CITY

For Charlotte, Adrienne, Mike and Steve.
With much love and thanks for evenings in, good food,
good wine, good company, and for always being there.

A LEISURE BOOK®

September 2006

Published by

Dorchester Publishing Co., Inc.
200 Madison Avenue
New York, NY 10016

ISBN 0-8439-5741-7

Visit us on the web at www.dorchesterpub.com.

Stony Stratford is a beautiful historic village in the county of Buckinghamshire, and also my hometown. The two pubs that still stand and trade in the middle of the high street, The Cock and The Bull, started their lives as coaching inns in the 17th century. It is from here that the phrase "cock and bull story" originated, from the tall tales told by passing travellers.

What better place to set a horror story?

PART I

PROLOGUE

I wish I could tell you that I saw lights in the sky. Or shooting stars that turned out to be alien spaceships falling to earth. That's how Armageddon stories normally start, isn't it? Some great portent signalling the oncoming doom, some clue that *They* have done this to us, whether the guilty party are the Russian *They*, the American *They*, the British *They*, or the all-time favourite, the *They* from outer space.

I don't *know* why it started. I don't know if it was the work of the government, a visit from space or an act of God. If I had to put money on it, I'd pick the first option; after all, they never stop adding chemicals to food and there was always going to be payback. But at the end of the day, I don't know why it started, and even if I did it wouldn't make a damned bit of difference now, would it?

My name is Matthew Edge, and at some point last year, the end of the world as we know it started. And I figure my version of events is going to be as clear a record as anyone's, so here goes. I hope that you'll read this through to the end. I hope there's a you out there to read it, and hell, I hope that I'm still alive when you finish, and I hope I get to shake your hand adult to adult, once you're born and grown into a person of this new world. Hope is all we have, after all, isn't it? Some things will never change.

CHAPTER ONE

"I can't believe it! I've put on three pounds!"

When Chloe called out from the bathroom I was still in bed, lazily enjoying the extra half an hour I had left before work pulled me into the outside world. I grinned at her indignant exclamation. She was hardly what anyone would call fat. Huffing, she padded back into our bedroom, dressed in only her knickers. She looked perfect to me, all slim curves and soft skin. Pulling the pillow next to me under my chin, I raised an eyebrow.

"Oh no, not a whole three pounds."

She flashed her dark eyes. "You're not funny, you know, Matt." A familiar twitch in her chin betrayed her humour. "That's five pounds I've put on in two weeks. God, at this rate not even my underwear will fit me in a month."

"Now that's a thought." And it really was an image that sent tingles down my spine. We'd been together for five years, outlasting all our friends' twenty-something relationships, and at the ripe old age of twenty-nine the sight of her naked body was still a glorious thing to me. To most men, I'd reckon. She was way too good for me, but until she noticed I had no intention of telling her. I ran my eyes over her. "Hmmm. I can just imagine you in a nice executive business suit with nothing on underneath. Except perhaps hold-ups."

A flying bra hit me in the face. "Don't you ever think of anything else?"

"I try not to. I am a man, after all."

She tucked her blouse into her skirt and smiled. "You certainly are. You're *my* man."

"Come here and give me a kiss, then."

She perched on the bed and I pulled her forward, ignoring her shriek and then giggle of protest as I rolled her underneath me. Her skin was glowing and as yet free of makeup. She looked gorgeous, smiling up at me with all that love, her hair spread out beneath us on the rumpled bedding, and my heart tightened.

"I love you, Chloe Taylor."

She touched my face. "I love you too, Matt."

I kissed her and she kissed me back, our tongues meeting, mine no doubt tasting of sleep and hers of toothpaste, but still within a second or two I could feel myself hardening. Still exploring each other's mouths as if they were new territory, I tugged at her blouse, needing to feel her naked skin.

"What are you doing? I've got to get to work. I'll be late." Panting the words, she made an attempt to wriggle free, but it was only halfhearted.

Her shirt undone, I kissed her slim stomach, mumbling my reply. "Yeah, but I won't. And anyway, I'm thinking of you. What better way to work off those extra pounds?"

"Bastard."

We smiled through our kisses and then made love. To my hands and touch there was no sign of any extra weight, not that I'd have cared. Not then. It was beautiful. I got to work five minutes late and she must have been half an hour behind time, but I'll tell you one thing: we were both smiling on arrival.

Often at night, that flash of memory still runs through my head, painful and sharp. I don't mind, though. I think it's important to try and remember Chloe like that. Like she *really* was. Before everything that came after. Yeah, for others it may have started earlier, but for me that day signalled the beginning of the end. I digress.

Back then, all fourteen months ago, when work and money were what counted in the world, I was a mortgage advisor for a small estate agency on Stony Stratford High Street. It was family-owned, which was its saving grace, and although I'd started out selling houses, Mr. Brown had soon seen that I'd want to move on and he pushed me to learn about mortgages and take over that side of the business. Seems funny to think about now, all that time sitting behind a desk calculating figures to see what people could afford, not ever suspecting that none of those loans would be getting paid back in full, and in the future that was fast approaching, there wouldn't be any banks left that would care.

The job paid quite well, I didn't have to travel far and I was content. I'd worked there since I was twenty-two, and although I occasionally felt bored and restless, I wasn't ambitious enough to move on. It was Chloe who had the big plans and dreams and the drive to fulfill them. She was already making a bit of a name for herself on the local legal circuit as a barrister to look out for, and her salary was more than double mine.

All that and six months younger than me, but I can honestly say I didn't care. I was proud of her. I wanted her to be happy, and as far as I could tell her work and me did that for her, and that alone made me the luckiest man alive.

We lived in a renovated cottage at the top end of High Street, close enough to walk to all the restaurants and pubs the old coaching town had to offer without either of us having to drive. We would sip wine and beer and laugh together about the days behind and ahead. As lives go, it wasn't a bad one. We had village life on the edge of a thriving new city, and London was only forty minutes away on a train, just in case we felt like trying to regain our early twenties. We were settled, and that may sound dull to some people, but then I suppose they never had the good luck to settle down with Chloe.

When I got in that evening at six, she was already home, sitting on our oversized, overindulgent sofa, her legs tucked under her, thick Mediterranean hair pulled back in a ponytail. She looked about sixteen, and that made the thoughts running through my head barely legal.

Undoing my tie and top button, I sat down at the other end. "Hey, gorgeous. You're home early."

Her eyes flicked momentarily at me and then back to the exposed brick wall above the fireplace. "I didn't feel well. I came home early. I wasn't in court this afternoon, so it didn't really matter."

She did look tired and pale, and I stroked her hair.

"You work too hard, babe. Why don't I get you a glass of wine and run you a hot bath?"

"That won't change it." She let out a weary sigh. "I went to the doctor on my way home."

Shuffling in closer, I felt the tension coming from her slim frame, and my heart tightened. Sometimes late at night, when she was sleeping curled up in the crook of my shoulder, I would quietly wonder when it was going to go wrong. It was too good, you see. She was too good for me, and what we had was too special. Maybe everyone in love feels like that, but when it's a first love that lasts, you can't help but wonder what may come along to destroy it. She'd been to the doctor. Doctors meant sickness. How ill was she? My mouth dried as a wave of suggested diseases flooded my brain.

"What's the matter?"

She looked at me and sniffed, her brown eyes impenetrable. Her bottom lip quivered as she spoke.

"I'm pregnant."

I'm pregnant. The world spun on its head for a moment, then froze as I tried to take it in. The words punching the air from my lungs, the best I could manage was a half-breathless laugh, my flesh tingling at every pore as I stared, no doubt with my mouth half-open and looking like a dribbling idiot, at her beautiful face.

"What?" At last I squeezed out a word. Not a particularly clever or appropriate one, but it was the best I could do, sitting there on the leather sofa, a month or so away from thirty and feeling like a big kid with my heart pounding too hard against my chest.

"I'm pregnant." Tears welled up, threatening to spill onto her cheeks. "And scared."

I could feel tears pricking at the back of my eyes,

too, and as soon as I could get my body to do as I wanted I pulled her closer to me. "What are you scared for? You're pregnant." I paused for a moment, needing to say the words to make it real. "You're pregnant." Real was good.

The grin on my face stretched until it almost hurt. "You're going to have a baby." I paused again. "*We're* going to have a baby." I laughed out loud. "We're going to have a baby, Chloe." The giggles wouldn't stop and I sat there chortling to myself. "That's fantastic!"

Staring at me, she pulled back slightly. "Are you sure about this? Are you sure you're happy about it? I thought you might...well, I thought you might want me not to have it."

For a moment, the fear crept back into my heart. I'd never really thought about children, not in any imminent way, but now that circumstances had overtaken planning I knew that I wanted this baby to come. It would cement everything that we had. But maybe she didn't feel that way. After all, it was a bigger step for her. It was she who had the big career ahead of her. Maybe she felt that her job was more important than a baby right now. The laughing stopped.

"Why? Don't *you* want to keep it?"

She smiled hesitantly, flashing her perfect white teeth. "Yes, yes, of course I do, I was just worried you might think it was too soon, that we should be married or—"

My mouth silenced hers and we kissed until the gentleness turned to passion right there on the leather, our child only a few weeks old inside her, our perfect day ending as it had begun.

CHAPTER TWO

The first month after that pretty much flew by in a whirl of baby name books and paint charts for the soon not-to-be-spare room. We laughed a lot that month, mainly over her strange food choices and what she considered my strange baby name choices. And there *were* a few strange choices according to her, although I still wonder how anyone could consider George an odd name. Even the fact that it had been my grandfather's name wouldn't sway her, but just made her laugh even harder, curled up on the sofa, her hand darting from the jar of pickled onions to the box of chocolates beside her, some old movie playing in the background.

She was nearly three months and the pregnancy was fine and so was Chloe. Apart from the weight gain. Which was odd, because she was still working hard, often not home in time for dinner, claiming to have eaten at work, and once the cravings had worn off, it seemed that we never ate anything together. And I know that pregnant women put on weight. I may be a man, but I understand the basics; however, this weight wasn't going in the right places.

One morning I found her standing in the bathroom, staring at her reflection in the mirror. Her greasy hair hung lankly over her shoulders, exaggerating the puffy face with dark bags around the eyes. In that grey light of dawn I could see the fat she'd accumulated on her thickened hips and thighs, looking lumpy and swollen under her pale skin. Her arms were dimpled and flabby, too, and I fought a wave of revulsion. There was something disgusting about the almost translucent texture of her skin. What the hell was going on with her? Surely this couldn't be right? Yes, she had a small firm bump at the front, but it was almost unnoticeable within the rest of the flesh she'd gained. And some of the lumpy fat seemed to be covering that, too. Her dressing gown was on the floor beside her and I picked it up, gently putting it over her shoulders. I looked into her sad eyes in the mirror in front of us. God, I loved her.

"Are you okay?"

Keeping hold of the dressing gown, she turned away from me. "I'm tired. I think I'll stay at home today."

"Good idea." And I did think it was. She needed to rest, to eat some healthy food and get her energy back. This pregnancy was obviously more difficult than she was letting on, and at last there was something I thought I could do. I followed her into the bedroom.

"Why don't I stay with you? I could be your servant for the day. I'll spoil you."

She kept her dressing gown on and pulled the covers almost over her head. Her voice was muffled. "You'll be needed at work."

"I'm sure they won't mind. Things are a bit quiet at

the moment, anyway." That was an understatement. It seemed that there had been a citywide slump in the housing market. For whatever reason people had just stopped selling and buying over the past couple of months. Although I was planning to work from home once the baby was born, it was beginning to worry me that there wouldn't be enough business out there to make it worthwhile. We'd agreed I'd be the house husband, but I had wanted something to do that would at least bring in some money. Male pride and all. Still, I consoled myself with the thought that these things never lasted. As soon as the good weather came it would be business as usual.

"I'll go and call them, shall I?"

She yanked the covers down, her eyes raging at me. "Go to work, Matt, and stop fussing. I just want to be left alone!"

Jolting backward a bit, not used to her being like that, I tried to touch her. "Look, babe…"

"Fuck off, Matt." Spitting the words at me, she buried herself back down into the bedding.

I sat there for a few moments waiting for her to start crying or come out and say she was sorry, but there was nothing but cold silence. Eventually, my heart aching and confused, I got up and did the only thing I could. I went to work.

The day passed slowly, with no business to speak of, just the odd follow-up call to clients. I spent most of the time staring at the small clock on my desk or watching the rain hitting the big glass front window. I didn't feel like talking and neither did old Mr. Brown it would seem, so we pretty much sat quietly, pretending to be doing something on our computers, drinking coffee and waiting for the day to end. I thought about calling her at lunchtime but left it. Maybe she'd be asleep. That's what I told myself, but really I just didn't want to hear her being angry again. I wasn't sure I could take it. Whatever was wrong with her, it was taking its toll on me, too.

At ten to five, I started shutting the system down and got my coat from the small kitchen at the back of the office. Mr. Brown was leaning against the draining board, holding a cup of coffee. It had a dark film on the surface, as if it had cooled untouched. How long had he been standing there? I'd been too lost in my own world to notice what he'd been up to.

"I'm off home now, if that's all right."

He looked up at me a little shocked, as if he'd only just realised I was in the room. "Oh. Right. Yes, of course, off you go." He attempted a smile, but it only heightened the wrinkles on his face, new wrinkles, the kind you get when you're tired; really, really tired.

"I suppose you'll be cooking something delicious for that lovely girlfriend of yours when she gets in. Tell her to take it easy. She should be relaxing in her condition."

I wondered if my own smile looked as awful as his. "She's at home today. Not feeling herself."

He shook slightly, and put the cup down on the drainer. "Peggy's not too well, either."

I pulled my coat on. There was an awkwardness in the air and I wasn't sure exactly why.

"Well, I hope she feels better soon. Give her my love."

"Yes. And to Chloe. See you tomorrow."

Opening the back door, I stepped into the drizzle, the ghost of the downpour not long past. "You will."

14

I considered buying flowers on the way home, but figured that would be extreme blokeism in Chloe's eyes and so decided on nothing. If she was feeling up for it, I'd get her a takeaway, or just cook her some soup. I just hoped that nasty anger was gone. It had had a tinge of hate in it, I was sure, and unwell as she was, I didn't want her to hate me. Selfish that might have been, but then all lovers are selfish.

I found her in the bathroom, under the glaring white light, standing on the scales and sobbing, hugging herself. Her tears were coming thick and fast, and as I appeared in the doorway, she literally fell into my arms, burying her head into my shoulder, soaking it. Her crying was coming from deep down in her chest, really terrible tears, and I squeezed her tight. What now? What now?

"What is it? What's the matter, Chloe?" Her matted hair smelt sweaty as I pressed my face into her neck. I thought of the baby. Had something happened to the baby during the day? Why hadn't I come home for lunch? Oh god, what had I done?

Her voice was thick. "I've put on a stone. A stone in two weeks. That's nearly three stone in the past two months."

Tensing slightly, I was shocked. I knew she'd put on weight, but I hadn't guessed nearly that much. That was about the amount all the baby books said she should put on in total, and she was only a third of the way through. Jesus. But still, I rationalised as I took a deep breath, trying to calm my nerves, it didn't mean anything. Maybe her body was just settling down. Maybe from now on, some of the excess weight would drop off. More than anything I just wanted her to calm down. I caught sight of myself in the mirror. Short blond hair and wide, frightened blue eyes above a tight mouth. Who was I kidding? I was as confused and scared as she was. Or nearly. I rubbed her arms and back.

"Well, you *are* eating for two, babe. You're bound to put on weight." It was lame, but it was the only thing I could think of to say. I didn't expect her reaction, the mix of laughter and tears that poured out of her. She stepped back from me, shaking as the fits of emotion took her.

God, I felt useless. She seemed like a stranger in front of me, and I wanted it to stop.

"What? What is it?"

I knew that whatever it was that was making her laugh so hysterically, it wasn't going to be funny, and for a small fraction of a second, I wished she'd never got pregnant, I wished we could just go back to how it was before and I wished I didn't have to hear her dreadful desperate laughter through her tears. It wasn't normal. It wasn't natural. And I couldn't deal with it.

Slowly, she calmed down and wiped her eyes, her breathing irregular. A last giggle escaped before she met my gaze.

"That's priceless, Matt. Eating for two. Oh, that's funny." She paused and sighed, rubbing fresh tears away with the sleeve of her dressing gown, leaning back against the sink.

"I haven't eaten anything for over a week. Not a single thing." A tragic laugh hiccupped out of her. "And I haven't even been hungry."

My legs were like jelly beneath me. What had she said? I could almost feel the colour draining from my face, my hands instantly cold.

She looked at me almost pityingly and whispered,

"So how can I still be putting on weight? How can that be? How can that be?"

We stared at each other for what seemed like hours, and in that moment we were closer than we'd been in a while. Both just looking and wondering if this was *the thing*, the thing that was going to end us, finally arrived. I bit my cheek to stop myself from crying. I looked at her face, still beautiful despite the weight, despite the fear, and I pulled myself together. There were a million reasons for something like this. There must be.

I haven't eaten for over a week. Pushing her words away, I straightened myself up.

"Get dressed. We're going to the doctor." I could see her about to protest. "And no arguments." The strength in my voice surprised even myself, and within ten minutes we were leaving the house. Whatever this was, we'd deal with it. Nothing was taking her from me without a fight. Not her, nor our baby.

The rain was falling heavily, dripping from the eaves of the old houses and trees, and by the time we'd got into the surgery just off Market Square, only five minutes or so from the house, we were both soaked. They still operated on an "emergency surgery" policy, so as long as you turned up after four P.M. and were prepared to wait awhile, you were pretty much guaranteed to get seen by a doctor.

Heading up the stairs, I wondered how long we would have to sit around for. The last thing we needed was for Chloe to catch a chill on top of everything else.

Surprisingly, the dimly lit building seemed pretty desolate, and the elderly receptionist gave us a plastic number and brought Chloe's details up on the screen before telling us to take a seat. From behind her bifocals, she watched Chloe carefully, almost warily, to the point where it was becoming uncomfortable and I was glad when we got into the waiting room. Maybe she remembered Chloe from a previous visit and was shocked by the change in her, but whatever her reason, the staring was just plain rude as far as I was concerned.

Far on the other side of the large open space lined with low chairs, an old man, easily in his eighties, coughed and shuffled in his seat. Apart from him, we were the only patients waiting. The rain beat at the windows steady and uncompromising, and I figured that must have been what kept the rest away.

There was no background music to break the tension, and feeling suddenly awkward and out of place I sat us down on a long row against the far wall, next to the magazine table. Neither of us picked one up. The air barely moved and I resisted the urge to whisper.

"Must be our lucky day, Clo. We'll be in and getting you sorted out in no time." I smiled at her, almost believing myself now that I was in the surgery, surrounded by *anything-is-curable-if-you-catch-it-in-time* leaflets. She smiled back, but it was almost lost in her bulging cheeks, less convinced.

A buzzer went off, a light flashing on the board in front of us declaring Dr. Carney was ready for his next patient. The old man pulled himself slowly to his feet and hung his number next to the doctor's name before disappearing down the corridor. It was number three.

We were seeing Dr. Judge, and I thought our number two meant that he had started late, but obviously it was just a very quiet night for the surgery. Spookily quiet. I'd never come to an emergency surgery without having to wait at least forty-five minutes, not for as long back as I could remember. Even as a child, when the town was smaller, you still had a good long wait ahead of you if you came after four. I tried to shake off my feeling of disquiet. There was nothing too odd about it. Out of thirty years, they were bound to have the occasional quiet night. This was just the first one that I'd ever encountered.

Chloe was quiet beside me, and with just the pounding of my heart in my ears, I was glad when the buzzer broke the silence and called us to our appointment.

Once in the impersonal office, I sat in a chair against the wall as the doctor weighed her, took her blood pressure and temperature, making all the expected noises, before finally peering into her nose and throat. She sat back down next to me and he took his leather chair on the other side of the desk, scribbling some notes down before speaking. With his head bent forward to write, I could see the bald patch that was growing at the back of his head, its edges flecked with dandruff. Dr. Judge had been here just about forever, and I supposed it was starting to show. I don't know why I was surprised. I guess I just expected him to stay the same forever.

He put down the pen. "So, you say you haven't eaten anything for over a week, and you're still putting on a few pounds?"

Beside me, Chloe nodded, her bottom lip trembling slightly.

"It may be that your blood pressure is fluctuating a little. Nothing to worry about. Quite common in many women. It should settle down by the fifth month and then everything will go back to normal." He moved some papers around on his desk, and for a moment I was dumbfounded.

What had he just said? I couldn't believe it. How could he say that this was normal? I'd expected something, but not this. I was no doctor, but even I knew that what was happening to Chloe was far from normal. Sitting there beside me, she seemed larger than she had been when we'd left the house, and that was just plain crazy.

She leaned forward, her eyes wide. "Really?" She sounded as shocked as I was. Shocked and relieved. "It's just that I've been feeling really strange recently."

Dr. Judge smiled at her. It was an almost genuine smile. "You really shouldn't be worrying. Just go home and relax. If there's no change in a month or so, then come back to see me and I'll give you something to sort out your blood pressure. Okay?"

"Great. That's great. Thanks, Doctor, I was beginning to worry. It's just all this weight and feeling so odd inside…" God, she was even beginning to sound a bit different. She sounded…*older*. That was the only way I could describe it. Perhaps there was a more gravelly pitch to her voice. Something.

"Like I said, nothing to worry about."

He already had the door open and before I realised it, we were ushered outside, my head spinning. He hadn't even checked the baby. Surely he should have put a stethoscope against her stomach or something. It wasn't right. It just wasn't right.

I stopped where I was in the corridor. "Chloe, I think we should get a second opinion."

She had already reached the stairs, and flashed an angry look at me over her shoulder as I trotted to catch up.

"He said it was normal. Perfectly normal. Are you trying to find something wrong with me, Matt?" Her tone was biting. God, her moods were changing so fast these days. A moment ago she'd been fine. Worried and upset, but not this new aggression that was rearing its ugly head again. Chloe was never aggressive. It was her cool head that made her such a good barrister.

"No, I just think we should be certain that he's right, that's all."

She snorted, tugging the outside door open and stepping outside. "You think I'm disgusting, don't you? You're repulsed by me. I see your face when you look at me."

I grabbed her arm and spun her round, my face flushed with searing emotion. "I don't know what's going on in your head, but I love you, Chloe. I could never love anyone but you, and I could never be repulsed by you. I just think we need to double-check his opinion with someone else. I'm worried about you. I want to make sure you're okay."

It was true. Standing there in the rain, I ached with worry. I wanted her back. The *her* on the inside. I didn't care about the weight, and yes, maybe she was right, sometimes its strangeness did revolt me, but never her, I was never repulsed by *her*. I couldn't be. Raising my arms in a gesture of peace, I made one more vain attempt to get through to her.

"Didn't you find it odd that he didn't check on the baby?"

Taking three steps backwards, she sneered at me. "That's all you care about, isn't it? The fucking baby."

Again, her non-Chloe words stung. "That's not true! What's got into you? Why are you being like

21

this?" I wanted to shake her until I got some sense out of her.

Her face was truly ugly as she reached into her purse and chucked a twenty pound note at me. Whoever it was that was talking, it wasn't my Chloe. It was whatever disease was growing inside her. The money landed at my feet, soaked in a puddle instantly. I stared at it, not wanting to look at her. God, I was tired.

"Go to the pub. I want some time to myself." She turned and started walking away and I couldn't help but yell after her barely recognisable outline, "That's all you ever seem to want these days!"

I waited until she had passed through the small archway at the end of the cobbled road, turning left and vanishing, before letting my shoulders slump forward. Jesus, what a day. How long had it been coming? How long had we been on the slow downward slide leading to here? I guess you just don't notice so much when the decay is gradual.

Is that how it is for all those old couples out there, still together but not knowing why, lying awake at night and wondering just how different it could all have been if they'd just been brave enough to leave? Or was I just judging the world by my own parents' standards? When your mother tells your father, as he's dying, that she'd spent the best part of the last forty years trying to build up the courage to murder him in his bed, it tends to leave a stain on your soul. But Chloe and I weren't like them and we never would be. We never argued. Not ever. This wasn't Chloe doing this.

The water invading my clothes through every gap, and feeling less than proud, I leaned forward and retrieved the soaking money, shaking it in a vain attempt to make it slightly less wet. If she wanted some time to herself, then so be it, and I couldn't think of a better place to spend that time than in the pub.

Tugging my jacket around me, I headed for The Crown, a hundred yards from the doctor's. It used to be a proper pub, all cosy snugs and alcoves, used in movies and that kind of thing, but recently it had been sold and was now a classy bar with a small restaurant. To be honest, I normally preferred somewhere more traditional, but Chloe liked it, and we probably spent a couple of hours a week sitting in their comfortable Chesterfields.

Aside from its proximity, I chose it because it wasn't a place I was likely to meet anyone I knew that well, as most I knew preferred the warmth and spit and saw-dust arrangements of The Vaults Bar on High Street. Not that I'd been out with the boys too much recently. Adulthood meant we'd all become too busy. In fact, I hadn't really seen any of them since the pregnancy had got underway. Not since all this fat business had really started. Nearly a month. God, didn't time fly when your world was falling apart.

I was glad to see that they had the small open fire lit, adding not only heat, but also life and warmth to the clinical whiteness of the décor. Once I had my pint in hand, I pulled up a chair close to it to dry myself out. The place was nearly empty, which suited me fine. I was in no mood for polite conversation. Instead, I sipped my drink and stared into the flames, lost in my own world of circling thoughts, veering from calm to gloom, but coming up with no answers for a problem that had yet to present me with a definite question.

I was just emptying my glass when out of the corner of my eye I saw a familiar figure sitting quietly on a bar stool, sipping a large glass of whiskey. My arm froze for a second, and then I slowly lowered it back to the table. It was Dr. Judge. Well, well, well. He didn't look so cheerful now, and he was drinking too fast for a man just relaxing after a hard day's work. Maybe it was time to get another pint.

He didn't notice me until I placed my empty glass on the smooth black marble bar beside his and placed my order.

"Evening, Dr. Judge."

Looking up at me from beneath his hunched shoulders, his eyes were momentarily glazed, then frightened.

"You."

"Yes, me." His reaction to me fuelled my need to speak. "I'd like to talk to you about what you said to my girlfriend, if that's okay with you."

He sighed. "The surgery's closed. If you're not happy with my diagnoses, then feel free to consult with one of my colleagues in the morning. I'm tired and I'm really not in the mood to get into a discussion."

The barman took my money and gave me my pint before moving away. I had a sip before ignoring the doctor's advice. I didn't really give a shit what he wanted. I needed to talk to him. I lowered my voice, but couldn't keep the desperate edge out of it.

"She hasn't eaten for a week and is still putting on weight. How can that be normal? How could you say that's normal? I've never heard anything like it, and trust me, I've been reading all the books."

Draining his large spirit in one gulp, he laughed and signalled for another, shaking his head into his empty glass. "Of course it's not normal. How is any of this normal?"

Confusion threw me into silence for a second, and then that same confusion made me angry. Angry and loud.

"Then for God's sake why did you say it? Surely you should be running some tests or something, whatever it is you do to find out what's wrong—"

His weathered old hand moved fast, grabbing the collar of my jacket and pulling me down so that my head was level with his. Spit hit my face as he hissed at me. "There are no tests. Not for this." His eyes were on fire. "Do you live with your head up your arse, son? Look around you. What are you seeing? Look at *the women.*"

My heart chilled in my chest. I stepped slightly backwards, letting his hand drop away, and I glanced around the room. There were no women in the bar, just a few men. Some drinking quietly, mainly by themselves, others paired in awkward silence. I didn't get it. I *couldn't* get it. What did he mean?

He was watching me with impatience, but the anger had gone out of his voice. "You think it's only you this is happening to? Poor Matthew Edge and Chloe Taylor?" He nodded his head in the direction of the busier side of the curved bar.

"Look at them. This is happening to all of them. *All of us.* And I can't do anything. I don't understand it. No one does. And when I say no one, I mean no one in the *whole world,* Matt. We're all just going to have to wait and see. That's all we can do. Wait and see."

He pushed back his bar stool, a little unsteady on his feet, and leaving his untouched drink on the bar, left me there. The world seemed too bright as I fought to get my breath, my eyes again running over the people around me. They all looked tired. Tired and frightened, just like me. Could this really be happening to all of them? Were there women like Chloe all over town? *All over the world?*

The landlord was cleaning glasses. He wasn't much older than me, maybe midthirties, but despite his wine bar surroundings, the lifestyle was taking its toll, and he was developing the red-nosed, large-bellied look, so typical in his profession. What was his name? Bill? Bob? Something like that. I caught his eye, and tried to keep my tone light.

"So, where's the missus tonight?" Normally, there was a blond, trim woman darting around beside him, making sure everything was running smoothly.

His eyes met mine for a moment before sliding away. "Upstairs. She's not been feeling herself lately." He moved to the far shelves and began taking bottles down to polish them. Well, whatever was wrong with his wife, he certainly wasn't in the mood to talk about it.

Taking a few long gulps of my beer, needing it to help calm me down, I took another look around at all the men who were concentrating on not meeting each others' eyes in the close confines. They were nearly all over fifty. Where were the young drinkers? At home looking after their women as best they could? Shit, the doctor had given me the heebie-jeebies. Despite the emptiness of the bar, it suddenly felt claustrophobic, and leaving my half-full glass behind, I stepped back outside.

The rain had stopped, the clouds clearing to let through some evening sunshine, but after what the doctor had said, it seemed that even that wasn't going to lighten my mood. The world suddenly seemed different, as if I was seeing it for the first time in ages. Maybe I needed to take the plunge and do what he said. Look around me properly. *Look at the women.* It wasn't as if there were any answers to be found anywhere else.

CHAPTER THREE

I started right there and then, on the way home. It was amazing how much detail we ignore in our day-to-day lives, how much we lazily omit seeing because we don't think it's important. I wondered how much longer it would have taken me to see the bigger picture of what was going on without the doctor's prompt. I wonder how long old Judge had known. I guess I'll never find out. I never saw him again after that.

Beneath the clearing skies, I wandered slowly out from Market Square to the main road. Normally, I'd just turn left and walk the couple of hundred yards to the cottage, but I wasn't ready to go back yet and I wanted to take a good look at my hometown.

The first thing I noticed was that there were no women about. I didn't see a single one. Stony Stratford High Street had a lot of restaurants, serving up food from all ethnic varieties, something for every taste, from Italian through Thai to Indian and back again, but each one I passed was either empty or closed. I paused for a moment, needing to try and take it all in, staring through the large glass window of The Passage to India into the unmanned darkness. My breath left a misty stain on the clean surface. Stepping back, I read the sign on the door. It said simply. CLOSED DUE TO ILLNESS.

The only nights that restaurants closed around here were Mondays, and this was a Friday, normally a busy evening with all-you-can-eat buffets dragging people in from all over Milton Keynes. How many staff needed to be ill or have sick relatives to close a restaurant? I gazed back down the deserted street and corrected myself—to close several restaurants.

My head rushed with blood and adrenaline, making me dizzy for a moment, and it took several deep breaths to get my feet feeling solid ground beneath them. This was crazy. Truly crazy. My face and the tips of my fingers were cold, my blood drawing back inside.

I think, looking back, that was the worst moment for my sanity. There were worse things to come, far worse, but at least by then I knew it was nature that had gone crazy, not me. Standing there at the bottom of the high street, I felt almost as if someone had slipped a small dose of LSD into my drink, unsure of what was real or not. I'd taken the drug once and that was enough. I liked to keep a grip on reality, to believe in what I could touch and feel, not just wild imaginings. I pushed my legs to walk and I tried to calm my thinking down as I turned up Vicarage Walk, strolling past the rows of houses, some showing the flickering lights of televisions reflecting large shapes on sofas, some with their curtains drawn despite the evening light. I shoved my hands deep into my pockets to warm them.

Maybe it was insane, but something *was* happening here. Silently, I listed the evidence. Chloe not eating and putting on three stone. Her personality changing. I rushed past that part in my head, not wanting to blur my thoughts with the fear I felt for her and for me. I remembered the disturbed and distracted demeanour of Mr. Brown earlier that afternoon. He'd said Peggy wasn't feeling too well, either. Neither was Bill/Bob's wife in The Crown. And the streets were pretty deserted. Definitely abandoned by the fairer sex, at least. And more than all that, there was the conversation with Dr. Judge. If I was going insane, then at least I had him for company. What had he said? *We'll have to wait and see.* It wasn't a comforting prospect. Not for me and Chloe and our unborn child. Maybe his lying to Chloe had been a kindness after all. I stared at the pavement, not needing to see into any more lives, and trudged forward into the falling darkness.

Finally, I found myself outside our little cottage and quietly let myself in. I didn't like the small wave of relief that I felt when silence greeted me and I realised that Chloe was already in bed. Getting a can of beer from the fridge, I cracked it open and went into the dark sitting room, leaving the lights off and flicking on the remote control.

Sophie Rayworth was delivering the news, and the can stopped inches from my mouth as her image glowed in the gloom. She was at least a stone heavier than she had been the last time I'd paid her any attention. Easily. Maybe more. I wasn't normally that great a judge of women's weight, but recently I'd become more of an expert. And was it my imagination or did she seem distracted, a little vague? She stumbled over two lines in the few moments that I watched. Not exactly her normal slick professional self. I wondered if she'd be giving us the ten o'clock news the next day, or would that show be "closed due to sickness?"

Turning the TV off, I leaned back into the armchair and shut my eyes, my temples throbbing with an oncoming tension headache. No great surprise there. I'm not sure how long I sat there like that in the silent dark, but eventually my thoughts and the headache became too oppressive and I sleepily climbed the stairs to our bedroom.

Without brushing my teeth, I peeled off my clothes as quietly as I could and climbed into bed. Chloe was sleeping curled up on her side, facing the other way as I lay on my back, gazing up at the ceiling hidden in the dark.

"Hold me, Matt." Her soft voice cut through my thoughts and into my heart. That was *my* Chloe speaking.

Rolling next to her, I wrapped my arm around her body, ignoring its unfamiliar feel. She pulled my hand up so it was under her face.

"I'm scared."

I pulled her close and said all I could that was true without admitting my own fear.

"I love you, Chloe."

The next morning was Saturday. When I finally opened my bleary eyes, still heavy from a fitful night's sleep, I realised the bed beside me was empty. Ignoring the vague thudding that was left of my headache from the night before, I called out her name, then listened for any sound of movement below. There was nothing. She'd gone out. Whether that was a good thing or bad, I didn't know, and rather than just lie there with only my morbid thoughts for company, I decided on a hot shower to blast away the cobwebs.

Outside, the sun was shining brightly and I opened the bathroom window a little, the spring breeze refreshingly cutting through the steam erupting from the hot jet of water, and despite everything, I felt my spirits rise. My headache lingered and my mouth felt as if it were covered in fur, but there was a hint of summer in the air, and that always made me feel good.

By the time I was dressed and coming downstairs, I was whistling and sure that whatever was going on, *they* would be sorting it out, and before we all knew it everything would be back to normal. The rustling of plastic bags escaped from the kitchen and I followed the sound.

My whistling stopped in the doorway, the dampness of my hair suddenly cold against my head, my scalp bristling with goose bumps.

"Morning, Chloe." I tried to keep my voice normal, but I heard the shake in it, and I'm sure if she cared, then she would have, too. Jesus Christ, what had happened to her? After those first two words, I just stood and stared, watching as she shuffled about the kitchen. I don't know if she even noticed my shock. She was bigger. Much bigger than she had been yesterday, and I had to resist the urge to laugh in shock. I was scared of where that laugh would lead. Madness? I didn't feel that far from it. Where was my Chloe in all of that excess fat and flesh? It was like looking at a nightmare distortion of the girl I loved.

She was wearing some floral tent of a skirt that she must have just bought, pulling my jogging bottoms out of a plastic bag and tossing them carelessly on the floor by the washing machine. Had they been that tight on her that she'd had to buy new clothes? Her upper body, bloated and shapeless, was covered with a large white T-shirt. God, she looked like some tragic reject from a reality TV show, the weight ageing her before her time.

Shaking myself, I took one of the shopping bags from her.

"Here, let me help."

The bag was half-full and heavy.

"Fridge." Her voice had more of that gravelly tone I'd noticed the previous evening, and I nodded awkwardly, pulling open the door. She was tipping a bag onto its side, and it looked like small wrapped parcels of meat. What the hell had she been buying?

Reaching into my carrier, I started to empty it into the fridge. More meat. I looked at the labels. Liver. Kidney. Heart. More liver. Tongue. More heart. We never ate this. Not even liver. My fingertips tingled with disgust.

"Jesus, Chloe. What have you bought all this shit for?" Unaware of her presence next to me, I stared at the shelves that I'd filled. She must have gone to more than one butcher to get all this.

"Couldn't you have just got steak and sausages like normal?"

Her growl made my skin crawl, and startled, I spun round to find myself staring at her face, pale in the reflected light of the fridge. The low animalistic snarl turned into a hiss, her mouth open, the sound coming from deep in her chest. I heard a low moan, for a moment not realising it was coming from me, frozen to the spot as I stared. My fear seemed to satisfy her, and the horrible sound ended, a twisted smile filling her face. As my headache roared back to life, sharp and nauseous, I wanted to cry. One of her front teeth was missing. *Oh, Chloe.* She touched my arm and I shivered inside, my stomach churning.

"I just need some protein, Matty." As she spoke, I caught glimpses of the black and rotting insides of her mouth, and I wanted to recoil from her, pull away, but I couldn't.

"For the baby. I was lucky. It was nearly all gone." Her eyes were glowing too brightly in her pale sweaty face, and suddenly I felt tired, tired in my bones, the pain from my head running straight down into my spinal column. I needed to get out of the house, right now, straightaway. My voice seemed to be coming from far away.

"I'm not a great fan of this kind of stuff. I'm going to go to Budgen's to get something for me." As excuses went, it was at least believable. There wasn't any food in the house. I hadn't felt much like eating recently, and when I had, I'd just grabbed a takeaway.

She nodded approvingly before taking her hand away, and I almost fell backwards, my legs like jelly. My fingers fumbled to pick up my wallet and keys from the breakfast bar. God, my head hurt.

Chloe was heading slowly into the sitting room as I opened the back door. She smiled unpleasantly over her shoulder. "Don't talk to any strangers."

I let the closing door be my answer.

I didn't find the spring air quite so revitalizing anymore, and rather than going down to the small supermarket, I decided to walk up to the big Tesco in Wolverton, a mile and half away. The confines of

Stony Stratford—so long a comfort zone in my life—
were becoming claustrophobic, and I turned my back
on it, my feet heavy in my trainers. Half my head was
numb with pain, but it thankfully eased as I finally
passed under the old bridge that signalled the boundary of the town, and I took in several deep breaths, relieved to have my thinking clear.

The streets were quiet, the odd car or bike passing
me, but no sign of any other pedestrians. I'd seen a
couple of people moving around Stony, but it seemed
that no one was strolling up to Wolverton this Saturday morning apart from me. On either side of the road
were fields, and they seemed to watch me silently as I
trudged up the mild incline. Although my headache
seemed to be going, I was sweating with exhaustion.
How could I be so tired? There was too much strange
shit happening way too fast for me to keep up.

Pushing myself onwards, I did my best to ignore the
pain in my limbs. There was just too much to think
about already, and at least the jabbing, sharp attacks
to my head were going.

By the time I got into the old railway town I was recovering slightly, but my soul still ached at the sight of
the nearly empty supermarket car park. I laughed
pathetically at my lack of surprise and stepped through
the sliding doors into the cool, brightly lit store. As the
door shut behind me, my headache dropped away a little more; it was still there, but it was at least tolerable.

Picking up a basket from the tall stack at the en-
trance, I began to wander up and down the empty
aisles, the tinny music filtering from above adding to
the eeriness of the ghost town atmosphere. I felt like I
was shopping in the middle of the night, not eleven-

thirty on a Saturday morning. My shoes whispered noisily as I walked, my eyes no doubt as wide as a child's.

The meat counters were all pretty much empty, some vac-packed bacon and frankfurters left unwanted on the shelves, the machinery humming hungrily as it kept them cool. Staring into the sterile shelving, hopelessness seeped into me. It seemed that Chloe wasn't the only one wanting protein today. I didn't care about the lack of meat. I found that since Chloe came home, I'd gone off the stuff. In fact, I wasn't sure that I was going to have an appetite for anything much in the near future.

The deli and cheese counter were closed and although there were no "due to illness" signs up, it didn't take a genius to figure it out. Not that there were many geniuses out and about to do the math. Going past the chiller, I took out a pizza and put it in the basket, adding two pints of milk. The sight of all this food was making my stomach turn, the image of Chloe's rotting mouth making unwelcome visits in my mind, but I couldn't go home with nothing. The idea of doing anything that might upset my girlfriend didn't appeal to me.

Turning away from the endless mountains of food, I headed into the toiletries section and grabbed two packets of paracetamol and the same of ibuprofen. There weren't many left on the shelf. It seemed that meat wasn't the only product in demand on this unusual weekend. Not wanting to wait until I'd paid for them, I ripped into the paracetamol and dry-swallowed a couple.

"Matt. Hi."

Jesus. The sudden voice jolted my jangled nerves. The pale face next to me attempted a smile and it took me a moment to place it, before it came to me. Mark. God, I hadn't seen him in ages. He lived just round the corner from here and we'd been to school together. We also used to play in the Stony pool league together. He wasn't a bad player and a good laugh to boot. He wasn't looking so amusing now, his eyes strained and bloodshot. I squeezed his shoulder.

"Hey, mate. How are you?" I glanced down and saw that his shopping basket was almost identical to mine. One meal's worth of food, tea bags and painkillers.

"You got a headache, too?"

He nodded very slowly, his mouth twitching slightly, as if he had to force the words out. "Shelley's not well."

Now there was a surprise. "Neither's Chloe." My own head pounded a bit harder. "You want to talk about it?" I stared at him, waiting for an answer. It was about time someone started talking about it, and it may as well be us over a cool beer.

Mark's hand shot to his head as he flinched, and the nod I was sure had been coming stopped. Leaning forward, he whispered painfully.

"Maybe later. Maybe when she's asleep." His face contorted slightly again. "It doesn't hurt so much then." Wobbling, he almost lost his balance and I grabbed him, keeping him on his feet.

"Are you sure you're all right?"

He nodded. "I have to go now."

He scurried away, disappearing around the corner before I could call him back. I stood there for a few moments, staring after him. What had he meant, it

37

didn't hurt so much when Shelley was asleep? Absently adding another packet of pills to my basket, *better to be safe than sorry,* I made my way to one of the two checkouts that was open and emptied my meagre load onto the conveyor belt, then stared down towards the exit. There was no sign of Mark.

The middle-aged man at the checkout smiled too brightly at me.

"Would you like any help packing your bags, sir?"

I almost laughed, looking at my few purchases on the counter. "No. I can manage." I wasn't sure where he was going to get this bag packer from. The store was operating with a skeleton crew, and the skeleton was missing a couple of limbs. The machine bleeped contentedly, oblivious to the changes in the world.

"That'll be five pounds ninety. Do you have a club card?"

I shook my head and handed over a ten pound note. His precisely gelled hair shone. Maybe this was his way of coping. Or maybe whatever was going on in his house, or his mother's house, or his sister's house, had driven him round the bend.

"Have a nice day!"

My bag filled, I raised a halfhearted arm in response, already walking away. Back in the fresh air, I had nowhere else to go but home, but at least I had plenty to think about while I walked. What had Mark meant, *it didn't hurt so much when Shelley was asleep?* I really hoped he'd ring me later, maybe go for a drink if we could find somewhere that was open. I needed to share this now, to talk it over with someone, just so I didn't turn into the crazy Tesco man. As I slowly made my way back to Stony, my headache pounded back to life, ignoring the painkillers I'd taken, making me queasy, as if I'd been breathing petrol fumes for too long.

By the time I reached my front door, I was throbbing with pain and frantically swallowed two more pills, despite exceeding the stated dose. Like they were going to help.

CHAPTER FOUR

The blinds in the kitchen were shut, and the cool darkness was a relief from the bright light outside, the slashing pain in my head calming slightly. I put the bag down and left it unpacked. The only things in it I was really interested in were the painkillers, and they weren't going to go off in the warmth. I was glad about that, as I didn't really want to look again in the meat-laden fridge, my stomach turning with the thought of all that offal.

"Chloe?" My voice wasn't much more than a whisper as I moved into the sitting room doorway. She was standing with her back to me, and the gloomy air was filled with a kind of half-light that came from whatever sunshine could filter through the heavy curtains, distorting shadows and haloing her new shape as if heaven were celebrating her awfulness. I waited for her to acknowledge me, and from the corner of my eye I could see dust particles hovering in the air between us, floating freely, released from fear of dust and polish. I don't think cleaning had been on either Chloe's or my agenda for quite some time now. As I reached for the light switch, her voice stopped me.

"Don't. Leave them off." She sounded muffled, and when she turned to face me, I realised with horror why. *Christ, what was she doing?* I stared, my own mouth agape, disgust squeezing at my guts. My hand dropped from the light switch, no longer wanting to brighten the darkness. I could see enough. More than enough.

Half-eaten raw meat hung sloppily from her lips, its sticky juice and loose lumps dripping down her large body to the floor below; looking down I could see a trail of dark stained splatter marks leading from the kitchen to here. She was chewing slowly, her eyes glazed as her lips and cheeks moved. *Jesus Christ, Jesus fucking Christ.* My stomach roiled and heaved, but despite the revulsion—and yes, it really was revulsion by then—I took a step forward. Even if Chloe was turning into god only knew what…at that point I wasn't ready to accept that she'd changed forever, *that she was leaving me,* she was still carrying our baby.

"What's going on, Chloe?" God, she stank. The skin on her face and arms shone and shimmered, dragging my appalled attention to it. Something like sweat was oozing from her; something *like* sweat, but not. This was thicker and foul-smelling, sweet and bitter all at once, the consistency of mucus.

Smiling, she raised her hand, ripping free another bite of the slimy flesh she was gripping. Smacking sounds filled the air as she chewed happily, mouth open.

"I'm talking to Helena."

Shaking my head, I raised my hands and turned away. I was tired. My head hurt. And there really wasn't much more of this I could take. Talking to Helena? What the hell was she saying? How could that be? Chloe and Helena had studied law together, and had been best friends in a way, before relationships turned up and changed things. She was a cheerful girl. Bright. Funny. Not a patch on Chloe, but a babe in her own way. But Helena lived in Birmingham, fifty miles away. *Fifty miles away.*

As I stood there, my head was filled with the image of another dark lounge, another fat and stinking girl, and another lost man hearing, *I'm talking to Chloe.* And then, as fear took hold of my imagination, that image multiplied and multiplied until there were a thousand girls, a million, in darkened rooms having secret silent conversations with each other. My blood chilled and Dr. Judge's desperately despairing face filled my mind, his words an undying echo I seemed to hear constantly, *This is happening to all of them. All of us. The whole world.* Christ, my nightmare image probably wasn't so wild. My shoulders slumped as I faced the stranger that was my girlfriend. She was staring intently forward. I tried to reason, to understand. For my own sake, if not for hers.

"But you're not even on the phone. How can you be talking to Helena?"

Giggling, she sprayed particles of blood onto our sofa. She didn't look at me. "Don't need a phone."

"Look, Chloe, this has got to stop, you can't go on—"

The force lifted me from my feet and slammed me into the wall five feet away, knocking the wind out of me, treating my body like a rag doll. What the hell was happening? Fear roared to life, my hip banging sharply into the skirting board behind me as I collapsed to the floor. My head was pounding and my neck was twisted slightly, but when I tried to move, I couldn't. *Oh shit, I've broken my neck, I've broken my neck and am paralysed.* Desperate for her help, I strained my immobile head forward and managed a pitiful mewl.

She flashed her eyes at me as if I were an irritating insect, and the sound in my throat stopped as my head banged roughly against the plaster, my vision filling with stars. She was controlling me, *controlling my body.* I tried to suffocate the thought that followed. *And what the hell is she planning to do to me?*

"Stay there. It'll be over soon." Grunting at me, she lowered herself carefully onto the sofa and went back to wherever that glazed look took her.

Time ticked by, my being immobile, pressed painfully against the wall, my head pounding away the seconds, pain and numb agony bleeding into every area of my body. The pressure was unrelenting and total. Not a single muscle in my body, outside of those needed to breathe and pump blood, could move, and the effects of that were more than anything I could have imagined.

First there were pins and needles, starting in my toes, working their way slowly up my calves and into my thighs. By the time they reached my hips and upper body, my feet had moved to the next stage and were raging at me, begging for some slight movement, and the sun had moved beyond the range of the lounge windows, lazily shifting into the cool afternoon, leaving us, the new Chloe and I, in the grainy grey gloom that was for now the confines of our existence.

About five hours in, after the first tingling of numbness, came the white heat of frozen agony, limbs screaming for release, for any kind of movement. My mind was a haze, the torturous agony more than I could believe possible from just being in exactly one spot for so long. All I could do was watch her, my bleary eyes drying beneath their open lids, and hope to somehow retain my sanity.

As night drew in I waited for her to sleep, prayed for it, Mark's words echoing in my dazed head. *It didn't hurt so much when Shelley was asleep.* Maybe that would work with Chloe, too. Maybe if she would just go to sleep, this awful hold she had over me would loosen, allow me some blessed movement. I didn't even think as far as leaving. Escape wasn't on my agenda, I knew I couldn't muster the amount of energy that would require, not even in my fantasies. All I wanted was to change position. To shift slightly would bring more relief than I could possibly imagine and I wanted it more than water or food or anything. I waited and waited, screaming with frustration inside my silent mannequin of a body, waiting for the first sign of weariness to appear in the monster that was my girlfriend.

But she didn't sleep. Not as far as I could tell from my position in hell on the floor, at any rate. Her huge, and god, she was huge by that point, frame filled our leather sofa, her legs spread slightly, no doubt in order to stop her thighs chafing. She seemed to be neither asleep nor awake, in some kind of trance. Occasionally, she let out a small giggle or undefined word as her body jerked slightly, the frame of the furniture creaking beneath her.

As the night wore on, I drifted into a nightmarish world somewhere between sleeping and waking, my brain almost hallucinating, my eyelids having no choice but to stay open. My bladder shrieked inside for release, but stuck there, become one with my living room, I couldn't even piss. Through the shadows and darkness, I thought at times that I saw shapes moving beneath her T-shirt, as if something was wriggling beneath her skin, and at some point, in the dark stillness a few hours before dawn, she pulled up the hem of her skirt and rubbed at herself, taking her pleasure loudly and animalistically. Mainly, she just ignored me.

It must have been about six o'clock the next morning that she heaved herself upwards and shuffled into the kitchen. In the cold grey light I could see the sweat and grease patches she had left behind on the sofa, both large cushions indented where she'd sat.

My head buzzed, my body beyond pain and totally exhausted, but when I heard the grunting and panting coming from the next room I mustered every ounce of remaining will to try and turn my head and see what was happening, but to no avail. *What was happening to her?* The sound of banging and beating on the units filled the house for at least ten minutes as she cursed with indefinable words, her tone violent and angry. Finally, she must have slid down the fridge freezer to sit on the floor, and then after she broke long and noisy wind, she settled down to snorting occasionally as she panted. After about half an hour, I heard something squelch, something wet perhaps, on the quarry tiles we had chosen together not that very long ago. And then there was silence.

I'd like to say that in that few moments I was worried about her, if she was okay, if she was even alive, but the survival instinct is an amazing thing, and if I'm honest—and now there's really no point in being anything else—then as I lay there the only person I was concerned about was me, Matthew Edge, nearly thirty and not ready to die. My heart pounded in my chest. What if she was dead? What if she was dead in there and I was going to be trapped here until I starved to death? How long would that take? Would I go mad before I died?

Rushes of panic drew my insides further in, my flesh recoiling from the idea, and then suddenly even *that* froze as I heard movement from the kitchen, the sound of Chloe dragging herself to her feet. New fears overtook those of only seconds ago. What had happened to her in there? Was she going to come back more nightmarish than before? I remembered the meat, the way she'd chewed at it, and wondered how much she had left. Was she going to come back *hungrier* than before?

She appeared in the doorway and stared at me for a moment before moaning and slumping into the door frame, her eyes shutting.

As soon as she made the noise, the pressure lifted from me, my bladder emptying itself instantly. I didn't care, shamelessly enjoying the pure pleasure of release, my headache gone. Oh god, it felt good. Even the pain of moving my limbs after such a long time immobile was welcome. I sat there on the floor, in a pool of my own piss, relishing the moment, almost unaware of her until she spoke.

"You have to get out."

Her voice was a monotone, but it was *her* voice. My heart leapt a little. So Chloe still was there somewhere in this mutated body. I blinked several times, trying to focus on her, my eyeballs painfully grainy and needing liquid. I rubbed them, trying to kill the numbness in my fingers at the same time. My hands were freezing, my whole body was freezing, and I shivered as I clawed myself upright.

"You have to get out." Her words were harder this time. I leaned against the wall that had held me prisoner, needing its support while my blood circulated, my limbs trying to steady themselves.

"What do you mean?" My throat felt like sandpaper, the dryness irritating as I tried to speak, reminding me of how thirsty I was. Pushing myself away from the wall, I took a few unsteady steps towards her, my heart and stomach aching. Despite the past day of hell, despite everything, I found I was desperate to stay. To stay with her. I was terribly afraid, but hearing her voice again, *my* Chloe's voice, I knew she was scared, too, and I couldn't imagine turning my back on her.

If I left her, that would be it. Everything over. And I didn't think I could do that. Not to her or our baby. I *needed* them. I needed them to make the world normal again. To put everything back just how it was. I raised a hand to reach for her, but she stepped back.

"There isn't much time. It's starting."

I stared at her. "I can't leave you. I love you. And our baby." I tried to smile, forcing the muscles in my face back to life.

She shook her head and sighed before meeting my gaze. I could see pain in there, as if she were fighting something, but more than that I could see that she loved me, too. Surely that counted for something.

"You still care for me, Chloe. You know you do."

"It doesn't matter, Matt." The words rang hollow around the room and she looked at me pityingly from those strange blank eyes. "I'm not me anymore. I'm... I'm something different. And I can't control it for much longer." There was something in her eyes that I couldn't understand. "And I'm not sure how much longer I'm going to want to."

Suddenly I wondered if her pain was caused by releasing me from the prison her mind had forced me into. Was she fighting her new self? Was I going to be slammed back against the wall any second? I didn't care, not while she was here. While she was back.

"We've got to try, Chloe. You've got to keep fighting. They'll have an answer soon, they'll cure you...." Man's old-fashioned faith in *they* again. We either think *they're* trying to kill us, or that *they* can find a cure for just about anything. That's what *they* do after all, isn't it? Kill or cure?

She barked a laugh at me. "There is no cure, Matt. It's too late. It's too late for all of us. So cut the shit and fuck off. While you still can."

I ignored the implied threat and stepped close to where she stood, blocking the doorway to the kitchen.

"We're having a baby, Chloe. Have you forgotten about that? Can't you fight for that, even if you can't fight for me?" She couldn't give up on our baby. Not my Chloe.

"There isn't any baby. Not anymore."

My world stopped as I stared at her, waiting for some evidence of a lie. "What? What did you say?"

Stepping backwards, she opened up a path to the kitchen. "Take a look."

I shuffled forward, needing to see, but not wanting to, knowing that this was it, this was the end of everything I knew and cared about. Behind me, Chloe retook her position in the doorway. Suddenly, all the panting and cursing I'd heard earlier made sense.

Tears burning my eyes, I fell to my knees on the tiles that were slick with blood. "Oh no. Oh no, no, no."

The tiny stillborn fetus was barely formed, but still just recognisable, one small arm developing a perfect hand and fingers towards its end, ears and nose beginning to take shape. My child. My beautiful never-to-be child. I sobbed openly, my vision blurred, but still I stared. I owed it to this little life. Horror mixed with indescribable anguish as I understood what I was seeing.

The other arm was missing, as were the legs, ripped away from the mutilated torso. I looked again at the congealing blood around me. *Something had chewed on my child. Something had eaten part of my baby.* Hearing my breath rushing in my ears, I felt completely cold, inside and out, and turned to face Chloe. She read the hatred in my mind.

"It wasn't me."

How could she sound so matter of fact, so uninvolved? I thought of the raw meat I'd watched her eat.

"You're lying." I spat the words at her, filling them with every lost hope I had.

"No. It wasn't me." Again that monotone sucked at her voice, and I realised she had been right. Our love didn't matter. Not anymore. It was too late for that. I dragged myself back to my feet, and we stared at each other hopelessly.

"There's not much time. Leave, Matt."

"If it wasn't you…then who?" I tried to keep the quiver out of my voice.

She paused before turning away and lumbering slowly back to the sofa in the sitting room, easing herself into the seat and staring forward.

"I think there's something else growing inside me." Some of that gravely non-Chloeness was coming back. "A different baby." She smiled unpleasantly into space,

49

rubbing her expanse of stomach. "A new kind of baby."

A wave of nausea ran through me and I clutched at the breakfast bar. The headache was coming back. I stared at her, and then at our dead future on the floor at my feet, and then back to her again. She was starting to convulse slightly, her huge body jolting and twisting, something happening under her skirt, something starting to emerge from there.

"Chloe?"

"Now! Fucking get out now!" Her head spun round to me, angry and venomous as she screamed, but I'm not even sure if the words would have been enough to make me leave, to move my shell-shocked and shattered body from that spot, if two of her teeth hadn't flown out as she screeched.

Watching their flight, almost in slow motion, I suddenly knew beyond all doubt that I had been a fool. There was nothing left to hold on to. She was right. She wasn't Chloe anymore, no matter how much I wanted her to be. And the last bit of my Chloe, the last pure bit of her, wanted me to leave, to get the fuck out of there. *While I still could.*

Turning my back on her, not wanting to see anymore, not wanting to *know* anymore, I fumbled at the back door, trying to turn the key, finally yanking it open and stumbling out into the light before the headache took over. The early morning air was fresh and new and I ran into it, my muscles burning with the sudden activity, sobs tearing from my chest, and I ran and I ran and I didn't look back. The houses on either side of the street loomed aggressively above me, and I turned down towards the river, running alongside it until I reached the old aqueduct that separated Stony from Old Stratford. My trousers, wet with piss, rubbed at my skin, but my mind was ablaze with the threat of madness.

Leaning against the worn stone surface, built so many long centuries ago, I stared up at the branches and sunlight above until the sweat cooled on my face and finally my stomach cramped. Twisting sideways, I tipped my head forward and threw up my madness.

CHAPTER FIVE

By the time I straightened up, my mouth and throat were aching and sore from the constant heaving, having retched loudly and angrily long after there was anything left inside me; but the hot white fear of insanity seemed to have passed. Shivering, I looked at my watch. It was nine o'clock. I'd been out here lost in shock and battling the onset of madness for over two hours. Jesus.

Looking around at the lush fields and the river with its neat towpath, nostalgia washed over me. I'd come walking down here all my life, but despite its familiarity I couldn't deny the newness in the air. What I *knew* couldn't be trusted. It was a brave new world I was looking at. There was no real human sound for a start, no cars, no children shouting at their friends, no hint of a passing conversation. I'd only experienced something like that once before in my life, on a holiday to Los Angeles. Tired with the shallowness of Hollywood, I'd hired a car and driven out to Death Valley, slicing through the silent red desert, a vast expanse that went on forever as far as I could see. I'd felt as if I were the last man on earth out there with just dust carried on the echo of wind for company, suddenly realising how fragile my existence was, how easily I could never be found should an accident happen. I drove more carefully after that moment of fear.

Standing there in the shadow of the aqueduct, I felt like that again, only this time for all I knew I *was* the only person left alive. The only sane one at any rate. Blocking out thoughts of Chloe, I remembered the horror of my frozen state in the lounge. Was that where all the children and people were now? No. I couldn't believe that. I *wouldn't*. Logic dictated that if I was here and okay, then other people must be wandering around shell-shocked, too.

The cool breeze drifted past, reminding me that I couldn't stay here, I had to move, to try and find out what the hell was going on. My jeans were acrid with dried piss and I was sure that I'd probably more than splashed myself with bile during my throwing up. At least that gave my journey a place to start. I needed fresh clothes.

Finding my legs steadier than I expected, I pushed away from the wall and followed it until I reached the steep stairs leading back up to the road that ran across the aqueduct. The gate squealed as it opened, the sound sending a shudder through my insides. The violence of the noise was out of place in this new, hushed world. Closing it behind me, I started to stride back to High Street, forcing confidence into my walk. If I allowed a noisy gate to make me nervous, then I was done for. Still, if I said that the dull thud of my shoes on the pavement didn't ring a little too loudly in my ears for my nerves, then I'd be lying.

I followed the curve of the wall until it bloomed into buildings—the mix of old and new shops and houses that made up the main street of the town—and then slowed down, nervous because of the silence. I couldn't believe all the people that filled the houses around me were dead and gone. If the local population *were* alive but not out here with me, then the alternatives were spine-chilling and I wasn't ready in my head to go there yet. There was only so far I could push my sanity in one morning.

To be honest, I wasn't even sure what had happened to Chloe, let alone anyone else, but I wasn't going to go back and find out. If she were still alive, then she wasn't my Chloe anymore.

Stony wasn't a town with many clothes shops. After going through a period of floundering without direction during the eighties, it had finally found a niche for itself in the retail world—small outlets and boutiques filled with gifts and knickknacks, glassware and ornaments. It was where people in Milton Keynes went to fill Christmas stockings and to buy that special something for a birthday present. But it wasn't a place to come to if you were looking for the latest in jeans or designer gear. In fact, it wasn't a place to come for stuff to wear if you were under retirement age. There was one shop that sold relatively good clothes for women; Chloe had been known to pick up a couple of things from it, but there was nothing here for men. Apart, of course, from Morris's Menswear, halfway up High Street.

It's funny the things you totally ignore in your everyday life. Morris's Menswear had been here for as long as I could remember, passed down through the family, surviving the cull of bankruptcies and repossessions that swept the town in earlier decades, but I had never even really looked at it, let alone considered going in. It still retained the same unassuming frontage that it had for years, its very blandness maybe the key to its success. It was aimed at a breed almost extinct, especially this far out of London, those kind of men who like to know their tailor, who like to buy their country casuals and business suits all in the same place, who like it that someone knows that "sir dresses to the left or right." I didn't reckon there were many of them under fifty.

Still, beggars couldn't be choosers, and my options were limited. I crossed the road at the churchyard and headed towards the tan awning, passing some of the smaller privately owned businesses, the pet shop, one card shop, a florist; all shut. No explanations on the door this time. By the time I reached the small co-op, it was obvious that Stony Stratford was not open for business today. All the doors were locked and the gloom behind the shutters and windows showed no sign of impending life.

The sun however, was beating down, keeping the air pleasantly warm. It was shaping up to be the best day of the year as far as the weather was concerned. It seemed that Mother Nature was oblivious to the problems of man, or maybe she just didn't give a shit, and who could really blame her? It wasn't as if we'd really played fair, had we? But that's a debate for another time.

Pushing my shoulder into the thick glass of the door,

I realised that it was going to take more than just a shove to get inside. There was no way I could just punch it and break it; it was too strong for that. Sighing, I squinted and peered along the empty street. I was going to need a brick or a missile of some kind and I wasn't sure where I was going to find it. Smiling, I saw the metal swing board of the butcher's—falsely advertising friendly service inside the abandoned shop— and jogged down to fetch it. It was heavier than it looked, and as I hurled it towards the glass window I flinched and cringed from the smash, expecting an alarm to rip through the empty air around me, heralding my descent into crime to any who cared to listen.

After the shattering of glass there was nothing. There must have been more pressing matters to attend to than setting the alarm for whoever was last to leave the shop premises, and I straightened up to get a good look at my first successful break-in. Not the most subtle approach, but it had worked. The models were wearing a dusting of glass bits, glinting in the sunshine, and the window was no more, a thousand pieces sprayed into the heart of the shop.

I climbed into the small room, carefully knocking out jagged shards that poked sharply at me from dangerous angles as I went, my eyes scanning ahead for any that might stab me as I passed. This was not a day to be getting injured. I doubted that A&E were up and running even if I could get myself there. I wasn't sure that I'd make the cut if it were survival of the fittest, but if it was survival of the wariest, then I was in with a fighting chance.

The shop was well lit from the sun outside, but the air was refreshingly cool as I brushed past the rows of suits. I needed new clothes, yes, but a shirt and tie weren't really what I had in mind. At the far side there was a rack of shelves with neatly folder trousers and jumpers filling them, and it was there I headed, ripping them out to find some my size.

Much to my surprise, I found a pair of pretty respectable chinos, a Levi's T-shirt and a crew neck jumper, all of which were wearable without disgrace. Coming across some Calvin Klein underpants brought me out in a full-blown smile. A pang of pain went through me as I imagined how pleased Chloe would be at my concern for appearance at a time like this, and I shoved it aside, peeling off my dirty clothes right there in the middle of the shop, dressing quickly in their crisp clean replacements.

Straightening up after re-tying my laces, I noticed a slimline portable radio on the counter above the till and credit card machine and my heart leapt nervously. Here was my chance to find out if anyone knew just what was going on in Stony and how widespread the problem was. Moving across the shop, my hand hovered above the On button for a second. Despite the horrors of the night before, there was still a certain amount of bliss in ignorance, and at the moment I could almost ignore the evidence to the contrary and believe that this was solely a local nightmare. I took a deep breath and pushed down on the thin steel.

Quiet static replaced the silence. Puzzled, I checked the frequency. 98.2. Radio One should have been blurting out some new tune or another, or at least reporting on all this. I turned the dial, slowly running the full length of the FM band. Still nothing. I could feel my own pulse throbbing through my body. Surely someone was broadcasting somewhere. *Surely* they must be.

Flicking a switch on the front I searched the medium and then long wave bands, my head lowered listening intently for anything, any sign of life. For a moment, a brief instant in time, I thought I heard the faint strains of an orchestra drifting in from a galaxy away, but it was gone before I could convince myself that it was really there. Despite creeping the dial backwards and forwards millimetre by millimetre trying to find it again, it was lost in the sea of white noise.

Turning the radio off, I mulled over the options. Either there was no one the length and breadth of the country attempting to broadcast, or something had happened to the radio signal. Maybe somehow it was being blocked. With that flash of thought, I stretched over the counter and grabbed the telephone, pulling the receiver to my ear. Instead of the familiar tone, again all I could hear was deathly static. Slowly, I put it back and leaned against the counter. My hands clammy, I gazed through the vandalised window at the bright day outside, staring at everything and nothing, and my skin tingled both inside and out. If there'd been a TV there, then I guessed that all it would be delivering was snow and crackle. So what was doing it? Some coincidental breakdown in *all* the communication networks?

Shivering, I remembered Chloe standing silently in the sitting room with that secretive smile on her face, her deadened eyes almost laughing at me. *I'm talking to Helena.* Maybe the new methods of conversation were blocking the old, all-inclusive ones. I sighed. There were too many maybes filling this morning, and I didn't have a concrete answer to any of them.

Perhaps if I went home I could find one or two, but the pain in my heart told me that there was no going back there. Shock was numbing my feeling of loss over Chloe, but I knew that what I *was* feeling was grief. Chloe was gone. I knew it in my soul. My Chloe was not coming back. Eventually, if no one started to emerge, I was going to have to break into a flat or house to face whatever was happening, but I wasn't ready for that.

Stepping back out onto the pavement, suddenly aware of the rumbling emptiness of my stomach, I realised that what I was ready for was breakfast. In fact, I was ravenous. Food hadn't been on the agenda yesterday, and any scraps lingering in my system had been vomited up down by the river.

I jogged across the road and through the small parade of shops until I got to Budgen's, but frustratingly the double doors to the small supermarket were locked and the shutters down, someone obviously taking their responsibilities very seriously before the world went mad. Cursing under my breath, I kicked the steel and turned outward, venting my anger at everything in that one blow. God, it felt good. I lashed out with my foot again. And then again, the noise echoing loudly, satisfying me that I was alive. Alive and angry and goddamned hungry.

If a shooting pain through the side of my foot hadn't paused my assault, then I probably wouldn't have heard the quiet running footsteps pattering away from me. Spinning around, I scanned the surrounding area for any sign or shadow of human life.

"Hello?"

I ignored both the creepiness of hearing my voice aloud and the warning voice in my head that advised quiet caution. Who knew what drawing attention to myself would bring out of the silent dwellings that surrounded me?

"Hello?" I called out louder this time, but there was no answer from the hushed walls and bushes. I waited, breath held, but no figure appeared or called back from their hiding place.

Still, unlike the vague hint of music on the radio, this was a sound I definitely knew I'd heard, and my spirits lifted. There was someone else out here other than me, and the fact that they were obviously scared of coming too close went in their favour. It certainly pushed up the odds of them being normal, at any rate. Only an insane person wouldn't be scared; not if they'd been through anything like I had with Chloe and then stepped out into this empty world. Fear was a healthy emotion and I was quickly learning to live with it.

Feeling buoyed by the almost-contact with another living being, I headed into St. Swythen's Court, tucked away behind the hairdresser's and bookshop. There was a little café there, and if I was lucky, maybe I'd be able to get my much-needed breakfast.

In the sunshine the tiny courtyard was picture postcard perfect, more so for the lack of people cluttering it and distracting from its peaceful charm. The small cobbles sparkled, the smooth stones reflecting the bright natural light as if they were glistening with moisture, and for a moment it could have been early on a perfect summer morning. There were even sparrows singing in the trees around me. They weren't too bothered about the lack of human company. Perhaps the whole of nature was heaving a sigh of relief at the respite.

My rumbling stomach threw any more philosophical wanderings out of my mind as I eyed the glass door and chintzy bay window of the small, whitewashed Old World café and smiled. This was going to be easier than Morris's Menswear; even my inexperienced burglar's eye could tell that. Unlike that thick plated window, the glass here was thin, and turning my face away I jabbed the pane immediately above the wrought iron handle with my elbow, relishing the sweet tinkling of the glass giving way. Once again, no alarm sounded despite the red box on the wall, and I reached my arm carefully through the gap and released the snib lock. With the gentle ring of the connected brass bell, the door swung open before me. The first hungry customer of the day had arrived.

Within moments, I'd lifted the wooden flap that served to separate the public from the workforce and found the kitchen, pleased to hear the humming of the fridge creating a sense of normalcy. Yanking the door open, I peered inside and pulled out some eggs and bacon and a loaf of sliced white bread that the management obviously kept in there to keep it fresh longer. I'd started to fill the kettle when I spied the coffee machine and grinned. Fresh coffee and a fry-up. I couldn't think of anything that would satisfy my grumbling appetite more, and if there was a morning for spoiling myself, then this was it.

Ten minutes later and the dirty pans were soaking in the large stainless steel sink. I sat down at a small round table covered with a chequered cloth, a steaming mug of strong coffee in one hand and a large plate of food in the other. After the second mouthful, my spirits had lifted further and I was almost humming to myself. I should have been tired; in fact, I should have been exhausted, but at that moment I think I was feeling the exhilaration of survival. For a while, my grief was suppressed, part of too big a picture to be real in itself, and all that mattered was that I was alive, that I'd heard the footsteps of another living soul, and that my eggs were perfectly cooked.

Having devoured my breakfast, scraping the last dregs onto my fork, I took my plate to the kitchen and then leaned against the counter, sipping my second cup of coffee and contemplating where to go and what to do next.

I was so lost in my own thoughts that at first I didn't hear the noise. It was almost not there, a furtive invasion, hoping for recognition rather than demanding it. Getting ready to step back out into the world, I'd just decided to make myself sandwiches to take with me when I finally noticed the gentle tapping coming from upstairs. Staring up at the white ceiling, I tilted my head, focussing on the sound; my body once again fully alert. Perhaps it was just the water pipes or the boiler. This building was old and bound to have quirky characteristics.

The coffee forgotten in my hand, I listened quivering with stillness, my breath short and raspy. There it was again, a rhythmic knocking above my head. It was too regular, too *intent* to be anything other than manmade. Slowly I put the mug down, ignoring the slight shake in my hand. What was it? Morse code? My heart thumping hard, I moved quietly back through the kitchen and gently opened a door that led into a small, carpeted hallway. A dull blue coat and tatty umbrella hung from a hook on the wall. Beside them, the stairs rose up to what was more than likely the owner's flat and home. The tapping was louder here.

Hesitating in the doorway, not wanting to investigate but knowing I really had no choice, my breakfast felt greasy in my stomach. The uplifted spirits of earlier were fading fast, each tap from above sending a slight bout of nausea through me, and cursing silently I pulled a large knife from the block on the counter and crept forward, leaving the door fully open in case I needed a hasty retreat. The carpet was soft beneath my shoes, and keeping my eyes focussed on the hallway above, I very slowly made my way up the steep and narrow stairs.

The flock-papered walls on either side of me were lined with family photos old and new, and the landing above was no different. A mahogany sideboard was covered with silver and wood photo frames. A dark-haired, plump woman of about forty-five and a balding man of about the same age smiled out from most of them, in the company of two teenage children. A happy family. I paused and absorbed them for a moment before dragging my reluctant attention back to the call of that morbid tapping. It was coming from the room at the end of the corridor ahead of me, no doubt about that, but the almost-shut door left me clues as to what I might find in there.

Flinching as a floorboard creaked under my weight, I gripped the knife handle and edged forward until I could peer carefully through the small gap where the door was open. The narrow field of vision betrayed nothing at first, just a patch of the same patterned carpet stretching out and the tiniest edge of a pale green velour sofa, but no clue as to where the surreptitious knocking was coming from, or *who* was doing it. Slowly, my throat dry and tight with fear, I reached out and gently pressed the chipped wood with my damp fingers until it crept open a few more inches, expanding my range slightly. I still couldn't see anyone, but something plastic glinted on the floor. *Oh God*. It was meat packaging. The kind of sealed plastic box that normally filled supermarket shelves with beef and joints of pork. It was empty, ripped open and tossed aside, but a small puddle of blood and meat juice still lingered at the bottom. *Oh shit*.

Unable to stay in this purgatory of unknowing any longer, I pushed the door again, allowing it to swing open but stayed outside the room, the knife uncertain in my hand. My mouth fell open as I stared, the door separating my rational world from the horror in front of me, framing it like a parody of the family photos I'd left behind in the hall.

A thin man lying on his side in vest and trousers, his body almost hanging off the sofa, dropped the spoon he'd been tapping with, his bare arm lolling to the ground. In the far two corners of the old-fashioned lounge the teenage children were pressed into the walls, unmoving, their eyes sluggish and dim. Something shone on them, covering their skin and clothes, and it took a moment before I realised it was like some kind of gossamer running up from them, shimmering on the ceiling and lights. Whatever the stuff was that was keeping them trapped, it wasn't the mental force that Chloe had used on me. This was real; it had substance.

My breath throbbed in my ears, drowning all other sound for the moment, as my eyes moved on to the dead woman sitting on the carpet, slumped against the TV. Her thick legs were spread, the lower half of her body covered in blood, loose folds of skin escaping from beneath her large floral blouse, reminiscent of obese Americans who suddenly lose all their weight, needing rolls and rolls of unwanted flesh removed.

Staring at the blood and intestines that hung from beneath the hem of her wide skirt, my head filled with the image of my poor dead baby on our kitchen floor, and Chloe's haunting words: *I think there's something else growing inside me. A new kind of baby.*

Jesus Christ. Were they *all* carrying something inside them? Is that what had killed this woman? Giving birth to something? Resisting the urge to turn and run I stared at her, needing more time to believe the horror of what I was seeing.

She too glistened with the light threads that covered her dazed children and most of the room, but in her case strands of it had erupted from within her, escaping through her nostrils, ears and mouth and wrapping round her body; even the corners of her eyes leaked it. Her dead body was cocooned, but done so from the inside. Had it been her last unnatural act, or had it happened postmortem?

The rasping moan pulled my attention back to the man who'd summoned me up here, his bloodshot eyes meeting mine and reflecting my own terror, urging me to step across the threshold into his nightmare world. His jaw worked silently before he finally got the words out, his body pushed forward on the edge of the sofa in an almost impossible position. How could he stay like that? Why didn't he fall off the side?

"Help me..."

I was about to move forward, God help me I was, when from behind him, from where slick sucking sounds drifted towards me, one milky, transluscent leg, thin and sharply jointed, came over his side, wrapping round him like a lover, and I froze. I stared at the shiny footless limb in disgust, as another crept over the man, and then another until four held his limp body in place, one at his shoulders, then his waist, his knees and his feet. *What the fuck was it? Jesus Christ, just what the fuck was it? And what the fuck was it doing to him?*

Looking over his shoulder, I could make out the smooth, curved edges of the creature's body pulsing behind him, completely inhuman, like some awful pale insect, huge and mutated.

"Help me...pleeasse..."

The desperate, dying man croaked out the words, a dribble of blood escaping from his thin anguished lips, and I couldn't imagine his agony. I couldn't see past my own fear, as the legs contracted tighter around him, pulling the prey closer, and the awful round body rose up slightly as if to investigate the distraction, its milky white surface shining like mother of pearl, as for a moment the sucking stopped.

"Pleaasee..."

I moaned as I felt it look at me, *really* look at me, from its bank of almost invisible eyes, their raised bump surfaces glistening with the same sickly colour as the rest of its body, each standing out only by the pinpoint of bright red at its centre. I knew in that moment, as it locked me in its gaze, that it was feeding on him, feeding on him while he was still alive, and the primeval fear at the core of me told me that this terrible huge spider thing was enjoying his pain. That it *understood* what it was doing.

I think there's something else growing inside me. A new kind of baby.

I remembered how Chloe had been when I'd left her, her body jolting and jerking on the sofa, something moving under her clothes, something pushing its way out of her, and staring at this monster in front of me, I let the scream that had been welling up inside of me out, let it rip free, and it released my own frozen limbs.

I didn't stay. I didn't help. I didn't even put the man out of his misery and save him from being eaten alive with a swift stab to the throat, which I think is the help he was asking for. No. I turned and fled down the stairs and through the kitchen, banging my thigh hard on a low shelf but not even pausing in recognition of the pain, my own scream echoing after me even as my shoes beat on the cobbles of the courtyard outside, during every second of my flight expecting to feel that thing touching me, catching me. *Devouring me.*

For the second time that day I ran in pure terror, my tired legs burning beneath me, but this time I didn't know where to go, where there was left to go. I came to a stop in the centre of the small roundabout at the corner of High Street and Wolverton Road, of all places, swinging round frantically, knife waving from side to side, raging in preparation for the attacking monster I was sure was behind me.

There was nothing. Just the empty streets and pavements. I spun in circles, checking over and over that I was alone, until finally my heart rate slowed down to somewhere near normal, my blood cooling slightly. But just slightly.

Only a couple of hours ago I was looking at my home like it was a ghost town. Now as I warily gazed up at the windows that looked down impassively, I realised I'd been a galaxy away from the truth. Stony Stratford was teeming with life. A new kind of life. It was a breeding ground for it.

CHAPTER SIX

I think it was the music that kept me sane. It started about ten minutes after my escape from the café, as I sat in the bus shelter alongside The Plough, my back pressed against the metal, my eyes watchful, letting it waft gently over me for an hour or so until I realised that I really had no choice but to follow it.

Standing up, I stared for a few more seconds in the direction of St. Swythen's Court before deciding that if I didn't turn my back on it then, I never would. My whole body shaking, I tucked the knife into my belt and faced in the other direction, biting back the conviction that the thing was instantly behind me, and stepped out onto the street. I pushed myself forward, concentrating on the sound, focussing my thinking away from the fear that bubbled through every pore.

It was distant, but it was definitely coming from somewhere in Stony. Even in this silence I doubted that I could hear anything from Wolverton or the other surrounding villages. It didn't seem to be coming from any of the estates on the south edge of town, so I turned onto Russell Street and headed north. It was light, fluffy forties Hollywood music, the slightly tinny quality of the recording becoming clearer as I walked. At least I knew I was heading in the right direction.

Blossoms dropped from the trees that lined the pretty street as I followed the tune like a rat following the pied piper, although I don't think his repertoire ever included anything by Frank Sinatra or those other old crooners. I passed the closed primary school and the high walls of the old folks home, and kept with the kerb of the road moving past the uneven line of cottages and houses. I was glad they were set well back from the pavement, mostly hidden by shrubs and weeping willows. I didn't want to see what was going on inside. I didn't need to.

Finally, the houses thinned out and the road curved right past the small path leading down to the ancient overgrown graveyard that sat forgotten in the heart of our town. Its sunlight was blocked by overhanging trees, leaving it in eternal twilight, the names on the stones long ago eroded, a true place of peaceful rest. I wondered how long it would take for the modern one on London Road to reach the same state. I doubted anyone would be popping in there with fresh flowers or a lawnmower in the near future.

The music was definitely clearer now, as ahead of me the high gates of the Stony Stratford Sports Club reared into view, one side of thin grey steel bars arched open wide, inviting me onto the gravel drive as Vera Lynn burst into song with "We'll Meet Again," from somewhere beyond. To my left, the empty tennis courts gleamed in the sun, and peering to my right I could see the huts a couple of hundred yards away that made up the cricket and football clubs, but all that was coming from their direction was a light breeze cooling the air.

I paused and stared ahead of me at the source of the sound. It was floating out from behind the neat hedgerows of the Bowls Club, the roof of the Club-house just visible from where I was standing, irritatingly blocking any view I might have of whomever was playing it. For all I knew, a madman was waiting there, his shotgun raised, ready to blow the life out of anyone who answered his call, and despite all that had happened, I wasn't ready for that. But still, if I wasn't willing to take a risk on someone, then it was going to be a lonely existence for as long as it lasted. And if the person on the other side of that hedge was still in control of their senses, then they were braver than I was, drawing so much attention to themselves. Or perhaps, they just hadn't seen what I had so far this morning.

Keeping my footfalls as quiet as possible, I padded up the neat path to the waist high garden gate that signalled the club's boundary. On the other side lay the pristeenly mowed green, pretty flowers growing in flawless beds set back against the hedges. It looked like a pensioner's paradise, and for a brief moment my heart ached for halcyon days it seemed unlikely I would ever have.

Lifting the latch, I took a deep breath and pushed the gate open, my legs ready to once again burst into flight in the opposite direction if I needed them to, and stepped onto the path, turning to face the clubhouse thirty or so feet away.

There was a chair on the raised porch and an old

man sat in it, dressed casually in a cream shirt and tan trousers, smoking a pipe, a relic of a record player on the table beside him blasting out the tunes of his youth. Seeing me approach, he waved a hand and stood up, leaving the glass he'd been sipping from down next to the gramophone and turning the volume down slightly.

Relief flooding through me, I took the wooden steps two at a time, and by the time I'd got to the shade of the porch my hand was out, ready to introduce myself. I knew that I'd wanted human company, but I hadn't realised how badly I'd *needed* it.

"Matthew Edge. Am I pleased to see you."

The hand that gripped mine back was dry but firm. "George Leicester. And likewise."

He was a tall man, over six foot, and although his hair was past grey and into white, his eyes were bright and focussed in his lined face. I took the knife out of my belt and placed it on the low table. George stared at it for a moment before speaking.

"Why don't we go inside and get a drink while we wait to see if anyone else arrives? I've made coffee, but there's a whole bar there if you fancy something stronger."

There must have been a hungry look on my face as we stepped into the cooler area of the bar and I stared at the optics, because George raised an eyebrow.

"Just the one though, son. I think we're going to need our heads straight today."

I nodded and smiled as he poured me a whiskey just like the one he had outside; then we went back and stood in the doorway looking out over the green and beyond. Vera had moved on to a less famous song, but

George hummed it quietly as he reached for his own glass.

I gestured in the direction of the music. "I thought I was the only person left alive in town before I heard that. Clever idea. Brave, too."

"Brave? Not sure about that. I just needed to know that the whole world hadn't disappeared on me."

I sipped my drink, enjoying the moment of heat in my mouth. Disappeared? I wondered just how much he knew about what had happened to our quiet village. Maybe there hadn't been too many women in his life to give him any clues. My knowledge was pretty limited, but my experience of my own mother before she died was that old people could live pretty lonely lives.

"Are you married, George?"

Leaning against the door frame, he shook his head. "My wife's been dead for five years. Still, we had forty good years. I miss her every day, but you can't complain after a marriage like ours. I've got a daughter living down in Bristol, Mary her name is, but neither her nor her husband have been answering the phone for almost two weeks now. To tell the truth, I've been a bit worried. No, to tell the truth, I've been a lot worried. She normally lets me know if they're going away for more than a day or so." His smile faded. "Anyway, I got up this morning and the phone wasn't working. Nor the radio or television." He took a long sip of his own drink, savouring it, before speaking again.

"And there didn't seem to be anyone but me about. I knocked on a few doors, but no one answered, even though their cars were in their drives, and then I thought of coming down here. To be honest, I couldn't think of anywhere else to go. Not that there'd been a lot of people turning up here recently."

He met my gaze. "I'd been so wrapped up in my worry over Mary and her family that I hadn't noticed how fewer and fewer people had been coming out. There's been a fair few matches cancelled this season, especially the ladies. But I didn't really pay it any attention. At least, not until this morning when they were all gone." He paused and stared out into the distance. "There aren't even any children out playing. Where are they all, Matthew? And why didn't I notice until it had got this far?"

I knew exactly what he meant. I'd been so absorbed with Chloe I hadn't seen anything else, either. I bet it was the same for that poor man in the café as well. I shivered. George didn't know how lucky he was that no one had answered the door to him.

"They're not gone. Not disappeared, at any rate."

"What do you mean? Do you know something I don't?"

"You'd better sit back down while I tell you this. It's going to take a little bit of believing."

Nodding, he took his seat, and I sat on the top step of the porch and hesitantly started to tell him my version of events, beginning with Chloe and ending with my arrival at the bowls green.

Speaking it all out loud, my words aimed mainly at my feet, was cathartic for my soul. By the time I'd finished, I was surprised by how much better I felt.

"I know it sounds crazy, but it's the truth."

Finally, looking up, I could see that George believed me. His face had paled beneath the worn tan of afternoons spent gardening, and his hand trembled slightly as he raised his glass and drained it. I may have felt better for sharing my story, but George Leicester was definitely worse for hearing it. For what seemed like a long while he said nothing, before finally leaning back in his chair, pulling a pouch of tobacco from his shirt pocket and refilling his pipe.

Sulphur blazed from the end of the match as he held it in the carved wooden bowl and sucked in, aromatic smoke rising up between us. I've got to give him his due, the shake in his hand was barely visible. I'd had weeks to adjust to the changes in Chloe, to get used to the madness, and still the things I'd seen this morning had nearly driven me to insanity. George had to take it all on my words and the evidence of the silent waiting world around us.

He puffed on his pipe for a few moments before speaking, his voice low. "So, your doctor told you this wasn't just local, this thing that's happened in Stony?"

I nodded. "He said worldwide. I don't know how true that is, but I think we can definitely say nationwide."

He sighed and nodded. "I guess that's probably right. But if it's okay with you, then I'm going to go on pretending my Mary and her boy are just fine and on holiday for a little while longer. Just for a little while longer."

He leaned forward, resting his elbows on his knees, staring out towards the gate, and I couldn't think of anything to say to that. I wished I could imagine that Chloe was sitting somewhere on a beach in Tenerife looking beautiful in her jade bikini, smiling over her shoulder and blowing me a kiss. My heart ached sitting there in the sunshine, early summer bees buzzing through the flowers in the borders. It ached for me, and it ached for George. He was too intelligent and long in the tooth to be able to fool himself for long.

We didn't speak, but grieved silently for our lost worlds and lost loves, strangers thrown together, listening to songs from an era long ago dead as time drifted past us.

I don't know how long we sat there, but I was absorbed in my own thoughts when George stood up.

"Well, well, well, Matthew. We've got company."

Suddenly back in the present, I was on my feet before I even knew I'd moved, my heart pounding inside my jumper, a smile cracking my face. Three men were walking awkwardly up the side path, glancing at each other occasionally as they approached, their clumsiness suggesting that they were as much strangers to each other as George and I were.

They certainly didn't look like friends at any rate. The one who'd taken the lead had to be in his late-thirties or early forties and was wearing an untidy grey suit with a grubby white shirt hanging untucked beneath it. His dark hair was receding, and even from a distance his exposed forehead gleamed with a layer of sweat. Slightly behind him came the other two, a gangly teenager in a baseball cap and a large fifty-something man in a sweatshirt and jeans.

What they all had in common were the wary expressions on their faces as they got closer, probably similar to that on mine when I had first laid eyes on George just a short while before. Standing tall and strong beside me, somewhat like Gregory Peck in his later years, he looked at me and smiled before waving at our new arrivals.

"Well, I think we'd better get a fresh pot of coffee on. And pour out a few whiskeys. It seems the world isn't quite as empty as I first thought."

Chapter Seven

Our guests had the fine idea of mixing their coffee and alcohol, and we were on our second cup of homemade Irish coffee by the time they were ready to share their stories. George and I had already told ours while calming them down and waiting for the coffeepot to stop bubbling, and we all sat round a table, two on the banquette and three on chairs and stools.

"It all went really crazy when I got in from work last night."

The man in the suit's name was Nigel Phelps, and even though we were sitting inside, his skin still oozed with fresh sweat. I was glad he'd kept his jacket on. I could only imagine the reeking patches of damp that were probably sticking his shirt to his flesh underneath.

"I mean, things had been bad before, but I hadn't really realised how much she'd changed until then. I just thought, well, hoped, that soon she'd get back to normal. I could even have coped with the weight she'd put on, just as long as she was back to being my Mandy again."

It was like listening to an echo of my own experience with Chloe, except Nigel hadn't had pregnancy to blame it on. His eyes flicked around the table as he spoke, not really settling on any one person.

"I've never been very good with dealing with women issues, and when she started, you know, becoming so different...well, I just threw myself into my job." He shrugged, and I thought I saw a slight wobble in his mouth, as if he were biting back tears.

"That was easy, because there were so many people off sick. I don't know why I didn't notice it. I don't think I've been noticing very much these past few weeks."

I nodded. "You're not the only one. I think we've all been in the same boat."

Sniffing, he gave me a half-smile before his eyes darkened, memories clouding his face.

"When I get in from work, I normally get changed and maybe go for a quick drink or so and then we have a late dinner, about eight. Yesterday, I didn't even make it upstairs. She was eating raw bacon, *eating it straight from the packet,* and when I asked her what the hell she was doing, she spat it at me. And then the next thing I knew, I was on the floor and I couldn't move. Paralysed."

George glanced at me, his mouth set grimly, recognising my own story in the other man's. Nigel took a shaky mouthful of his fortified coffee, his voice trembling.

"I was there for hours. All night, stuck to the same spot, not able to move or speak. I've never been so scared in all my life. She'd taken to spending a lot of time in our bedroom, just sitting on the bed and staring at nothing, and for most of last night that's where she was. I just sat there in the dark, wondering if I was going mad." He paused again. "And then eventually she came back down and sat on the sofa, right in front of me."

Tears were flowing down his ruddy face as his voice dropped to a whisper. "She was shaking. Shaking and twisting and turning, and laughing. Somewhere between laughing and crying, anyway. And something was happening inside her...blood leaking from her... and then...and then...this, *this thing* came out of her, this huge white thing, covered in some kind of birthing sack smeared with her blood. It wriggled out of the membrane and unfolded itself. God, it was awful, horrible, like some awful monster spider...." He buried his head in his hands, sobbing freely. "And it had come out of her...my Mandy. It had been growing in her all that time....God, I'd been sleeping in bed next to her with that thing growing."

I'd had the same thought myself, but tried to ignore it. We waited in silence until he'd composed himself, but it was George that asked the question.

"How did you get away?"

Nigel kept his head low, his voice slightly whiney. "For a brief moment after it came out of her, she lost her hold on me and I got up and ran. Ran for my life." His words were hollow.

I patted him on the back of the shoulder in support. Not that I thought it was going to really make him any better. I didn't know what could make things better for any of us. "It might not feel like it now, but you were lucky. We all are, given what we've seen today." I smiled at him. "You must be pretty fit, because when Chloe let me free, I could barely stand, let alone run."

His eyes flashed at me, and I could feel him bristling beneath his clothes.

"Well, that's how it happened. Are you saying you don't believe me?"

His manner turned almost instantly, his voice a snarl. What the hell had got him so defensive? Raising my hands up in front of me in a gesture of surrender, I shook my head. "No, no...not at all, I was just trying to say you were lucky to get out. I just keep thinking about that man in the café. That's all."

His shoulders slumped. "Sorry. Sorry. Don't know what came over me."

George refilled his cup. "It's okay. We've all been through a hell of a thing. Tempers are going to be frayed. We've just got to keep a check on it."

Dave Randall, the older man, leaned back in his chair, shaking his head slowly. "Well, after what I've heard from you two," he nodded at Nigel and then me, "I think I got away lightly. My story's pretty mundane. I'm not married, never have been. I prefer the bachelor life of golf and beer. It's less complicated."

Unlike Nigel's had been, his gaze was open and direct.

"Well, anyway, with no women in my life in any significant way, I didn't have anything at home to raise any alarm bells, and I run a garage, so my workforce is all male. A couple of them have been having a lot of time off with sickness recently, and it's been getting so bad that if they hadn't been married with young families I'd have considered letting them go. I guess that must have been down to all this business."

Leaning forward, he rested his arms on the table.

"I'd like to say I noticed the changes in women, but I just didn't. I'm quite shocked, you know. I never realised just how little attention I pay them until now. And I have been having a lot of headaches—I guess that's been distracting me. I almost went to the doctor last week, that's how bad they've been." He idly massaged one temple. "I don't have one today, though. In fact, I woke up feeling fantastic, only to find the world had disappeared. Thank God for your music, George, otherwise Christ only knows what I might have wandered into."

He pulled a packet of cigarettes from the back pocket of his jeans and lit one. I'd given up over five years ago and thought I was past the cravings, but it took all my willpower not to grab one myself and suck in the nicotine. Suddenly lung cancer and heart disease didn't seem like such a threat. I watched him jealously as he smoked and I talked.

"I think the headaches were caused by the women. I had them, and I know others did, too." I remembered Matt in Tesco's and wondered what had become of him this morning before pushing it away. Too much imagination could be a bad thing. "Maybe you were getting them from women around you."

He nodded. "Could be. I live in one of those big flats in that converted house down by the river. The one next to me is shared by some young women." He smiled slightly, but it was a smile haunted by the knowledge of what they must have become.

"I always wanted them to lure me into their flat and divide me up between them. But I didn't expect it to be as dinner. Jesus." The reality of the situation seemed to be dawning on him and he sunk into a reflective silence, mulling it over.

A delicate hand reached out and dipped into Dave's cigarettes without asking, the pale fingers slim and long. From beneath the baseball cap, a plume of smoke rose up. I watched the enigmatic young man who'd only spoken one word since his arrival, and that was to give his name.

"So what about you, John? Do you want to talk about it? You might feel better for it." I tried not to sound patronising, but it was difficult. He was only eighteen or nineteen and dressed in over-baggy jeans and a *The Darkness* T-shirt. I couldn't even guess at what was going through his mind.

"I'll tell you. I guess it doesn't matter anymore." His voice was surprisingly deep and calm. "I had the headaches, too. I live…," he corrected himself quickly, a tremor hanging in his voice. "I *lived* with my mum. Just me and her. My dad cleared out years ago. She's been changing, too. Got fat. Well, she wasn't exactly thin to start with, but she got fatter. And nastier."

He drew hard on the cigarette, pulled his cap off and ran his hand through his short dark hair before replacing it.

"I killed her three days ago. Hit her over the head with a hammer in the bath. Over and over. She'd left the door unlocked and I went in for a piss and saw her laying there, something moving under her fucking awful stomach, and I knew it couldn't go on. *I* couldn't go on." He shrugged. "She just wasn't my mum anymore." Pausing, he stood up and went to the window overlooking the bowling green. "I haven't been out since. Just sat in the house not really knowing what to do. I'd pulled the shower curtain round her so I could take a piss and have a wash without having to look. I don't think I ever intended going out again. Time was moving in a haze. And then I woke up this morning and the TV and phone had gone off. Then I knew I had to go out, just to see what was going on."

The rest of us sat dumbstruck, listening to his gentle voice. Jesus, his story was as chilling as mine and Nigel's. This kid was stronger than I'd first thought. He glanced back at us, and I could see the pain in his face.

"Nothing came out of her, though. I must have killed that, too. I'm glad about that. I'm really glad about that."

Leaving the window, he went behind the bar and pulled out four or five packets of crisps and threw some at our table.

"I don't know about you, but I'm fucking starving."

I stared at him a minute before ripping open a packet and crunching on a handful. I'd had a decent breakfast, but my body was ravenous for more food. George refilled his pipe and stepped back out onto the wide porch, and we all followed. Placing the needle back on the record that had been silent for a while, he turned the volume down slightly so we could hear ourselves.

Leaning on the pretty white wooden railings, Dave contemplated the contents of his bag, chewing slowly.

"So, what do you think that thing was doing to the man in the café?"

"I think it was eating him. In fact, I'm pretty sure it was eating him."

Pleease...help me.

The memory of his plea itched at me, lodged itself in my conscience, and I was glad when George joined in.

"Or maybe mating with him. Who knows how much of their original hosts have survived in them? Do they still need us to reproduce?"

It was a horrible thought, and Dave screwed up his half-eaten crisps. "Or maybe both. Maybe it was mating with him and *then* eating him, like some kind of black widow spider."

I raised an eyebrow. "Oh, that's much more cheerful."

Dave peered at the skyline of uneven houses that marked out High Street in the distance. "God, there must be thousands of them out there."

John was still in the doorway. "Isn't it preying mantises that do that? Eat their mates?"

George ignored the boy's remark and smiled. "Widows. I like that. I think that's what I'm going to call them. Widows. What do you think, Matt?"

"You haven't seen them. That's far too human for what they are. And anyway, they're white. Or near enough." I shivered at the memory, my stomach clenching.

"Sometimes you have to give your enemy a human face. It's makes them less terrifying. And if that thing *was* eating the man in the flat, then 'widows' isn't that inappropriate, is it?"

I nodded at the old man. "I'll take your word for it." We had to call them something, so if he was taken with that, then I didn't give enough of a shit to argue the case. And he was right. We couldn't go on calling them *things* or spiders. They sure as hell weren't spiders, not entirely at any rate. They were something new. Something different.

"What the fuck is that?" Nigel gripped at my arm, staring into the far corner of the bowling green near the gate.

"What?" I followed his gaze, and sure enough there was a slight quivering in the hedge far down on the left.

"Do you think it's one of them? The widows?" The whine was back in his voice and there was something about it that I found unpleasant.

"No, I don't. Not unless they've taken to wearing clothes." Leaning forward I could just make out a flash of colour here and there. Whatever was hiding in there it was wearing jeans and a T-shirt. Nigel, however, wasn't taking my word for it and scurried back into the clubhouse behind John's lanky frame.

"It's okay!" I shouted over the music at the brief glimpses of clothes. "We're all okay! Come out. You'll be safer with us. I promise we won't hurt you."

A moment of silence passed and then two figures emerged nervously onto the path.

"Well, I'll be." George muttered from behind his pipe, and inside I echoed his sentiment. It was a young woman and a little girl. They approached cautiously as we stared, the woman gripping the girl's hand.

Both wore jeans and had their long chestnut curls pulled back into ponytails. As they came up the stairs, the young woman stared at us cautiously, but her eyes seemed to flicker slightly with recognition when she glanced at me and I thought I knew why.

"Was it you that was following me earlier?"

She nodded, and I tried not to notice how pretty she was. It didn't seem right to even think about it, not so soon after Chloe. But still, I found myself staring at her smooth skin and wide eyes just slightly too much, drawn in by the blend of green and hazel that flickered there. She could only have been about twenty-one or twenty-two. I felt a pang of delicate hope. If she were alive, then maybe this hadn't happened to all women. Maybe there were more that were unaffected. *Uninfected.* The thought was so good it terrified me. I just needed to focus on these two. These two girls and us. There was too much to think about and I was pretty sure that we'd find out what state the world was in before too long.

George handed her a coffee and she took a sip before speaking.

"Yes, that was us. We'd come down from Wolverton. The only person we'd seen up there fired an air-gun at us and only just missed. He was yelling at us like he hated us." She frowned slightly. "After that, we weren't in a hurry to make friends quickly. We almost approached you, but then when I saw you kicking that shop grille, well, you scared us a bit. We couldn't take the risk."

"Yeah, I can see how I must have looked." I tried my best winning smile on her, but she didn't look convinced. "Matthew Edge." I held out my hand and she took it and shook it, which was a start.

"Katherine...Katie Parker. And this is my little sister, Jane."

The girl couldn't have been more than eleven or twelve, and she hid slightly behind her sister's slim body, her wide suspicious eyes peering out at us. She seemed to calm slightly as George held his hand out to introduce himself and it didn't surprise me. There was something very reassuring about George Leicester that went beyond his age.

"Well, we're very pleased to have you among us, Jane."

I nodded in agreement. "Why don't you join us? We're not really sure what we're doing yet, but whatever we decide, you're welcome to come along if you want." I was eager for their company and I could see George was, too. What would Katie and Jane be to him? A replacement for his lost daughter and grand-children? Perhaps what they represented to us didn't really matter. Perhaps the crux of it was that no matter how much we had moaned and complained about them in the past, a world without women seemed like a bleak place to exist in.

"You lot must be fucking joking!"

Nigel barged past John and Dave, forcing his way up to us, and Jane recoiled from his outburst.

"They can't come with us!" His face was red with aggression and small darts of spit flew from his mouth. "That man with the airgun had the right idea. They'll turn into those things...the widows. They can't fuck-ing come with us!"

There was a quiver of fear in Katie's strong face at the mention of the widows, and I realised in that moment that I didn't like Nigel Phelps too much and I doubted I was ever going to. My disgust must've showed on my face, because he hesitated for a second and stared at me before his eyes sought reassurance from the others. He didn't find it.

"I admit I don't know much about women and chil-dren, but even I can see you're scaring the child." Dave's voice was quiet and controlled. "And they both look pretty healthy to me."

"Those things could be growing in them. Don't you get it? You didn't see them." Sweat dripped from the damp curls at the nape of his neck.

George smiled gently. "In those waists? I doubt it."

"They're staying with us, Nigel. It seems the ma-jority are in agreement."

"I'll go along with that." John's words escaped with a mouthful of smoke from somewhere just over my shoulder.

"So that's everyone but you. Of course, if you're not happy with that, then you can go off on your own. You're not obliged to stay with us."

His gaze darted hesitantly around the group, and for a moment the awkward silence hung so heavily in the air that I thought only a rumble of thunder from above could break it. As it turned out, it was Jane. She had crept out from the cover of Katie and climbed the first two of the wooden stairs.

"Aren't you Emma's dad?" Her words were almost not there as she stared at Nigel.

"What?" Spinning round, it was like he was really seeing her for the first time, as a person, a little girl rather than some potential monster.

"Emma Phelps? I was in her class. 7M. I came to a sleepover at your house a couple of months ago and you took us all to McDonalds." Her sweet face broke into a hesitant smile. "It was really nice that day, Mr. Phelps. Thank you."

His cheeks wobbled with emotion as he stared at the child, tears welling up once again. I felt a frown pinch my forehead. Why hadn't he mentioned having a child? And where had she been during his final day with his wife?

Jane glanced around. "Is Emma here?"

Nigel moaned and turned, his slouched frame heading back into the clubhouse. We let him go. Whatever story he had to tell about his daughter, this obviously wasn't the time. Still, despite everything he'd been through, I couldn't bring myself to like him.

"No, honey." George crouched on the stair. "Emma's not here."

Jane just nodded as if she really hadn't expected any different, and then sat on the bottom step staring into the distance. Dave came out and gave her a bottle of coke, which she took without saying a word as the rest of us gathered on the porch. George turned the music off.

"I think that's done its job now. Anyone else out there obviously doesn't want to join us, so I guess this is it." He lifted Gracie Fields carefully from the record player and slid the vinyl regretfully back into its sleeve before putting it with the others on the small table.

"Now all we have to do is decide what we're going to do from now. We can't stay here forever."

He was right. This had been a good gathering place, but it was time to move on. It was almost half past two and the day was ebbing away from us, and I for one didn't want to find myself outside and unprepared tonight. Who knew what the widows would do when night fell?

Dave must have been thinking about the new species amongst us too, although his voice was lighter in tone than I was feeling.

"Well, at least we haven't seen any out and about yet. That's got to be a good thing." He seemed to take comfort in that until John shook his head, resting his thin body on the railings.

"I wouldn't read too much into it. They're new-born. How many newborn animals do you know that just get out into the world the minute they arrive? None." He paused. "And these don't have any mothers to show them the ropes. Not of their own kind, anyway."

I nodded, the memory of that flat above the café flashing again unwelcome in my head. "And they've got a supply of food. At least for a while."

Despite the sunshine, I think we all shivered.

John threw down his butt and ground it out. "They're going to take a little time to adjust. But personally, I want to get the hell away from here before they start exploring their new world."

"I second that." George picked up the dirty glasses and coffee cups to take inside, as if it made a difference now.

"We should go up to the city shopping centre." It was the first time Katie had spoken. "Get some supplies, like sleeping bags and things. They should have everything we need there."

She was right. The city centre would be a good place to go. I certainly didn't fancy working my way through the Stony shops. "That's a good plan. And there shouldn't be too many widows around. It's a working place, not a living place. From what I've seen so far, most people got trapped at home."

George emerged with Nigel in time to catch the end of the conversation.

"Just one problem there, Matt. I don't have a car, and to be honest, its years since I've driven. Probably won't be much use to you there."

I grinned at him. "Don't worry, you can be the navigator."

"But he has got a point. What are we going to do for cars? I walked here." Dave shrugged, a little embarrassed by his obvious bachelor lifestyle. "I've got one at home, but it's a little sporty thing. Not really ideal for carrying stuff."

"We need four-wheel drives. They'll be the best. Range Rovers or Land Rovers. Who knows where we'll have to take them, and they've got plenty of space." My adrenaline was starting to pump again with the thought of moving, of *doing* something.

John pushed his hat slightly back on his head, revealing sharp blue eyes. "Well, we'd better go and find some then. Stony's not a poor town. I bet there's plenty dotted around. We've just got to find three or four and then get the keys."

The idea of getting the keys wasn't pleasant. That meant getting into peoples houses, and although I could see the necessity, it was a sobering thought.

Moving slightly forward, Nigel glared at the young man. "Can't you hot-wire them or something?"

"Just 'cos I'm under twenty and don't wear a suit doesn't make me a criminal. Sorry to disappoint you." He turned away, but the dangerous snarl was visible. It seemed that it wasn't only me that had taken a dislike to Phelps.

CHAPTER EIGHT

Having arranged to meet up again at the large round-about at the top end of the village in an hour, we split up to find some transport. George had paired Katie with me and, despite the wave of guilt and grief that followed it, I felt a small thrill surge through me when she smiled. Maybe she was pleased to be with me, too. I couldn't help it. I liked that thought.

We walked silently in single file, Jane protected as best she could be between us, and in Katie's firm grip was the knife I'd fled from the café with. There'd been a moment when it had looked as if Nigel was going to argue that he and George needed it more, but he'd wisely shut his mouth, his bottom lip trembling and moist. If he hadn't kept himself quiet then I might have forced him into it. However, Jane seemed to unsettle him and make him edgy, and that silenced him. His eyes couldn't rest on her. It was strange; you'd think she would bring out his paternal side and make him more protective, but as far as I could tell he just wanted to stay as far from her as possible.

Small flies gathered buzzing around my head as we cautiously passed The Plough, and I could see them forming haloes above the girls ahead of me. Jane swatted around her impatiently, but Katie ignored them, her slim frame striding forward like some kind of jungle huntress, out of place amongst the brick and concrete surroundings. Although, as the encroaching oppressive heat of the afternoon promised to end this first day of our changed world in an angry downpour, I wondered if she was that out of place at all. There was no safety left in the walls we'd built to protect ourselves. The Englishman's home was no longer his castle. It had become a nest of widows.

We paused at the narrow cobbled road that led into Horsefair Green. In the long summer days, rock, jazz and folk bands would play on makeshift stages, entertaining lazy crowds relaxing on the grass, and in the cooler months of April and May it would be host to numerous fairs and fetes. The green with the bandstand was a sought after living area, the small terraces that surrounded it fetching huge sums for the charming but very small living space they provided. And I should know. In that past life of less than a week before, someone from the Green putting their house on the market would set my heart racing. They sold themselves and it was an easy bonus.

Along with the smaller properties there were also several very beautiful larger houses, some almost medieval cottages, and others more Georgian in look, with their large windows peering down from impressive whitewashed walls. They were all terraced, and as we stared ahead of us, what had only a few days ago been a beautiful, if slightly quaint, view, was now claustrophobic and brooding. It seemed as if the houses were glaring at us threateningly, daring us to come forward. The small roads at the far two corners seemed a long way away. Too far away.

"Well, I don't want to sound paranoid," Katie's voice was low and soft, "but I'm not sure I want to go in there." With her free hand I noticed she'd reached for Jane. The child looked up at her sister, and there was more than a little fear in those wide eyes.

I glanced from the women to the green and back again, mulling it over. If I were honest, I wasn't keen to wander into such a densely populated part of the village myself, not with only one small weapon and a woman and a child. The memory of that man in the café flashed again in my head and I shivered, a ripple of nausea and fear twisting my nerves. If the widows ambushed us, then I doubted there would be much we could do. I wondered how fast they could move. On eight legs, however pale and spindly, I figured they could easily keep up with us. Too easily.

I wasn't talking myself into going forward, that was for sure, but this was the part of town we'd agreed to check out and I didn't want to let the others down. Hell, I didn't want to let myself down. And a very small part of me didn't want to look like a coward in front of Katie. I guess when you think there's only one grown and normal woman in the world and she happens to be gorgeous, then the built-in need to impress tends to take over.

So I stood there and dithered until Jane's small voice broke into my hesitation.

"What about that car there? It's like a pickup truck."

Turning round, I found myself facing her ponytail as

she looked the other way, pointing across the road. I scanned the street.

"Where?"

"There." Her finger stretched. She wasn't pointing at the pavement, but behind it, at the small tucked-away piece of tarmac that served as the car park for The Plough, and I could see what had drawn her attention. Sticking out from the red brick rear wall of the deserted car park was a large shiny black tail end of a beast of a car.

"That looks perfect." Grinning at the girl, I patted her firmly on the shoulder. "Well done, Jane." She smiled back at me and it was good to see. "Let's go and take a look."

Re-crossing the deserted road, the girls waited on the other side of the low wall while I scouted round the side of the building. There were no signs of any widows and only two cars; the old battered Ford Escort with the tatty paintwork parked in front of the back door, which must have belonged to the landlord, and then the glistening silver and black bodywork of the imposing Mitsubishi Animal that cast its shadow far over the tarmac ground. The wheels were huge, raising it far up from the ground and the height of it appealed to me. Anything that would improve my viewing range seemed like a good idea to me. The rear pickup area was covered over with a hard black roof that looked easy enough to remove, but tough enough to protect the contents from whatever we had to face. At least *I hoped* it would be tough enough. If it wasn't, then neither would anything else.

Peering through the tinted glass I could make out two large seats in the back and two in the front, and it seemed to have all the mod cons. The petrol gauge dimly pointed close to the full mark. As far as luck went, we couldn't really have asked for more, apart from maybe having the keys sitting neatly in the ignition, and that they certainly weren't. The number plate gleamed up at me. H5 SNK. Personalised. But meaningless now.

I trotted back to the others, and Katie pushed a few loose curls behind one ear, impatient as she spoke. "Well?"

"Yeah, it looks perfect. No keys, though. And I don't have the first idea how to start a car without them."

The sun glared at us from above, and Katie was still squinting, even with her hand shielding her eyes.

"Maybe whoever owns it is still inside."

I weighed the likely outcomes of that scenario and wasn't pleased with any of them. Getting my hand into the pocket of a cocooned man was not tops on my list of preferred actions and I hoped it wouldn't come to that.

"Maybe, but maybe not. The bloke that runs this place is really tight on drunk driving. He's known for taking keys from his customers when he thinks they've had too many. He's been like that ever since one of them drove into a couple walking down London Road. Killed the man outright and left the woman in a wheelchair."

I looked back at the building behind us. "It could be he's just hung the keys behind the bar and sent the owner home on foot or in a cab."

Katie sighed and shrugged. "I suppose there's only one way we're going to find out."

"Correction. There's only one way *I'm* going to find out. You two can wait out here." Katie hadn't been forthcoming with her and Jane's experiences of the widows, but I doubted they'd seen anything like I had in the café. And I didn't want them to. Especially not Jane. She may not have brought out the paternal streak in Nigel Phelps, but I had a bank of building father feelings for my own never to be born child, and they were finding an exit in her.

"Oh right. Like we're going to stay out here on our own. I don't think so. And anyway, we have the knife."

"I was hoping to take that with me."

She smiled sweetly. "If you think I'm letting go of this, then you've got another thing coming. Now come on. I'll try the front bar door."

Jane rolled her eyes at me as if this stubbornness was something that she was used to, and we both watched as Katie strolled away. That chin-up determination reminded me of Chloe, and that wasn't helping me fight the attraction. She disappeared for a second round the corner and then returned, shaking her head. "Locked."

I figured we could break in if we had to, but I wasn't keen on making too much noise anymore. Not now that I knew there were probably inhabitants. I nodded towards the wooden archway of the side bar. "You try that one. I'll try the back door."

Leaving them there, I trotted back into the shadowy rear of the building, past the huge car that was our target, and came to a stop in the small gap between the battered Escort and the dusty, neglected chipped black wood of the door. Twisting the handle, expecting to feel the resistance of the lock, I held my breath in surprise as it pushed open with ease, silently slicing through the dark air inside.

The footfalls behind me seemed far too loud, and without turning I whispered to them, "It's open."

I'd taken my jumper off on the walk from the bowls club and now I untied it from my waist and quietly pulled it on. The heat was still sticky, but I wanted as much protection as possible and the thought of going in there with bare arms made my stomach turn. I stepped over the thin wooden lintel into the gloomy hallway, the girls following me. To our right there was an open door leading into the industrial metal gleam of the pub kitchen, a faint smell of stale oil drifting from it, and to our left was the door leading to the downstairs bar. Ahead were the stairs leading up to the living quarters, two dog leads hanging over the side. I didn't wonder where the dogs might be. There was no need to. The answer was obvious, staring at us from everywhere we looked.

"Oh shit." Katie breathed behind me. "Oh shit, oh shit, oh shit."

It looked like winter had settled in there, every surface covered with pale, shiny strands, like cobwebs covered in frost, but not quite, too thick, their heavy substance stretching from stairs to walls to tables, with no sense of rhyme or reason and none of the intricate beauty and structure of a spider's web. The translucent colour, so like those awful legs, shone in blues and pinks in the reflected light, and they left trails of some kind of slime wherever they had been, darker and more glutinous than the strands themselves. I wondered what would happen if you touched it, but I wasn't keen to find out. When Katie's soft hand gently brushed my shoulder I almost screamed.

"You know what you said about you coming in here on your own?"

I nodded.

"Well, you know, on second thought I think that sounds fine by me." Her whisper was so quiet I had to strain to hear it. "I'll even give you the knife."

"You're too kind."

"Think nothing of it."

Reaching back, I took the offered weapon, the handle slightly damp from where it had been gripped so tightly in her hand. "Stay here in the doorway. If you hear anything moving upstairs, then call me. Not too loud, though." The last thing I wanted was us drawing attention to ourselves.

"Okay." Her breath tickled the back of my neck.

"If you *see* anything on the other hand, then scream."

"I wouldn't worry too much about that. I don't think a scream will be much of a problem." A finger poked into my ribs. "Now stop stalling."

Unconsciously sucking in a deep breath, I took a small step to my left, ducking low to avoid my head touching one of those slimy ropes, and slowly moved as quietly as possible through the doorway into the bar. The murmur of my trainers on the lino below seemed like a shriek in the silence as I looked carefully round.

The dark green curtains were pulled across the windows all along the far wall creating an empty, false dusk, only occasional shafts of light from the gaps hitting dusty tables, some still littered with dirty ashtrays, and one with a glass, an inch of beer stale in its base. Multicoloured lights from the machines flashed at me, teasing and tempting any potential customer to part with his money in an attempt to win the elusive jackpot. It was going to be waiting a long time.

For a moment I had a glimpse of that machine blazing away for decades until its parts slowly gave out, grinding down to stop, waiting so patiently in vain for someone to play with it. I shivered, and moved on. This was no time for chilling imaginings; there was enough in the here and now, *right above my head,* to keep my imagination and fear fully engaged. Looking around at the abandoned pub, I figured that although the landlord may have locked the doors, he certainly didn't have his mind on the job last night. The drip trays were dirty beneath the pumps, and dishes of drying sliced lemon still sat on the sides. I felt as if I'd stepped onto a ghost ship.

Thankfully, there were less of the shimmering strands in the bar, although sludge covered most of the bottles against the mirrored back walls next to the till. Making sure I didn't touch it, I crouched down to duck beneath one thick thread that had spread like a creeper of ivy in through the door. I heard my knee click and cursed as I pushed myself up from the squat, my thighs aching slightly. Something told me that if I was going to survive for long, I was going to have to have to get fitter. And quickly. It didn't help that the tension had my muscles wound so tight that they felt they were going to snap. The knife safely in my grasp, I could have tried cutting through the strands, but something stopped me; I was shit-scared of what would happen if I did. What the hell did I know about these new nightmarish creatures? What if there was some kind of sensory link between this sticky web-like substance and its creator, who was probably only a few feet above my head somewhere? I didn't have any intention of finding out; unless I had no choice that was something I was going to avoid.

Letting my breath out slowly, I moved onwards.

The pub had originally been divided into two completely separate rooms, and although several years before it had been opened up to become one large one, the serving area still had a dividing wall with an archway running between them. It was on the other side of this arch that the key hooks were, nailed into the wall. Only a few feet away, it seemed to be taking me forever to reach it, my heart thumping and my mouth dry. If one of the widows chose now to come downstairs, then there was no way I would make it .back to the door. I'd be cut off from the others, trapped. And I wouldn't blame them for not sticking around to help.

The thought spurred me on and I took three long strides to reach the arch. Peering round, I was relieved to see this part of the pub lounge as empty as the rest, no creature ready to pounce on me, nor any cocooned half-alive helpless people; just a sea of chairs and tables dozing in the stale air behind bar stools that wouldn't be filled this lunchtime, or any time in the foreseeable future.

Keeping my body in the archway, I twisted to see the hooks and my heart leapt, a small hiss of air escaping me. There was one set of car keys hanging alone, the metal key ring declaring it an Animal. That was our baby. Less cautious now, eager to get away, I grabbed them, ignoring the metal jangling they made as they tried to cling to the hook rather than my sweaty fingers, wrenching them free from the wall as I turned back. Ducking under the creeping strand, my joints feeling more flexible this time, something caught the corner of my eye.

"Fuck it." I muttered under my breath, and thrusting the Mitsubishi keys into my pocket, pulled forty Benson and Hedges from the narrow stacked shelf above the till. After a moments hesitation I grabbed another pack, and also the dated eighties-style Harley Davidson Zippo lighter resting on top of an open packet of Sovereign. That strange rebellious exhilaration that only smokers know overtook me, and for a brief moment I almost smiled, as if by voluntarily screwing with my health, I was somehow screwing with the order of this new and unpleasant world, giving the widows the universally acknowledged victory salute with attitude. And anyway, this was no time to be an ex-smoker.

Reaching the doorway, relieved to be getting out, I grinned at Katie as she came into view. Before I could speak, she raised an arm, and I froze where I was. Her eyes were staring up the stairs at something I couldn't see.

"Katie?" My voice was low, but the urgency in it was obvious. "What is it?"

"Move very slowly and come behind me." She still kept her eyes locked on their frustratingly-out-of-my-view target. "Keep your head down and don't speak."

Biting back my questions, I did as I was told, and taking as tiny and as smooth steps as I could, stared at the stained and grimy floor beneath me, and slid out into the corridor behind Katie's arm. From somewhere above me came a wet, angry hissing sound, and I fought the urge to run as the open back door got closer, glimpsing Jane waiting outside in the sunshine, her fearful expression no doubt a reflection of mine.

"Go and open the car and get Jane in. I'll be there in a minute."

Unable to resist, and needing to know just what the fuck was going on, I threw a quick glance over my shoulder while the top of the stairs were still in sight. I couldn't help but shudder. Half a widow was curved round the top banister, its bank of pinprick red eyes glowing angrily as it hissed, long spindly legs pawing at the dull carpet, whatever substance that flowed through its veins almost visible through their revolting milky surface. Its mouth, *its two mouths,* if they could be called that, clacked wetly as the two sets of mandibles mashed into each other.

Jesus, it seemed so full of hate, so ready to attack, except that something was stopping it, and that something was Katie. How the fuck was she doing that?

"I said go!" her voice growled at me, and I didn't need asking twice, no matter how fucking strange all this was. Dumping the cigarettes on the enormous black bonnet, I groped in my pocket for the key, pressing the unlock button before I'd even wrenched them free.

"Get in!" Yanking the back door open, I pushed Jane inside before grabbing the Bensons and getting in the driver's side. The key slid into the slot and the beast of an engine roared to life.

"Come on, Katie. Come on." The seconds seemed to be ticking by too slowly, and I couldn't see her from where we sat. Pushing the gear stick into reverse, I turned the truck, ready to pull out of the car park.

"Is she going to be okay?" Jane sounded so much younger than her years, her fragile voice like glass.

"Sure she is, honey. Sure she is." I hoped so. I really hoped so. Ripping open the packet, I thrust a cigarette into my mouth and lit it, sucking in a choking lungful of poisonous smoke and chucking the rest on the vast expanse of dashboard. My head swam as I resisted the urge to both cough and throw up, the nicotine speeding through my capillaries, and I opened the electric window slightly. God, I'd forgotten how shit cigarette smoke tasted. I could only hope it would improve with practice because I sure as hell was intending to practice.

"There she is!" Jane squealed into my ear as she leapt forward in her seat behind me. "There she is!"

My heart skipped a beat as Katie appeared from the doorway and pulled it shut before jogging round to the front passenger side of the Mitsubishi and climbing in. She stared at me for a second before reaching for a cigarette of her own.

"What are you waiting for? Fucking drive!" The lighter shook in her tiny hands, and it wasn't from the movement of the car as I pulled out onto the deserted road. I gave it a couple of seconds while she took a first stress-relieving pull and leaned back in her seat to exhale in a sigh before I spoke. Maybe she'd bite my head off, but I needed to talk about it. To find out just exactly what had happened while I was getting the keys.

"So how long had that widow been there? I thought we'd agreed you'd scream if you saw anything, not take it on head to head." I was hoping that my light tone would coax her into conversation, but when she answered there was a definite defensive edge.

"It came round the top of the landing pretty much straight away. I didn't scream because I was too damn scared." She didn't look at me but turned her face away and stared out of the window. "I would have yelled if it had started coming down the stairs, but when it saw me it stopped. And then I was too scared to move, take my eyes off it or anything."

"How weird it didn't attack. I can't believe it let us go like that."

"Maybe it just wasn't hungry."

I didn't miss the sharp snap in her reply.

"Yeah. Maybe." Neither of us believed that lack of hunger had anything to do with it, both aware that the widows were more likely to stockpile their food, but she didn't need me pointing it out. I pulled down the visor to block out the glare of the hazy afternoon.

"Anyway, I don't want to talk about it." She glared at me. "And I don't want you telling the others about it, either."

"No problem. I won't tell a soul."

She was obviously scared and confused by the experience, and I could understand her wariness of someone like Nigel hearing about it, but when she'd calmed down I'd try broaching the subject again. If she could ward the widows off, then that was something we all needed to know to use against them. Still, insensitive man or not, even I could tell this wasn't the time for that conversation.

Jane giggled behind us. "Have you seen *Doctor Who*? It's an old sci-fi series. I've been watching it on Bravo."

I nodded sagely into the rearview mirror, suddenly feeling my age as memories of hiding behind a cushion on my parents' sofa awoke behind my eyes. "Yes, thanks. I remember it the first time round."

"Well, maybe the widows are like the Daleks. They can't get down stairs."

I smiled slightly at the ludicrous idea, and when I looked at Katie I was pleased to see that colour was returning to her cheeks and some of those dark clouds had cleared in her eyes.

"Actually, young lady, the Daleks couldn't *climb*

stairs. They were always left at the bottom while the doctor and his lovely lady assistant escaped upwards."

Jane sighed. "Well, logic would dictate that if they couldn't get up the stairs, then they couldn't very well get back down them, could they?" There was a slight pause before she hit me with her final shot. "Geek."

It was enough to make us all laugh, and I wanted to turn round and kiss the girl for easing the tension, even if it was only slightly.

We pulled up at the roundabout, and even though we were well before the agreed time, it seemed that everyone else had been lucky finding four-wheel drives, because there were two Range Rovers parked up on the road. Stepping out, I was pleased to find everyone alive and well, if a little sombre.

"TVs are still off. We tried a couple and the radio in the car. Seems like we're on our own for now." Dave was leaning against the brown bonnet of one Range Rover and Katie had gone to stand next to John, where she offered him a cigarette. My heart sank slightly. I must have blown my chances. I tried to convince myself that that wasn't such a bad thing, but I couldn't fight the pang of loneliness that hit my stomach, all mixed up with Chloe and the mad new world. I needed to get away from here. It was time to leave home.

"Let's go then. City Centre?"

George handed me a sheet of paper.

"I took the liberty of making up a short list of things we might need. I thought perhaps that you, Nigel and Dave could go and see if you can track down these items, and the ladies, John and myself will take on the food halls. Drive round and meet us there when you've finished. What do you think?"

"I think that sounds fine." I glanced over at Katie,

but she was already climbing into a car next to John. Jane turned and waved at me with a big grin before she scrambled in, too. I grinned and waved back. At least someone still liked me.

Turning back, I saw that Nigel had taken the front passenger seat. "So, are we going or what?"

Dave raised an eyebrow at me as he got in and I could see that Mr. Phelps was going to be the weak link in our chain. There was something about him that just rubbed you the wrong way, and I wondered if that had been the case in his life before today. Turning the engine back on, I decided it probably was. You could bet he was the know all bloke in the pub who just joined in conversations and never realised that his company wasn't wanted because he was too thick-skinned to read the signals.

"And drive carefully. The last thing we need is an accident."

I bit my lip. "Of course I will. Although I doubt we're going to have to worry much about oncoming traffic." Turning my head I tried smiling at him, but he was scowling out the window, patches of sweat oozing down his shirt sides and onto the leather of the seat. What had pissed him off, I didn't know, but I hoped he'd get over it. We didn't need any rows. We all needed each other whether we liked it or not.

CHAPTER NINE

It had to be said that George's list was pretty comprehensive; sleeping bags, camping gas, outdoor clothing, rucksacks, wire cutters and tin openers for a start. At the bottom he'd added in a small note not to forget anything we could think of that would work as weapons. Old he may have been, but I was glad we had him.

We parked up at the top of the T-shaped shopping complex and pushed through the swing doors into the glass and marble vastness. At least there weren't too many houses on this side of the centre, but we all glanced round warily. We hadn't discussed each other's experiences of getting the cars, but I could bet they'd both seen plenty more evidence of the widows. Not that Nigel had needed it. He knew all about them firsthand, just like me. Still, I found it hard to find any sympathy for him and was slightly self-disgusted, but that didn't change the way I felt.

I shivered in the chill of the air-conditioned emptiness and we padded forward towards John Lewis. The huge store was likely to have pretty much everything we'd need, and if it didn't we'd start exploring further.

"This is too strange. I've never seen this place empty." Dave wasn't whispering, but as soon as his first words started to echo around us, he lowered his voice to an almost reverential hushed tone.

I knew what he meant. Tesco's had been weird, but this was definitely worse. The Milton Keynes Shopping Centre had been the first of its kind in England, a mammoth construction of glass, marble and stainless steel that had been added to as the years passed, its huge walkways filled with every branded shop you could imagine, and a selection of individual boutiques and small stalls of jewellery, ice cream, cookies and frozen yoghurt. People came here in coach loads, and even during weekdays it was always busy. Christmas was a nightmare, but every day was busy. Until today. Today it had become a giant empty mausoleum. We were like ghosts walking amongst the ruins of a past civilisation, and for another brief second I felt a shiver of nausea as the reality of it all once again took hold and the world shimmered too brightly.

Nigel sniffed. "In some ways, this is the best I've ever seen it. No kids tripping you up anywhere and mums getting in the way with their damn pushchairs and screaming brats. I never could stand it up here."

"You're something else, aren't you?" Dave shook his head in disgust, and stepping a little away from them, my heartbeat quickened slightly. Nigel had better watch himself. Dave may have been older, but I'd have bet he was in better shape and knew how to handle himself.

"Doesn't this bother you at all?" He snarled at the other man, who ducked his greasy head. "The place is fucking deserted. There is no one fucking left but us. Everyone is dead or worse. Don't you get it?"

The echo added to the ferocity of his attack and Nigel glanced up at me for support, his confidence gone and his chin wobbly. "Everyone has their own way of coping." He whined, his wide red-rimmed eyes shaking slightly, "You were lucky, Dave. You didn't have to go through what Matt and I did. A thing like that changes a man. Doesn't it, Matt? You know what I'm talking about, don't you?"

Keeping my gaze forward, I didn't answer. I didn't like him trying to pull me in as an ally in his little battle with himself and the rest of us. He was nothing like me, and I hoped that whatever happened I would never be anything like him. As it was, something else caught my eye.

"Hey, Dave, it seems we're not the only ones left, after all. Someone else has been here."

The closer we got to the large front of the store, the clearer the thick sheets of broken glass that covered the ground in front of it were, and we jogged the final few metres, Nigel panting a few steps behind. A large television lay in the window display. Dave whistled as he surveyed the scene.

"Well, well, well. Someone's saved us a job, anyway." He grinned at me. "Maybe they're still here. They could join up with us. Safety in numbers. Yeah, that'd be good."

I smiled back at him, my own spirits rising. It was good to know that we weren't alone in this desolation. That there were other people out there determined to survive.

"I suggest we go cautiously. We don't know what they're like. They might be dangerous." Nigel had quickly regained some pomposity, but this time Dave didn't bite, and just ignored him. It was all he deserved. I sure as hell didn't want to speak to him. No wonder the world had got itself into this state with people like him filling it with paranoia and suspicion. Nigel looked put out by our lack of response but didn't say any more, and instead just hung back and muttered something to himself as we made our way into the store.

"Hello?" Dave called out into the vast expanse of perfume and makeup counters. "Hello? Can anyone hear me?"

He called again as we moved further inside to the central block, where the escalators and lifts were, but no one called back. Middle age seemed to sink back into Dave's features and I gripped his shoulder.

"We'll call out for them on every floor. We may find someone. Or maybe they were here this morning and left a while ago. The important thing is that someone *was* here. It shows we're definitely not on our own. Who knows, there may be thousands and thousands of small groups like ours out there." I grinned at him, buoyed by the optimism of my own words, even though I could sense the emptiness of the building around me. It was true though. It was enough to know that despite everything, people were still trying to survive.

"I won't be calling out for anyone. If I see someone, that's fine. But I'm not shouting out." Nigel's voice was sullen rather than defiant, and his tone spoilt the value of his comment. "I don't want to let any widows know we're here." His final words were muttered under his breath as he stepped towards the frozen escalator. "Not that you'd have thought of that, no *the important thing is that someone was here.*" His face twisted as he mimicked me, and I fought the burning desire to punch him hard whilst pushing back the thought of how pleasant it might be if Nigel did come across a widow and save us all a lot of strain.

"Good point. Maybe we'll be better just looking out for ourselves for now and keeping the noise down." Dave's jaw was clenched as he stared at Nigel; his meaning wasn't lost on me. "But God, I hope we bump into some new allies."

Nigel was already climbing the steel stairs that someone had thought were important to turn off.

"I need some new clothes. These stink. Shall we start there?"

"Tell you what," I called up at his retreating figure. "Why don't you get the outdoor clothing, sweaters, thick socks and walking boots and meet us down here in half an hour? I'll get the camping equipment, and Dave can get the rest." I glanced at Dave. "If that's all right with you, mate."

The older man nodded. We both needed a little down time from our companion and this seemed the best way to do it. We were stressed enough without having to cope with Nigel on top of everything.

"Fine. That's what we'll do then." I'd walked off before Nigel's shocked brain could get a whine out about how stupid splitting up was. And maybe he was right, but at that moment I truly didn't give a shit.

The great thing about John Lewis was that it really did sell just about everything, and good quality everything at that. I had no doubt that we'd get all the items we needed there, and as I trekked up four flights of stairs I was glad that it wasn't likely that I'd have to go exploring any further into the vast glass wilderness of the shopping centre. Despite my anger at Phelps, the soft *shwup* of my trainers on the ground beneath me were a reminder with every step that perhaps my idea to split up wasn't the sanest.

As my breath wheezed in and out, sounding like a poor Darth Vader impersonation in the silence, I ran through the film files in my memory banks, searching for one in which the main characters split up and they all survived. *Alien, The Thing, Event Horizon, Scream.* Scanning through the relevant scenes of each movie, I didn't find anything to comfort myself in them. As far as I could tell, if this were a film, then I'd become the character that every audience in the world screamed at to *not be so bloody stupid.* Right then I was feeling bloody stupid, letting my dislike of Phelps jeopardise my personal safety, not that I was particularly sure that the three of us together would have much more chance against a widow than me on my own, but I preferred the idea of having others around me. *Let's split up.* The oldest cliché in the horror film world. And I was the prat that had said it. Still, I had to remind myself that this wasn't a movie and those rules didn't necessarily apply. As I finally found myself in front of a range of tents and camping gear, the thought that this was reality and not fiction wasn't particularly comforting.

As it was, the three of us passed each other a few times as we carried our goods down to the front of the building, silently depositing our heavy loads just beyond the broken glass, nodding with sweating faces when we crossed paths. No one spoke, all of us intent on just finishing off the job as quickly as possible.

I wasn't sure how much to get, but I erred on the side of safety, and within about forty minutes I'd brought down eight large rucksacks, ten thick quilted sleeping bags neatly folded away in their own carry cases, and three large tents. I didn't figure anyone would be too insistent on privacy in the nights to come, even the girls. Company was a calming influence, even if it couldn't guarantee us our safety. I'd found some camping stoves, and after breaking into a safety cupboard managed to find the gas canisters to go with them. The focus and exercise had calmed me, and despite having found no trace of the people that had saved us the job of breaking in, I felt satisfied by our raid and relieved that I hadn't come across any widows. Relieved was an understatement.

Finally convinced that we'd got just about all we could carry, including a fine array of golf clubs and kitchen knives and choppers rooted out as weapons by Dave, and to be fair a good selection of clothes and boots deposited on our mountain of booty by Nigel, we stood there, as if round a bonfire, panting and glowing.

Dave sniffed, wiping sweat from his forehead with his sleeve. "Right. We'd better get this lot loaded into the truck and meet the others."

I nodded, and my tired arms reached down to load up.

"I'll just go and get changed then." Nigel was still in the same stained suit that he'd arrived in the bowls club in. "I didn't see the point in new clothes before the sweaty work."

If I hadn't been so eager to get out of there, I'd have suggested that we wait for him before starting. Dave looked like he could use a rest and I sure as hell felt like I needed one, and lugging all this equipment out to the Mitsubishi was going to be hard work. Nigel knew that as much as I did and that's why he'd left finding some new clothes until now. I found that his selfishness was no longer surprising me, and that stopped me getting so annoyed.

"Just be quick," I grunted, as I shoved the camping stoves, gas and sleeping bags into the large rucksacks and hoisted four of them over my shoulders, leaving my arms free for more.

Ten or so minutes later, as I was heading back from the car after the last trip, Dave stopped me coming the other way, shaking his head.

I stopped, both of us still in the increasingly close warmth outside. "What's up?"

He glanced over his shoulder, his hands tucked into the pockets of his jeans. "Seeing is believing, Matt. I'm not sure what to make of it myself. I think he's gone a bit mad. Come on. Have a look for yourself."

Speeding up to a jog, we passed through the automatic doors into the cool air inside and I turned into the large hall slightly ahead of Dave. There were just a couple of items left to carry outside, and Nigel stood beside them as if debating whether to pick them up.

I paused, confused, and the words came out before I could think of anything more subtle. "What the hell are you wearing that for?"

He turned to me, his expression puzzled. "What do you mean?"

"Well, it's not exactly what I was expecting. Don't you think something more comfortable might be better? Something a bit more hard-wearing?"

Standing there, he pushed his chin defiantly in the air and looked every inch the pompous businessman. Having ditched his tatty and stained suit, I'd expected him to find some jeans and trainers, but I'd been wrong. Instead he'd just upgraded his original outfit. The sharp suit, probably an Armani, housed a crisp striped shirt, and beneath the jacket I could make out a flash of brightly coloured braces. Shining beneath the hem of his trousers was a pair of well-polished black leather shoes. Perfect for a day in the city, but no grip on the smooth soles. No good for running away quickly, and running away was something I was sure we were going to have to do at some point in the future.

"I'm sorry if you don't approve, Mr. Edge, but I don't see how what I wear is any of your business." The corners of his mouth had turned down slightly in that pout that was becoming unpleasantly familiar. Just what was his problem? Didn't he realise we were all on the same side?

"Look, I don't give a shit. You can dress up as Wonder Woman for all I care, I just thought something else might be more comfortable for travelling in."

Mildly placated, he shrugged and crouched to pick up a sleeping bag. Just one of the three left on the floor that he could easily have managed.

"Well, I feel comfortable in *this*. *This* is who I am. So I'll thank you not to mention it again." The sleeping bag tucked under one arm, he drew himself up and strode past me. His forehead still shone with sweat, but under the artificial lights it seemed to gleam more than previously and it wasn't until he'd gone by that I realised what it was. He'd put Brill cream on what remained of his hair. That or some other kind of gel.

Dave had come alongside me and picked up the remaining bags. "So, what do you think?"

I watched the departing figure, searching for the right words.

"I think he's fucking barking."

"I couldn't have put it better myself."

"Come on. Let's get back to the others." I pulled the car keys out of my pocket and followed Phelps outside, my brow furrowing. That was all we needed—one of our number to start unravelling beside us.

CHAPTER TEN

The dark windows of the flats a hundred yards or so behind the shimmering modernity of the food hall glinted at us like angry eyes as the Mitsubishi purred into the car park. I ignored them and pulled the truck to a stop at an angle, neither in one bay nor the next. I didn't figure it mattered too much. Who the hell was going to complain?

George was hoisting a tray of cans into the back of the Range Rover and, looking at the various jars and packets that filled the large boot, I could see they had been busy. He paused as I approached and pulled a handkerchief out of his pocket to wipe his face with.

"It's getting very sweaty out here. I reckon there'll be a storm tonight. How did you get on?" He nodded in the direction of the pickup. "Looks pretty full."

"Yeah, we got most of what was on the list, and a few things that weren't. We should be okay." Glancing over my shoulder, I made sure that the others weren't too close.

"We may have a problem with Nigel, though. He

seems a little..." I wasn't sure just how tactful to be, hesitating over the words. "Well, I think he's cracking." There it was. Out. And not very tactful at all. "His moods are all over the place, and have you seen what he's got on? He *chose* that to change into."

George's eyes wandered casually over to where Dave and Nigel stood. "Oh, I see. Yes, I see what you mean. That's not right at all, is it?" His expression clouded over for a few moments, before clearing slightly. "Well, there's not really a lot we can do about it for now apart from keep an eye on him. Maybe it'll pass. It might just be shock." Raising an eyebrow, he smiled and slapped me gently on the shoulder. "That's a nice suit he's got on, though. At least the man has some taste."

Signalling for Nigel and Dave to follow us, we headed back into the large supermarket.

"We're just about done in here. John and the ladies are loading bottles of water into trolleys, and that's the final thing. It seemed to me that we'd better bring some. I'm sure the water systems are okay, but we don't want to get stranded somewhere with nothing to drink."

Once again, George Leicester made me feel glad he'd found us. God forbid anything should happen to him, whatever was waiting for us in the future. I wasn't sure just how well any of us would survive without him. He was the calm in our storm.

"I don't suppose you found any signs of anyone else being here, did you? The window of John Lewis's was smashed, but we didn't come across anyone. Wondered if they might have come here as well." Up ahead I could see Katie and Jane struggling with a case of plastic water bottles, Dave rushing to help them and

Nigel a couple of paces behind. She smiled when she glanced up, but I couldn't be entirely certain that it was aimed at me. Jane's enthusiastic wave was, though, and I raised my arm in response.

"No, unfortunately not. No signs of life here. Although we haven't been to any of the other supermarkets, so maybe Sainsbury's wasn't their first choice." He smiled. "Still, it's always nice to know we're not alone. I'm sure we're bound to come across plenty of others as the days go by. Law of probability would dictate that we're not alone."

As the days go by.

George's words shuddered through me as I watched him head off to tell the others to stop collecting water from the aisles. I couldn't imagine this new world going on for days and days, stretching out ahead of us into infinity. Somewhere in my subconscious I'd been clinging to the hope that I'd wake up the next morning and everything would be just about back to normal. No Chloe, perhaps—and I wasn't ready to face the pain of that yet—but I'd been hanging on to the idea that *they* would have sorted the widows out. *They* would have put their master plan into action and saved us all. Standing there in the cool air of the deserted supermarket, my slow masculine brain finally accepted what the world had been screaming at me since Chloe came out of the kitchen in the early hours of the morning. The world as I knew it was over. Kaput. Never to be the same again. It was just a matter of survival now. Keeping alive and seeing what happened.

Taking the front end of a full water trolley, I steered it back out to the car park, John pushing from the rear. The boy looked better for having been busy, and the slight pang of jealousy I'd felt earlier now seemed childish and stupid. We were all we had and we needed to stick together.

The others followed in a convoy of wobbling and weaving unruly steel, as if even the shopping trolleys knew they were about to be abandoned to remain unused forever, and were making the most of their last moments of movement. They and we finally arrived at the cars, though, and it wasn't long before all available space in the vehicles had been filled and three two-litre bottles placed in the foot wells of each car.

"Shall we get out of here?" John pulled off his baseball cap and ran his fingers through his sweaty hair before putting the hat back on.

George nodded. "Nigel, you come with me and Matt."

Not giving the other man time to argue, he steered him towards the Animal. As much as I disliked Phelps, I knew why the old man had done it. We needed to keep an eye on him, and it was too much of a job for John and the girls. Dave could take the other Range Rover by himself. As it was, Nigel didn't seem to mind.

"Do you want me to drive?"

I shook my head. "No, you're all right. You can take the next leg if you like."

"If you're sure." He slid into the back, and I couldn't help be relieved that it was George that would be up front with me. The oppressive heat was making my skin itch and I couldn't wait to be started just to get the air-conditioning on. The passenger door slammed shut, and George leaned back in his seat, tugging his seatbelt on.

"Shall we head out towards Buckingham? Get out of the city a bit, and then we can think about where to aim to."

"Sounds fine to me." I pulled my own safety belt on, despite the fact that there was no one out there to enforce the law. In a world where it was unlikely any ambulances would come to save you if you ran your car off the road, the *Clunk-Click* campaign suddenly seemed sensible.

As I turned the key in the ignition, the engine groaned, but failed to roar into life.

"That's odd." I tried it again, letting it turn over, waiting for the sluggish rumble to turn into a healthy purr. "Sounds like there's some kind of blockage." Twisting the key more aggressively, I swore quietly under my breath. This was all we needed. "I don't understand. It was working perfectly. It's a bloody new car."

"Oh shit."

The words drifted quietly in through my open driver's window, and I looked up to see John, his mouth a wide O backing away round to the other side of his Land Rover, just as the suspension rocked slightly beneath us.

Signalling furiously, Dave climbed out of his four-wheel drive, his voice a blur, shouting from too far away. Staring at him quizzically, I finally figured out the last three words

"*...under the car!*"

The car shook again.

"What the fuck was that?" Nigel leaned forward, filling the small gap between the two front seats. "Just what the fuck did that?"

I didn't know, and I didn't want to know. "I think something's under the car." *Something*. The word hung in the air. We all had a pretty good idea of what that something might be. Without thinking, I pushed down the lock on my door, and George did the same on his side.

"Oh Christ." The old man's normal calm trembled. "Look at that."

Two white, slick limbs appeared on the bonnet in front of us, tapping and scratching on the paint, the clawed translucent end screeching like fingernails on a blackboard as it dragged itself towards us.

"This might be a good time to do your window up." He didn't look at me, just stayed staring ahead.

"I can't. The electric's not working." To make my point I jabbed the button next to the shift stick a few times. It was no good. Struggling with the keys, my hand shook as two more shiny limbs stealthily appeared, followed by the first angry row of red, unnatural eyes. Again the engine could only moan. Nigel made a similar noise as he pushed himself as far back into the rear seats as he could, yanking at the door.

"It won't open. It won't open."

George pulled at the button he had only just pushed down. That too refused to budge. "What is going on? How can it do that? How can it stop the car from unlocking?" Panic was rising in his voice, and with my head filling again with Chloe *talking* to Helena in our darkened living room, with the knowledge that we barely knew what these things were capable of, my stomach cramped with my own dark fear.

The bank of eyes grew like hateful rising suns, and beyond them was the smooth rounded surface of the thing's body. "Come on, come on." I turned the useless key again and again, hoping for something.

Hissing, all stealth forgotten, the widow leapt upwards, slamming itself into the windscreen, its mandibles clacking hungrily at the glass. I don't know who screamed first or whether panic overtook us all at the same time, but amongst the others, I could hear my own cry as I raised my hands to protect my face. *Jesus Christ, Jesus Christ.* It was coming for us. It wanted us.

Pulling back, it launched at the glass again with such force that its grotesque lower body should have burst on impact. Instead, it quivered like a distended water balloon as the legs sought purchase, one clinging to the inside of my open window, the creature's furore finding release in an unholy high-pitched wail that seemed to come through its damp skin rather than mouths.

"Oh shit, oh shit..." Sweating, my shaking fingers pulled too hard at the key ring and the ignition key clattered to the foot well beneath me. The shrieking stopped as the widow twisted, suddenly aware that two of its legs were creeping inward; it froze on the bonnet for a split second before turning, realising its advantage. A small gust of wind caressed my cheek, as if teasing me through the gaping hole in our armour.

"Just close the fucking window! Just close the fucking window!" Nigel's warm spit rained onto the tips of my ears as he screeched from the rear, his fist pummelling into the back of my seat.

"I fucking can't, all right?" As I yelled my frustrated words at his reflection in the rearview mirror, the disgusting thing on the bonnet took a small, terrifyingly agile jump to the right, still pressing itself into the glass, shifting towards my window, the legs that were close enough stabbing inside, trying to find the leverage to haul its repulsive body in and upon us.

"Christ." Releasing my seatbelt, I wriggled to the

left, pushing myself over with my feet until I was wedged in beside George. As two spindly legs hooked into the driver's door, a third reached for me, stopping only two or three inches from my sweating face, stretched almost straight from each of its joints, some clear gel-like substance starting to ooze from its pointed tip turning white in the air before dripping onto the driver's seat and controls below.

In the corner of my vision I could see the burning eyes seeking me out through the thin protection of glass, and there was intelligence in them; angry, hateful intelligence, calculating the attack, taking its time, knowing we were no match for it.

Fumbling hastily beside me, George flipped open the dashboard and scrabbled inside. "There's nothing in here. I can't find anything." The frustration screeched in his trembling voice as the mundane and useless bits of life gone by tumbled out onto the floor. His elbow nudged into me as he reached desperately further within the dark recess, pushing me a breath away from the spewing legs that stretched out dripping their almost-liquid juice millimetres from my jeans and face. I allowed my eyes to flash at him for a second, the heat of fear burning my face.

"Jesus, George!"

"Sorry...sorry..."

Beneath me, I could feel the thin brittle bones of his legs as I pressed into them, my body almost sitting on his lap, the sweat from my terrified skin no doubt melting into his. Behind us, Nigel scrambled to the other end of the backseat as the window became filled by the bulbous midsection of the nightmarish, sectioned, translucent torso.

"It's coming in, isn't it? This isn't exactly how I saw

126

this all ending. Not quite so soon." The brutal futility in George's voice was inescapable, and I stared at the pulsing alien, which slowly twisted and bent itself in front of us so that its eyes dipped into view, pausing to enjoy its moment of power.

It hissed at us in victory, filling our vision, and as we flinched and pulled back against the locked door, eyes squeezing tight, it mirrored us in preparation for the final attack. My heart pounding, I waited to feel its awful skin against mine as it came through the window.

Instead, the hiss turned into a screech and my eyes flew open in time to see the widow twist angrily around and leap from the car. Behind it, everything was happening so fast that I couldn't take it in. Flames and smoke leapt from something in Dave's hand, and despite my shock I heard myself yelling at him to back away, the thing was too close, it was far too damn close to him, twisting and turning and lashing out, and then for a second the man was lost in a blur of limbs and people and smoke, and all I could see was John beating at it with a golf club and Katie coming in close, creating flames of her own with a large aerosol can and a lighter, her pretty face tight with grim determination. From beneath them a dark, thick smoke rose upwards, spreading its putrid aroma into the atmosphere. The insides of my nostrils burned, as the screeching finally stopped.

For a moment none of us moved, and all I could hear was the panting of those outside, and the pounding of my trembling heart inside, until eventually there was a bout of dry coughing from ground level and Dave pulled himself to his feet.

With my fingers chilly at the tips and clumsy with numbness, where no doubt the blood had withdrawn in mortal terror, I tried the lock. The button slid up smoothly and I stepped outside, looking down at the mangled leftover of the widow on the ground, my guts turning.

His lungs clear, Dave sniffed. "Well, at least we know the pissed off bitches can die." His smile was wan and I could feel that the one I returned wasn't exactly confident. George appeared quietly beside us. "What happened to your wrist?"

Following the old man's gaze, I saw that Dave had one arm held carefully in his other hand. A small patch of blood crept through his shirt, staining it brightly. He shrugged. "I think it bit me. Doesn't hurt much. I don't think it was deep."

George nodded. "That's as may be, but I think we'd better get it cleaned up and bandaged before we go. We can't take any risks."

Dave didn't fight the suggestion too hard, and I had a sinking feeling in my stomach as we sat subdued and silent, watching Katie and George work, that Dave had lied a little about the pain. The thin veneer of sweat on his pale face hinted that the bite was bothering him more than he let on. It was bothering him enough not to fight Katie's suggestion that she drive his car, at any rate.

Above us the clouds were darkening, giving the afternoon the impression of being much later, and it seemed to me that we had all aged a little in that twenty minutes or so. Just how long would we survive in this new world? And just how long would we be able to keep trying? Finally ready to get moving, I slid back into the driver's seat of the truck, not taking much comfort from my quiet passengers, and this time when I turned the key, the engine purred into life without a hitch.

As we pulled away from the glass and metal city, heading out of the manufactured grid system and into the older, wilder Buckinghamshire, I resisted the urge to look back. In fact, none of us turned in our seats. Perhaps we all realised that to look back was pointless. There was nothing there for us now except lost dreams and lives and loves. To look back meant death.

There was one thing I was beginning to be sure of— if we were going to survive this thing, then we needed to concentrate on the future.

CHAPTER ELEVEN

We'd been driving for about twenty minutes when the clouds roared and ripped themselves open, releasing their heavy wet cargo. The noise of the water beating against the windscreen was a welcome relief from the silence. None of us felt like talking, and although I'd put a CD on when we'd first left Milton Keynes, the haunting sounds of the past were too much to bear, and when I turned it off, there were no complaints from my passengers.

I peered through the rhythmical sweeping of the wiper blades. The water seemed to be coming in sheets, whole puddles falling from the skies rather than drops, as if even the forces of nature were trying to wash us from the face of the earth. The world beyond the glass was a constantly shifting blur and I slowed down, dropping a gear. "This is all we need," I muttered, leaning forward slightly, my eyes squinting.

The wide dual carriageways of the new city had started to weave into the smaller darker roads that led into the outlying villages, and with the rain and clouds blocking out the natural light and evening slowly coming upon us, we could have done with the benefit of street lamps. Beside me, George was equally alert, scanning the road ahead and its borders for any sign of widows, and I could feel the tension in his body. I glanced in my rearview mirror for a moment to check that the others were still close by. Katie was driving the car behind me, and I didn't like the idea of her getting into any trouble whilst I was too lost in my own thoughts to notice. From her hesitancy when pulling away from the supermarket, I'd guessed that she didn't have too much experience in handling a big four-wheel drive, and although Dave would be talking her through it, in his injured state I wasn't sure how much comfort or relief he would be.

"So, where are we going to go?" Nigel's voice was calm, none of the irritating whine I now associated with him present. In fact, he just sounded the way I felt—tired to the bone. Maybe the shock of the attack had knocked that pretentious defensive-aggressiveness out of him. Glancing behind me, I reckoned I'd still be happier when he finally loosened that ridiculous tie. I reckoned he would be, too. I couldn't see ties featuring heavily in the immediate dress code of our new society.

"I don't know. Right now, I'm just heading out of Milton Keynes. You got any suggestions?" I hoped he had, because despite having lived around Buckinghamshire all my life, my brain was pretty empty on ideas.

"London?" He leaned forward. "Maybe the government's got some kind of control of what's going on there."

The good old faith in *they* again rearing its head. It seemed logical, but the thought of that teeming London population, half of it evolved and hungry, turned my stomach. What if we got there to find widows spewing their sticky trails over Downing Street? All I could see for the moment was a vivid image of Tony Blair, cocooned and terrified, as the unrecognisable Cherie approached for an afternoon snack. Perhaps we weren't quite ready for London yet.

"I was thinking more along the lines of an army base or something. Somewhere with relatively good defences where there may be some more survivors."

He nodded, but there was a small flash in his eye at the disagreement. The kind of look that said, *You're talking shit, and if I wasn't so dependent on you right now and if I wasn't so fucking tired then I'd so enjoy telling you where to shove your better ideas.* Maybe the pain in the arse Nigel was still alive and kicking in there after all. But right now, I didn't have the energy for him.

"It's just a suggestion. Maybe London is the best place to head."

"I've got an idea." George twisted in his seat so that he could see both of us, and his ancient face was very much alive, his eyes bright. "There's a place out by Hanstone. It's a government place, Foreign Office, I think. A lot of the guys down at the bowls club used to work up there. It must be pretty secure, I mean it's surrounded by barbwire and high walls, and I think we can't ask for much more than that." Listening to him, I felt my own tiredness lifting a little.

"But the best thing is," as he spoke he allowed himself an optimistic grin, "it's a communications centre. That's what the old boys at the club used to specialise in, anyway. So if we can get some contact with the outside world anywhere, then we've got a good chance of it being there."

The grin was infectious and I allowed myself a brief look away from the windscreen to share it. Even Nigel was smiling. Maybe he didn't mind George having the best suggestion, as if he was beginning to realize our survival was not some kind of boyish competition.

"Sounds good." Hanstone was north of Milton Keynes, just across the border of Northamptonshire, pretty much back the way we'd come, maybe five or six miles from Stony Stratford. I'd been idly heading south, so we'd need to turn round. "Shall I go back through the city, or take the scenic route?"

All of our spirits risen, I think I wasn't alone in not wanting to invite depression by going back to such familiar territory, and so despite the treacherous weather, we opted to take the country roads and work our way through the villages. As I came to the next T-junction I veered to the left to start our circle back. Behind me, the other two cars followed like obedient children, no questions asked, but I had no illusion that it was me they had the faith in. George was the quiet, calm leader of our assorted band, and I was happy with it being that way.

Despite the slightly renewed energy granted to us by having a destination, within fifteen minutes the weather was so bad that our speed dropped to about ten cautious miles an hour. The wind had picked up, driving the rain into us, making visibility worse, and the deluge of water collected rapidly beneath the wheels, occasionally sending us sliding heart-stoppingly out of control towards the fields on either side. It was getting darker too; the twilight was almost unnatural. My eyes began to hurt from squinting.

"Perhaps we should have gone back through the city." Nigel's murmur sounded like an accusation, and I bit my tongue to stop the angry retort that burned there. George said nothing and we slipped into silence once again as we crawled through the miles. It was a relief when we drove under a small pool of light given off from a lone street lamp about half a mile outside the village of Pickford, the metal pole guarding a solitary one-story building, my vision for a brief second given a moment to relax.

We were about thirty yards past it when behind us Katie flashed her headlights several times, her own vehicle stopped. Carefully reversing back up the dark road, I came to a stop in front of her bonnet, and jumping out of the car, ran the few steps to her driver's window. The water soaked me instantly, but the shock was its warmth. I felt as if I were standing beneath a hot shower, and the wind was barely cooler than the liquid. As the force of air threatened to push me over, I felt a vague inner disquiet at how tropical the world around me felt. Not like England at all.

Katie wound down her window, her tired face looking thin and even younger. "We've got a flat, rear left. We've had it for about half an hour but there didn't seem to be anywhere safe to stop."

She was right. Standing outside alone in the darkness, with this wild weather cutting through my clothes, I didn't feel safe at all.

"You want to change the tyre here?" My heart sank, but she shook her head.

"No. I thought we could rest up a bit here, in the scout hut. It seems far enough away from any houses or anything."

I looked behind me at the building we'd just passed and saw she was right. It was a solid old stone building with a thick oak door, small and secure. A worn wooden sign proclaimed it the Pickford Scouts Meeting Place, but from the state of the chipped lettering, it didn't seem to me that the scouts were a thriving business in the little village. Staring at it, however, the idea of a rest was appealing. At the rate we were going it would take us half the night to get to Hanstone, and we'd still need to sort out Katie's car. If she drove on it much longer she'd damage the wheel, especially with all the weight in there, and then we could be stuck in a much worse situation.

She was still waiting for an answer, and I nodded. "Sounds good to me. I'll tell the others."

Behind the wheel of the third car and on his own, I could tell John was relieved even though he was trying not to show it. He pulled his Land Rover up onto the verge and turned it off before stepping out.

"Shit, it's warm out here." He protected his face from the wind, but his surprise was obvious.

Nodding, I led him past the street lamp and through the small gate. Away from the immediate light, the gloominess crept in threateningly.

"Let's worry about the weather later. How the hell are we going to get in?"

John pointed up at a small window just above his head. "Can you give me a leg up to there? I think I could get through and see if I can open the door from the inside."

Crouching down, I locked my hands and his wet boot stepped into them, jumping up as I pushed. He wasn't as heavy as I expected, but I hadn't given anyone a leg up since my teens and the awkwardness of it made me wobble slightly, John's thin hands digging into my shoulder occasionally to steady his own body as we weaved in the wind, a pathetic human totem pole.

"You okay up there?" Warm water sprayed into my mouth as I twisted my neck round and I spat it out, the abnormal tepidity unpleasant.

"Yep," he called down. "Now keep us steady and keep your face down! I'm going to break the glass."

Turning my face away from the rain was a welcome relief and I squeezed my eyes shut. My feet slipped slightly as John banged his elbow into the small pane, the shock of the hard contact echoing down his legs and through my body.

"Fuck, that hurt. This glass is fucking tough."

As his muttered words drifted down from above me, his weight shifted back to central. Despite his slimness, the constant liquid made it hard to grip and I could feel my fingers slipping apart with the pressure.

"Anytime now would be good." I tried not to make my voice sound too much like a grunt, but it wasn't working. My teeth were gritted together with the effort of keeping him up.

"Hang on, old man. Here goes."

I pressed my back against the wall, not wanting to disturb his efforts with my own lack of stability. The idea of having to get back into the car and keep driving was even less appealing now that I was soaked to the skin and my arms ached.

I didn't have to worry. This time John was taking no prisoners, and his knee involuntarily dug painfully into my neck as he launched his elbow for the second time into the window. Small pieces of glass mixed with the rain and showered me from above, but most of the big shards fell inwards into the dry hut.

John tapped out the dangerous jagged edges clinging to the frame. "Okay, Matt. Give me a shove."

As I pushed and he hauled himself up through the window, his weight disappeared from me, and listening to his clumsy landing on the other side, I rested for a second, letting my aching arms relax. Suddenly I regretted all those times I'd found an excuse not to go to the gym. I was going to have to get stronger quickly if I was even going to start feeling safe in this new terrain.

The handle turned and the door was pulled open in front of me, revealing John holding a key. "Dib, dib, dib. Be prepared. It was hanging by the door. Must be a spare." He winked. "Welcome home, mate." John's face shone with boyish adventure, and for the first time since we'd met I could see the resilience of his youth picking his spirits up, and I gave him a wry smile.

"You need to go on a diet. I think my arms are broken."

"Whatever." His hand darted to his side, and he flicked a switch. Dull yellow light ebbed into the building from a single bulb hanging from the centre of the ceiling. The boy grinned.

"Well, it's better than nothing. Come on, let's get the others." He slapped me on the arm as he passed, trotting happily back out into the rain. Peering into the room, I wasn't overly impressed. There was no carpet on the grey concrete floor and the walls had been painted with a similar eggshell colour, the shade and sheen giving the small space the feel of a prison room. Still, on the upside, there *was* a door marked TOILET on the far side and a two bar electric fire pushed against the wall, alongside a row of tatty chairs and a dusty bookshelf with a few tattered paperbacks leaning listlessly within.

My eyes came back to the fire. If the lights were working then logic would dictate that the plugs were. But logic could be a fucker sometimes.

George appeared in the doorway carrying a large container of water, putting it down heavily on the floor before slowly straightening up. He sighed, one hand massaging his lower back.

"The girls are digging out the camping stove and Nigel's getting the sleeping bags from your car. The general feeling is that we just bring what we need in, and leave the rest stowed."

I nodded. "Sounds good to me. I don't know about you, but it feels to my bones like it's been one hell of a long day."

"Add on another forty years, sonny, then come and talk to me about what kind of day it's been on the joints."

I grinned. "Point taken."

Nigel came past us carrying three sleeping bags and a rucksack with can shapes bulging through the soaking canvas, and I wondered how comfortable that neatly done-up tie and shirt was now that the rain had hit. It didn't seem to bother him, though, as he dumped his burden in the middle of the room. Beneath the sickly yellow glow, I couldn't tell whether his exposed forehead was dripping with sweat, as it had been when we'd first met, or just wet from the flood outside. He glanced around without bothering to wipe the liquid from his face.

"Could be worse." The sneer that twisted his lips hinted that as far as Nigel Phelps was concerned, the likelihood of actually finding somewhere less pleasant was almost an impossibility. He peered at the broken window. "How are we going to block that up?"

George and I both turned to it as Katie and Jane came into the hut beside us, the first carrying a camping gas stove and the second barely visible beneath a final bundle of sleeping bag holders. Both managed a wan smile before adding their loads to Nigel's pile. Dave followed behind them, a bag of aerosols slung over one shoulder and his good hand carrying the first aid box. A fresh bloom of pink was visible through the layers of bandage coming loose on his injured wrist.

"It's not cold out there and the window's pretty small. Can't we just leave it? We're only stopping overnight." George must have been tired, because it wasn't like him not to want to dot the *i*'s and cross the *t*'s. Not where our safety was concerned. Leaning forward, Dave grimaced as he twisted his upper body, letting the bag slip onto one of the chairs against the wall.

"Well, I'm as shattered as the rest of you, but that window is going to be sealed before I relax. I don't care how we do it."

Looking at the pain etched on his face, I agreed with him. No matter how far we were from other houses, I didn't fancy trying to sleep with one eye on whether any of those awful legs were silently creeping in. Dave's face had paled since we left Milton Keynes, and the redness in his eyes suggested that his temperature was rising. He was running a fever and I hoped it wasn't going to get any worse, but for the first time since the attack I wondered if there may have been some kind of poison in that bite. The thought made my skin cool and I shivered some of my tiredness away, focussing on the source of our unease.

"Yeah, you're right. We can't leave it like that. But what can we use? This place is hardly teeming with two-by-fours."

Katie opened the rucksack that Nigel had come in with, searching the tins for something we could heat up quickly.

"What about the parcel shelf from the Range Rover? I almost threw it away since it was taking up most of the backseat. That'd probably cover that space, don't you think? Do we have any tools?"

"Yes. There's some in the Animal." I said another silent prayer of thanks for George and the list of necessities he'd sent us shopping for. "A box of the basics at any rate. Hammers, nails. Plenty to do the job. Chuck me the keys and I'll go and get it."

Kattie smiled gently at me, one can of Sainsbury's all-day breakfast in her hand. "It's not locked. I didn't exactly see the point. I doubt there's too many joy riders out tonight. Especially not for a car with a flat tyre."

I grinned back, glad that we seemed to have reached a kind of truce after this morning in the pub, and risked a joke.

"Get my dinner on, wench, while I do the man work."

One delicate eyebrow raised at me. "Let's just take a moment to remember who was stuck in the car not so long ago, and who was killing the nasty monster."

Swallowing another couple of pills from the first aid box, Dave laughed. "She's got you there, mate."

"Okay, point taken. You win. I'll just get out there and do the manual labour and hope for some crumbs when I get back. That's if you heroes can spare me a bean."

"We'll see what we can do. Now go!" She shooed me away with a can opener.

With a slightly lighter heart, I headed back out into the night rain, breaking into a trot.

CHAPTER TWELVE

We ate our dinner of beans, sausages and bacon on paper plates, and then finished off with tinned peaches, evaporated milk and coffee, all of us huddled round the fire, sitting on our sleeping bags, listening to the wind that was building up outside, mostly too tired to speak. It felt to me as if we had travelled back in time to the second World War, just a group of ordinary people holed up in their air raid shelter, waiting for the worst to pass over their heads, not knowing what the blackness of the night held in store for them.

Jane was virtually asleep sitting up, and Katie took her plate and gently eased her into her padded bed, still fully dressed, the little girl putting up no resistance. George opened a bottle of expensive red wine and the rest of us sipped it quietly, letting its rich warmth soothe and dull our heads a little. By the time I was halfway through my first glass John had drifted off, emotional and physical exhaustion claiming its second victim and reminding us all just how fucking tired we were.

Still shivering, Dave pulled on another fleece before sinking inside his sleeping bag for the night, only his freshly bandaged arm visible. Nigel disappeared into the small toilet for several minutes, a washing bag under one arm, and when he emerged he wore pyjamas and looked scrubbed and clean.

"If you go in there, be careful of my contacts. They're on the side in their solution. There's not a lot of space, so try not to knock them over." He looked at me with slight disdain, as if he could tell I really had no intention of scrubbing myself clean. Where the hell had he gotten lens solution? He must have gone and found it while we were sticking to George's list in John Lewis. Nice of him to check whether anyone else needed some.

Still sniffing in my direction, Phelps put his washbag down in the corner. "I've left spare toothbrushes for everyone in there."

George had moved his sleeping bag to the wall and was sitting up skimming the blurb on the back of an old paperback he'd taken from the shelf. Smiling, he raised his topped up glass at Phelps. "Thank you kindly, but I may wait until the morning before I take advantage of your kind offer. This is a very fine wine, and I don't want to spoil it with mint."

"Suit yourselves." Nigel's pinched expression acknowledged that he knew George spoke for the rest of us that were awake, and turning his stiff back on us, he arranged his suit carefully on one of the chairs. "I just don't see why we should let our standards slip. You can always judge a man on his personal hygiene." Still muttering to himself, he spread out his sleeping bag in a little space away from the rest of us and climbed inside. "You can turn that light out whenever you're ready."

We left the light on for a further twenty minutes, until the collective irritation had cooled enough to realise we were being childish. Eventually it was Katie that got up and flicked the switch, before coming back and sitting with me. It seemed that she wasn't ready for sleep anymore than George and I, but rather than chatting, we sat together and yet apart, each lost in our own thoughts and memories, until the rhythmic rustle of paper brought both Katie and me back to the present.

"What are you reading?" I kept my voice low as I peered across through the shadows to the red glow of the fire where George was turning the pages of a tatty paperback.

"You ought to be careful reading in that light. You'll damage your eyes." Smiling at the older man, Katie leaned in closer to me, and I have to admit it felt pretty good having her so near.

The creases in his face, elongated by the semi-darkness, became caverns of blackness, making George almost unrecognisable apart from the kind, intelligent twinkle in his eyes.

"Thanks for your concern, but at my age, your eyes aren't too much of a worry." His smile widened. "They're about the only part of me that doesn't complain if I move too quickly in the mornings." He turned the yellowing book over, reflecting on the cover. "John Wyndham, *The Kraken Wakes*. Have you read it?"

I shook my head and so did Katie.

"Well, you should. It's a damned good book. I read it the first time about thirty years ago, and it's as good this time round as it was then. Good books are time-less." He raised his glass. "Like good wine." Pausing, he took a sip. "Anyway, this time it's more of a re-search project. You see, it's a kind of end-of-the-world book. I'm wondering if Mr. Wyndham has any better ideas of what we can do than we do." Smiling, he re-turned his gaze to the text and lost himself in it.

Across the room, Nigel murmured and called out something from beneath the zipped quilted covers, his body twisting slightly in the casing. However much Nigel thought he was holding it together in daylight, his sleep had been pretty much constantly restless since he'd gone down for the night, and whatever was cracking up his conscious state was having fun with his unconscious one.

"I don't like that man." Katie stared over into the corner, her voice hard.

"I'm not too keen, either. But he may shape up. We'll have to wait and see." After what Nigel had said about the man with the air rifle having the right idea for shooting at them, I couldn't blame Katie for her dislike. But there was more to it than that. Phelps just didn't like women, and I doubted he'd had that much respect for them when they were all normal. I won-dered what kind of life the late Mrs. Phelps would have had. Dull, dreary and patronised, more than likely. I bet there was one pissed off widow out there that really wished she'd got her man.

"But I do like *him*." Katie nodded in the direction of Dave. "And I'm worried about that bite."

"He looks like he's running a fever."

"Yes, I'm sure he is, but I'm not surprised. That bite was looking a lot worse tonight."

Our eyes met, and the fear in hers made me remember how young she really was. She was looking at me as if I could somehow make things better. As if having reached the almost old age of thirty, I had some infinite knowledge that could cure him. *Oh yes, mutant female spider bite. I know just the thing....* But behind that hope was a twenty-year-olds slowly unwrapping knowledge that all that was just a pipe dream of childhood. No one had the answers. In fact, no one had a fucking clue.

"How do you mean? Do you think there's poison in there?"

She shrugged slightly and sipped her wine. "It wouldn't surprise me. Would it you?"

"No, not really. Looking at Dave earlier, I figured there may have been something more to that bite, but I was hoping that there wasn't." I paused, looking at her green eyes, which seemed to flicker yellow in the warm light, and wondered what they hid. "What about you? How are you doing?"

Lowering her head, she avoided my eyes and tucked a long curl behind her ear. "Oh, I'm okay. As long as Jane is, I will be." Looking over at where her little sister slept, the lines of tension that had begun to form around her mouth softened. "It's funny. I don't really know her that well. I mean, there's ten years between us. I was a late baby and I guess my parents thought their days of being able to have children were over, and they became a little less careful with their precautions." She grinned, not at me, but at the memory of people that I would never meet.

"My mother was in the throes of the menopause when she fell with Janie. She never tires of telling people that one." A small flinch went through her as she stumbled over the use of the present tense. We both let it pass without correction. "Anyway, the age gap was such that as much as I love Jane, we've never really done much together. Not once she started school, at any rate. And then by the time she was nine, I'd done my A levels and was off to university. Bit of a waste of time, really. I graduated this summer and look at the world now. I wish I'd stayed at home and had more time with my family."

I could feel the barriers she was putting up and squeezed her arm. It felt so fragile through the thick fabric of the man's sweater she was wearing.

"Hey, foresight is something all of us wish we'd had a bit of right now." Glancing over at George, lost in his old book, I wondered how he was coping with the loss of his family. Probably the same way as I was coping with the loss of Chloe. By ignoring it. By putting the grief out of reach for now and by doing those we'd lost proud by surviving. Or at least attempting to for another day or two.

"She's a good kid. I think she's dealing with all of this better than some," I said.

"Yes. Yes, she is. I think my mum would be proud. I certainly am."

Even with the sleeping bag beneath me, the ground was hard, and I lay down on one side resting on one elbow and took a long gulp of wine, draining my glass.

"Do you want to talk about it?"

This time her gaze met mine, straight and strong. She didn't need me to spell out what I meant. She shook her head.

"No. The past couple of days are private to me and Janie. If she wants to talk about it when she's ready, than that's fine with me, but I'm not like that. I need it inside me to keep me strong. I don't expect that makes a lot of sense, but that's how I am. What about you?"

The idea of retelling my pain for the second time that day weighed my soul down, and I shook my head. "I think we can both live without that story right at the moment."

Nodding, she said nothing, and we sat in silence for a few moments, until eventually she lay down facing me. Again, her beautiful eyes intrigued me; staring into them, I was so glad that they weren't brown, so glad they couldn't make me think of Chloe.

She chewed her bottom lip delicately. "Can I ask you something?"

I lowered my voice so it matched her whisper. "Sure."

"I don't mean this in any funny way, but..." Her eyes slipped away from me. "But will you hold me while I go to sleep? I...I think I need the contact."

Saying nothing, not wanting to embarrass her or make her feel more uncomfortable—and also knowing my own innate ability for saying the wrong thing, which came with the territory of maleness—I moved across as she slid into her sack, her body facing the other way. Unzipping my own bag I got in and then curled up behind Katie, one arm around her waist. Holding my hand, she pulled it upwards so that it was under her chin, her face warm and soft, and making my heart ache for reasons I was too tired to analyse.

"Good night, Matt." Her breath brushed over my fingers.

"Good night, Katie. Sleep tight."

I'm not sure how long I lay there listening to the rain outside and the rhythmic breathing around me, occasional moans and sounds coming as dreams and pain injected themselves into the night, my mind numb to thought. All I know is that somewhere after Katie and before George, I eventually drifted off into my own restless sleep.

I woke up suddenly with fear making my breath catch in my throat, my survival gene ahead of the rest of me, shaking me free of the grip of my dark dreams of Chloe and widows and the inescapable mixing of the two. I stared at the others in the glow of the fire.

"What the fuck was that?" Dave sat bolt upright. George was already out of his sleeping bag and Nigel was on his feet, standing awkwardly in the middle of the room.

From outside, mixed in with the increased level of the wind and rain, glass smashed angrily and something hard thudded into the wall to my left.

"Jane! Get over here!" The hiss in Katie's voice alone was enough to make the small girl scurry into the arms of her older sister.

"What is it?" John coughed, hauling himself sleepily in my direction. He pulled a crumpled pack of cigarettes from the back of his jeans. "Shit." Rooting inside the box, he found one that wasn't too damaged and lit it, sucking in hard. "What's happening?"

I shrugged, my body tingling with adrenaline. "I don't know." I tried not to whisper, but failed.

"There's something outside. Isn't there?" Nigel's voice was almost a snivel, and he huddled in with Katie and Jane in the centre of the room.

"Shhh." George moved to the door and quickly pushed the bolts across at the top and bottom, slamming them home as something on the other side angrily clawed at it. The smashing from outside got louder, coming from more than one angle, and I ducked instinctively as a thud came from the roof above, followed by an unpleasantly close scuttling that scratched over our heads in fits and starts.

"Yes. I think we can definitely say there is something outside." George wasn't whispering, but his voice was low.

"Should we turn the fire off? Maybe that's attracting them. Maybe they know when we're using electricity or something. Like with the phones." Standing now, Katie had managed to extract herself from Jane's grip and held a large aerosol, but from the slight shake in her hand, I would guess it wasn't bringing her any comfort. It pleased me, though, that someone had thought to bring them in earlier when all I'd been mainly concerned with was food and sleep.

Outside, the rain was drowned out by the screeching and crunching of metal, and my eyes focussed with dread on the small window that we'd bandaged up with parcel shelves. I tried to remember how hard we'd hammered those nails home, and how many we'd even used, but it was all a tired blur.

"It's them, isn't it? The widows." Jane's words came in a series of rushed, panicked breaths.

"Shit!" My heart beating faster, I jumped as the mended window shook with an impact from outside. I wasn't the only one with the jitters, Dave letting out a mumbled expletive that I couldn't quite make out.

"Yes, darling," George's soft words answered Jane. "I think it is them. But we're safe in here. This building's stood firmly for longer than I've been alive, so I think we can trust it to keep us safe now."

I glanced back up at our repairs. "Well, that may be, but I think I'd still feel a little safer with a few more nails up there. Someone pass me the tools." I pulled a chair out and climbed up, instantly feeling the breeze that squeezed through the gaps, reaching out for me and making me shiver, my skin crawling with the idea that one of those *things* was probably only inches from me, red eyes desperately seeking out a chink in our armour.

Something scraped the ground of the hut, and looking round I saw Katie climbing onto a chair beside me. She held up a lighter and the can, her gaze firm and direct. "Just in case."

I smiled, but a sudden scrabbling on the other side of the carpeted plastic made me wobble backwards, almost losing my footing completely. "Fuck."

"Whenever you're ready, Matt. Take your time. Personally, I'm loving it up here."

Taking a deep breath and ignoring her sarcasm and the less than pleasant sounds on the other side of the wall, I placed three nails in my mouth as I hammered in the first. We actually hadn't done a bad job the first time round, and by the time I stepped down, there were nails only about two centimetres apart all the way round.

"Well, if that doesn't hold it, then nothing will."

"Very comforting. What should we do now?" Nigel had regained some of his arrogance, which gave me slight comfort. If he thought we were in any immediate danger, then I was sure that now-familiar grating whine would have taken control.

Turning away from the door, George lit the small camper stove. "We just sit and wait until the morning. There's nothing else we can do." He looked down at his watch. "It's only three-thirty. I suggest Jane and Dave try and get some more sleep. The rest of us can take it in turns to watch the window. I'll make some coffee."

There was nothing more to say to that, but tired as we were, despite George's apparent calm, there was no way anyone was going back to sleep with all the irate activity outside. My nerves were too alive to relax, and they weren't helped by the strong coffee being brewed up.

Occasionally our silence was broken by the sound of a cigarette being lit—Dave even managing one or two, his fever seeming to have abated slightly—but in the main we just sat in a huddle in the middle of the scout's hut and listened to the sounds of the new world outside.

Chapter Thirteen

As dawn crept into daylight the sounds outside became more sporadic, filtering away, the noise less intrusive and aggressive; but we still sat in our group, staring at the walls, barely whispering to each other. By six-thirty, although our limbs were numb and stiff, nerves had unwound enough for Katie to take Dave to one side and re-dress his arm, talking softly to him, while George made fresh coffee—that great spiritual healer of all things—and heated up some golden syrup Oats So Simple for breakfast in a large pan. Despite everything, the hot smells made my mouth water, and as the silence outside approached forty-five minutes, I found that my fear had subsided.

Still with a cigarette in his mouth, John helped George dish up the food onto paper plates while Nigel packed away the sleeping bags and equipment, before heading into the bathroom, his suit and shirt tucked under his arm.

John nudged me as he passed me my breakfast, and

nodded at the closed WC. "What the fuck is all that about? Why is he wearing that stupid suit?"

I took a leaf out of George's book of experience and tried to make light of it. "Each to their own, John. Maybe he needs that to feel normal at the moment."

"If you say so, Matt, but I'm not convinced that's making anyone feel normal. Now tuck in."

We ate quickly and hungrily, scraping our plates clean, but as I got to the bottom of my coffee, I noticed that Katie and John had started to sip more slowly. I looked at the door.

"So, time to go out and face the damage?"

Jane's eyes darted up above her cup. "But what if they're not gone? What if they're still waiting out there for us?"

"I don't think they are, honey. It's been quiet outside for a long time now."

She didn't look at all convinced, and her hand gripped Katie's arm tightly.

Leaning towards her, I squeezed her knee. "I promise we'll be very, very careful. We can hardly stay in here forever, can we?"

Shaking her head, she was still doubtful. "We'll be careful?"

"More careful than ever."

"Okay."

The little girl's courage seemed to spur us, and within five or ten minutes we were gathered beside the door. George slid open the bottom bolt, his free hand gripping the golf club that had come in so handy the previous day, and I held my breath, waiting to hear some kind of reaction from outside, but as much as my ears buzzed from the strain, there was nothing.

"So far, so good." I met the old man's eyes and nodded at him, holding my can and lighter up. John and Nigel did the same alongside me. Katie stood behind the door with hers, Jane tucked behind her, so that if anything did burst through then she had the best chance of being protected. Although armed with hairspray and lighters, I wasn't convinced how much protection we'd be.

Pulling the top lock back, George opened the door an inch or two and I peered through. The air was still unnaturally warm, especially given the early time of day, and because of the damp heat a fine mist seemed to cling to the hedges and trees. But I couldn't see any sign of living creatures.

Taking a chance, I pushed the door, swinging it open wide. Nothing moved except the slight breeze that nudged past me, eager to set free the stale odour of tired and scared humans that filled our temporary sanctuary. I stepped forward onto the gravel, checking around me for any widows, relieved to find none, but still ready with my makeshift weapon.

"Holy shit."

Turning round, seeing what had caused Dave to swear, I almost dropped the can from my hand. I certainly forgot about it. In fact, standing there with my mouth open, I don't think I'd have noticed a widow if it came and tapped me politely on the shoulder before ripping my head off.

"Jesus, we must really piss those things off." Katie passed me, walking almost to the end of the short path, where the gate glittered with moisture. In fact, everything shone with drops of water, the humidity so much that although the storm of the previous night was over, the air itself felt wet against my skin. But the weather was a worry for another time. Right now, I could only stare at what was left of our careful foraging from yesterday.

The windscreen of the Animal was smashed completely, as was the window on the passenger side; the load of clothing and tents was ripped and strewn across the road in untidy clumps, sodden and useless. The windscreen wiper stuck out at an angle from the bonnet, as if something had been halfway through tearing it off when it had become distracted by more tempting prey.

Behind it, the Range Rover was in a far worse state, tipped completely over on its side, all the water containers emptied on the ground around it, and the bonnet was yawning wide open, revealing its mutilated innards. The final vehicle was in a similar state to the Animal, but the wheels sunk hopelessly into the earth, gouges in the thick rubber tyres having stolen the air from them, just in case we dared to think about trying to drive the wrecked body away.

Still trying to get my breath back, I left the gate behind and walked into the road. For a hundred yards or more in either direction, our food and goods lay damaged, dented and abandoned. I took care not to touch anything, not because it was the scene of a crime and the police would be here any moment to dust for fingerprints, lovely though that thought was, but because there were shimmering sickly strands of widows's webs covering every surface, running between each item of evidence like a trail of spit from a psychotic madman, twisting and linking into each other with no rhyme or reason. The breeze lifted and with it came a vague odour of rot that could only be coming from the gift the widows had left behind for us.

"Can you smell that?" The others had followed me

out onto the road, so they were close enough to hear my low whisper, although in the silence of this new world I'm sure the sound carried almost into the village. No one answered and I took it as a yes, peering round at them. "When I went into The Plough in Stony to get the keys for the car, the bar was covered in this stuff. I don't remember that smell. I don't remember it smelling of anything."

"Neither do I." Katie stepped past me and turned round. "So, what does it mean?"

I shrugged. "I'm not sure it means anything." What the fuck did I know? I barely recognised the countryside ahead of me, hiding its secrets in the mist.

"Oh, yes, it does." John paused to light another cigarette, the focus of all our attention. Rather than lecturing him on the health risks of nicotine, I took the opportunity to light one of my own, needing to conquer the invading stench with a friendly acrid one of my own choice; and on top of that I didn't like the slight dread in his tone.

"What it means is that things haven't finished settling down yet. We're still in the *beginning*." He looked at each of us as if that were enough.

George eventually spoke for all our confusion. "Explain."

"It's simple. The widows haven't fully developed yet, so like yesterday, when they were newborn, this shit they spew out didn't smell, but today, one day later, it does. And who knows what else it does. I'm not going to touch it unless I have to, anyway. What we've got to remember is that this has only been going on a day. The rules aren't set yet. We've got to not take things for granted."

Nigel stared at the desolation in front of us. "So, if

we chose to look on the bright side of the idea that nothing's set yet, then things could actually get better. The widows may only have a life span of a couple of days. Maybe the smell is the sign of sickness or weakness." He smiled, a wild hope in his eyes.

"Or it could just get a whole lot worse." Dave just got the words out before he broke into a hacking cough. The light in Nigel's expression went out, and scowling, he turned away.

"And speaking of worse, I don't want to be a pain in the arse, but my arm hurts like hell. I think I need some stronger antibiotics or something."

"So, where should be go? The village? They may have a chemist's there." Katie was clinging to Jane, and I wondered who was comforting whom. Her hair had come loose from her ponytail while she slept, and her wild curls hung free down her back. Again, my urge to protect her was suddenly confused with other, more primal instincts, and I swallowed hard trying to focus on our situation rather than the sudden tingling sensations that ran through me.

Dave nodded at something in the distance. "There's a farmhouse over there. I think that's where we should go first. They may have a couple of shotguns we can have." He leaned against the wall a little, revealing his weakness. "I don't fancy taking on any more of those bastards without something a little more substantial if we can help it. I can manage another couple of hours on the pills we've got."

From the look of him I wasn't so sure, but there was sense in what he was saying and I could see agreement on the tense faces around me. We did need better weapons, and the farm was the best bet. My heart sank a little at how we were toughening up. "Okay. Let's go."

The building looked deceptively close, but had to be at least two miles away, and that was heading over the fields. That was going to be hard work, given the amount of rain that had fallen.

"How are we going to get there?" The answer to Nigel's question was so obvious that no one answered it for a moment, until George filled the silence.

"Our only option is to walk. So I suggest we get started."

Our mood sombre, matched by the thick grey sky above, we loaded up rucksacks with what we could carry and tucked supersized aerosols and lighters into our belts within easy reach; then we began walking.

We finally trudged through the gates at the bottom of the farmhouse drive just over an hour later, and despite our slow pace, I was sweating and tired. The clouds were hanging low, the weight of their load obviously getting too much to carry, and I didn't need a weatherman to tell me that it wouldn't be long until another downpour was upon us. With the stifling humidity, our thick fleeces and the bags on our backs, making our way through the fields had been hard work, and it hadn't only been Dave that had needed rest stops. None of us had argued when the suggestion had been made to take a breather, and at least in the open we could see what was around us, even if we didn't have the energy to run from it.

"Any sign of life?" George pulled a handkerchief from his pocket and wiped his face, grimacing slightly, the walk obviously having taken its toll on him despite his lack of complaints.

I peered around. Alongside the large old-style farm-house there was no garage, but a car port had been built onto it, and there was no sign of any car there. I didn't know if that was a good thing or a bad thing. No car meant it was likely that there was no one home and that was definitely a positive, but it also meant we had a long walk back to town.

"Doesn't look like it."

Deciding that I was too tired to be terrified, I swore quietly under my breath and strode towards the front door. Twisting the handle, I shoved my shoulder and backpack into the thick wooden door and almost fell into the hall when it flew open, unlocked.

"Shit!" Scrambling backwards on the worn red car-pet, I steadied my feet and gripped the door frame, breath racing in my ears, eyes darting around wildly, sure that something was going to leap out at me. Katie and George must have been of the same mind because they were suddenly by my side, aerosols raised.

"Shit." The repetition was calmer than the original, but my breath was still quick. The hallway stood deso-lately empty in front of me. Smiling humbly, I shrugged at the others. "Don't panic." The irony in my words wasn't lost on me, and my grin became sheepish. "I know, I know…the only one panicking here is me."

Katie nudged me. "It's all right. It didn't show."

"Thanks."

"Much." Giggling, she evaded my sideswipe, and this time I felt much perkier as I crossed over the Hoovered threshold.

"Any sign of that white stuff?" Dave's voice carried in from out on the drive.

The interior of the house laid out in front of me was tatty but clean, the faintly cool smell hinting at no central heating. Checking the kitchen on one side and the pantry on the other, I moved forward. There were none of the widows's trails in sight. "It seems empty. I think we're okay."

Relaxing slightly, George went into the pantry and pulled open the fridge. "Well, at least the electricity's still on. There's bread and cheese in here. And some ham. I'll make sandwiches." The rustle of his back-pack sliding to the floor followed his cheerful words out into where I stood in the hallway.

Katie's attention had been grabbed by something in the kitchen, and her elfin features sprang to life. "Wow! An aga. How cool is that!" Flicking her hair over one shoulder, she jumped up and down in child-ish excitement. "I'll be making coffee, if that's all right with everyone."

This time it was my eyebrow that rose. "No prob-lem. You two make house. I'll get on with the serious business of finding weapons, shall I?"

"Good man." She winked at me before disappear-ing, and for a moment my heart skipped a beat. I tried to calm it down, but it was difficult. Possibly the last normal woman in the world, and she was winking at me. *And* she was gorgeous.

Watching us, Dave managed a wan smile. "Easy, tiger." With his good arm he helped me off with my pack, resting it against the staircase before tapping me gently on the shoulder. "I'm only kidding, mate. It's just nice to see some flirting going on. Shows that not everything's changed." He leaned against the wall, al-lowing space for Nigel to pass us, his pack left by the door. There were four more doors ahead of us, and af-ter peering cautiously through the doorway he silently disappeared into one of them. The lack of screams or terrified shouts led me to believe that there was nothing to be concerned about in there.

I searched Dave's too-pale face, and the question was out before I could help myself. "So, you reckon there might be some flirting going on then? From her side?"

The belly laugh that erupted from him was enough to drag Nigel back out into the slender hallway.

"What is it? What's going on?" His voice was irritated and he held something behind his back. Glimpsing it briefly, I had a sinking feeling it was a bottle. Dave, however, didn't notice, still giggling to himself, his head resting against the wall. He slowly let out a sigh. "You wouldn't get it, mate. Don't worry about it." When he opened his eyes again, the contempt he felt for the other man was only too visible and the moment was lost. For a moment we just stood there in awkward silence before Nigel retreated, muttering to himself.

I nodded in the direction of an oak panelled door. "I'll start in there." Moving away, I was suddenly glad to have a few minutes alone, the company of strangers vaguely claustrophobic, all of our fear so obvious. Our need for unity, whether we liked each other or not, was just a touch too desperate, and I couldn't wait for the time when we could settle down and relax slightly, or at least know each other well enough to be able to be honest about our feelings. I hoped we all lived that long.

As it was, it only took a few minutes to conclude my search. The room I'd entered was more formal and better kept than what I'd seen of the rest of the house thus far: the panelling of the door carried into the walls, their darkness offset by the array of shelves filled with books of various coloured spines and the deep red crushed material of the two oversized sofas on either side of the huge fireplace. It stopped me in my stride for a moment or two, its presentability too out of place in comparison with the hallway and what I'd glimpsed of the old kitchen. Perhaps the house had recently changed hands and this was the first room to get a makeover, or perhaps this was the main living and entertaining space and all efforts had been made to preserve its beauty and dignity. It was like a formal drawing room in a manor house.

Shaking myself, I started to examine the surfaces and walls more thoroughly. Musing over its existence wasn't going to get us anywhere, and again I was reminded about how much more focussed I was going to have to become. I was supposed to be finding much-needed weapons to protect us, but instead I'd let my mind wander off into unimportant thoughts that had no space in this new life.

I found the plain cabinet I needed behind the door, unlocked. Bingo. Sitting neatly inside, proudly polished and upright were two full-length shotguns. Slightly warily, never having handled any kind of firearm before, I pulled them free. The weight surprised me and I tensed my grip, the long barrels wobbling slightly. John appeared round the door and grinned. "You look like the Terminator. Here, give us one."

Swivelling it round so that the stock and not the barrel was facing him, I held out my left hand. "Do you know anything about guns?"

He shook his head, and I was pleased that once he was holding it, he looked slightly nervous. "Nope. Not a thing. Are they loaded?"

"Not sure." Fumbling with the catch at the top I finally cracked it, so that the gun fell open. "Empty. Yours?"

"Empty too. Are there any shells in there?"

The gun cupboard was pretty bare once the weapons themselves had been taken out, with no drawers or hidden compartments. So maybe that's why the farmer had left it unlocked. Without the bullets, they were pretty harmless. Still, I doubted the gun lobby would have been pleased with this guy. "Nothing."

"There's a dead cat in the dining room." Dave's face was sweating slightly again as he joined us, but he seemed to be ignoring his pain pretty well for now. "Nigel found one in the den as well. Nothing apparently wrong with them. Just dead where they're sitting. Weird. Oh, good. You found some guns."

John disappeared, no doubt his teenage curiosity engaged by the mysteriously dead pets. As much as I was fond of cats, however, the shells were still my main priority.

"Yeah, but no bullets. I'll go upstairs and have a look. My money's on them being in the bedroom. I'll be back in a minute." Resting the gun against the wall, I went back into the hallway and took the uneven stairs two at a time. Despite knowing that the others were just below me, when I reached the landing and stared at the various doorways spread out ahead I felt a moment of unease that wasn't helped by the creaking of the old floorboards under my feet.

Unhooking the aerosol from the belt of my trousers, I pulled a lighter from my pocket before checking in each of the rooms. The bathroom was clean and cold and I thanked God that the shower curtain was pulled neatly open and not drawn across the bath, leaving me to wonder what could be hiding behind it.

There was a small, sparsely decorated third bedroom, and at the end of the corridor were three more rooms, two without enough clutter to be lived in, and the master bedroom, where the missing occupier obviously lived. A large double bed was covered with a perhaps homemade patchwork quilt, and there was a chair by the window, over which some working clothes had been slung rather than put away in the oversized oak wardrobe. The washing basket was overflowing slightly and I was glad to see no evidence of a woman living here. The dressing table top was free of lipstick and perfume, as the bathroom had been.

I was about to start rummaging when a noise from across the corridor caught my attention, freezing me. I turned around slowly, my heart once again thumping hard. The corridor was empty. Despite the urge I felt to run back down the stairs, I crossed the landing and peered into the large spare room. For a moment there was nothing, and then I heard it again. A crumbling sound.

Keeping against the wall, suddenly very much believing in monsters under the bed, I slid round to the other side of the double to see what was causing it. The sound of dust hitting tiles came again, and this time I could see, with relief, what was causing it. Against the far wall was a small fireplace, probably directly above the one that dominated the lounge on the lower floor, and small bits of soot were coming down from the inside and landing in the grate, the clumps scattering as they hit the hard ground. Small flecks of dark dust had spread on the carpet. Smiling slightly, the muscles in my shoulders relaxed a little. The wind was whipping up again outside and the storm the previous night had probably loosened some of the muck collecting in there. Or birds had taken refuge in it. They still seemed to be surviving pretty well. *Not like the cats.*

Turning away, I padded back into the main bedroom. There were two bedside cabinets and I pulled open and peered in both. In one was a selection of magazines and videos mainly aimed at the male marketplace, and the other was empty. Ignoring the clutter on the small shelf below the bedroom mirror I pulled open both top drawers of the large chest. One held neatly folded underwear and paired socks, but it was the other one that made me smile. There were four large boxes of cartridges, and lifting the lid to check if they were full, my grin stretched to see the metal gleaming back at me.

"Got them!" I yelled, pulling the boxes free and stacking them.

It was then that I caught a glimpse of something moving in the reflection from the mirror. A quick, darting action as something crossed the corridor. Putting the final box down and picking up the large can of hairspray I'd momentarily let go, I slowly turned round, knowing what was going to be there, and praying to God that I was wrong.

Blocking the doorway, about a foot inside the room, it hissed, some of its awful shiny surface covered in black dust, suddenly leaving me in no doubt as to what had been disturbing the soot in the chimney, those red eyes all focussed on me as they shone. Raising itself up onto its rear legs, it waved the others almost delicately forward, as if it were reaching out to embrace me. My mouth falling open in horrified disgust, I stared at its revolting underbelly. I thought I was becoming hardened to their physical presence, but that illusion fell away as my eyes tried to take in the sight of the monster's guts: a moving mass of suckers, peering through from a smooth pearlescent coating that would no doubt work like a foreskin, pulling back to allow those greedy mouths access to whatever they sought. I tried to call out, to get help, but as if in an awful dream, I couldn't get any sound out of my throat.

Mandibles clacking, the widow hissed, a loose spray emerging with the sound, and with sweating hands I finally managed some movement of my own, squirting the can and squeezing down on the lighter. Nothing happened. The flint clicked, but no flames erupted. "Shit, shit, shit..." With slippery fingers, I tried to keep my grip and flick the small lever down again.

Dropping itself back down, the widow took a slow step forward, as if sensing its advantage.

"Help me, pleeeaseesssss..."

The words sounded wet and in no way human, but rang clear in my head. A chill ran up from my spine and through my guts as I stared in horror, my fingers freezing on the nozzle of the can.

The widow took another step towards me and paused, the words coming again, seeming to ooze out from its surface rather than out from its moving mandibles.

"Help me...pleeeaseeesssss...."

Lost in fear and confusion, my brain desperately tried to work, grasping at what I was hearing. What did it want? Did it *want* me to kill it? How could I help? Suddenly, as I stared into that bank of redness, the cold truth washed over me. They were the words the man in the café had spoken, that he had so desperately tried to spit out at me, the words that I had ignored and run so hard and fast away from. A low moan escaped from me. *But how could it know? How could it possibly know?* As those foul legs crept closer to me, I stared into those awful pin-prick pupils at the depths of it tumourous eyes and saw something new there, something other than rage. It was taunting me. It was enjoying my fear. More importantly, *it was enjoying my shame*. That sense of victory glowing from it, it crouched, preparing to attack, to finish its destruction of me.

"You fucking bitch." Rage at the memory of that poor bastard eaten alive on that sofa, and rage at the poor bastard that had been me, running terrified, awash with crushing guilt, gave me the incentive I needed, and holding the can out directly I pushed the nozzle down and firmly ran my finger over the lighter.

The widow leapt into the roar of the flame, screeching as it realised, and I stepped backwards, the ledge beneath the mirror digging sharply into my back as I cowered away, taking all my resolve to keep my arms forward, burning it.

The flame I was producing was nowhere near enough for the job, and although I had stopped the creature mid-flight and sent it to the floor, it twisted angrily there, darting around the flame, trying to get to me, lashing out with its limbs, hisses and squeals escaping from it. The fire from the can was fading, getting thinner, and the nozzle was hot between my fingers. Part of the widow was burning, but instinctively I could tell that it still had enough energy to kill me before I could destroy it.

Through the smoke and madness another shadow filled the doorway, and my heart leapt. John was there, flame erupting from his own large can, raising the widow's hiss to a shriek as its rear legs caught fire. With the creature distracted, I reached for the dressing table, my fingers fumbling into one of the boxes, grabbing desperately at some of the cartridges. Two within my grasp, I turned and launched them at the creature, not sure what, if anything, was going to happen. As soon as the metal had flown free of my hands, I squeezed back down on the lighter, sending the remains of my aerosol fire to help John's.

One cartridge fell redundant on the carpet and rolled under the bed, but the second exploded like a firework, making me instinctively recoil, the power of it taking two of the widow's legs off, and for the first time I heard agony in its wail, and what I hoped was fear. My own heart surged with the thought of surviving.

Unable to move, it lashed out with its remaining legs, squirming on the floor, until eventually the hissing died and it stopped moving. On the other side of the room John kept on burning it until the surface of its body popped and melted, all those alien eyes melting into one. The smell that erupted from it was like that we had encountered coming out of the scout hut. For a few moments we both just stopped and held our breath, as if waiting for it to leap back to life.

"Jesus." John was panting, his eyes shaking slightly.

"Cheers, mate." Dropping my can, I picked up the boxes of shells. "Come on. Let's get out of here."

He still stood, staring at the sizzling mass on the carpet. Stepping past it, I grabbed his arm, shaking him until he met my own gaze. "You just saved my life. You killed the bitch. Now let's go."

He stared into my eyes for a few seconds and then nodded before his stare moved slightly beyond me.

"Matt. The curtains are on fire."

Turning round to face the room, I could see where the bottom of the thick old material was losing the battle against the fire. The flames were also slowly moving up the bedspread.

"Fuck it. We'll leave it." Tugging his arm, I pulled him out of the room and towards the stairs.

"Wait."

Eager to be gone, I snapped impatiently. "What?"

"What did that thing say? Did it speak to you?" His eyes were full of dread, and it sapped my anger. The whole thing had run in crazy time for me, and I hadn't realised that he'd been close enough to hear it.

"We'll talk about it on the way to town, okay?" It had to be okay, because I wasn't ready to discuss that yet, my thoughts spinning too fast to focus. Once again, I was drawn back to that memory of Chloe in the darkened living room holding a conversation without a telephone. The likelihood of the dead widow being the same one as I'd seen in the café in Stony was highly unlikely, so how could it have known about the dying man's words?

At the bottom of the stairs, George held out my backpack to me and loaded the guns while I put on the pack.

"I can use one of these. Not a brilliant shot, but I was good in my day. National Service and all that." He filled his pocket with more shells and then did the same with mine. He met my eye and lowered his voice. "You carry the second one. Nigel's not reliable and John's too young. Dave's outside throwing up." The old man's expression was grim. "I don't know what that bite did to him, but it's not good. We need to go on to Woburn. It's a couple of miles on from here, but

170

they are more likely to have a good chemist there than that little village. We're also going to have to find some more cars." Squeezing my arm, he glanced upstairs. "Is it dead?"

"Yeah, it's dead. I fucking hope it is, anyway. We blew two of its legs off." Smoke was starting to appear at the top of the stairs.

George slapped me on the shoulder. "Well, we'd better be going then."

Following him back out into the humid air where the others had gathered, Katie and Nigel supporting Dave, that image of Chloe lingered, and things seemed to slot a little into place. Could the widows have some kind of collective consciousness? It would make sense that if they did before they evolved, then maybe they did after. Following George's lead, I trudged silently back onto the gravel track, not feeling much more secure for the shotgun resting across my shoulder. Within a few steps, the first heavy drops of rain began to fall.

Chapter Fourteen

The rain was still coming down steadily when we entered the historic, idyllic town of Woburn, a haven of thatched buildings and antique furniture shops, awash with the spirit of Miss Marple, tea shops and twitching net curtains. Although I was thankful that, as we walked warily towards the main road, none of those thin voiles moved to signal prying eyes. I was pretty certain that if they did, it wouldn't be just nosy old ladies trying to peer out at us.

We'd actually been closer to Woburn that we'd originally thought, and by braving the roads rather than attempting to navigate across the fields, it had been a much easier walk than our first of the morning, despite the weight of the bags and the clouds emptying onto us from above. Plus, this time round, no one even attempted a conversation. I led silently, my gun ready even if I wasn't, and George brought up the rear, his weapon held hopefully with a little more confidence.

The main street of the town was wide, the middle

section made up of two lines of parking bays to accommodate the shoppers that converged there during the daytimes and especially on Saturdays. These were normally full, but as we turned the corner I could see only three or four cars stranded there, and it would seem that as with most of the rest of the animal kingdom, the human race had stayed in the comfort of their own homes to die. Or *change*. Which pretty much amounted to the same thing for those of us that were left behind.

"Where's the chemist? Does anyone know?" Katie sounded tired, and I'd noticed dark circles gathering under her eyes as the day wore on. Nigel had taken over her role as support for Dave as the older man had got progressively weaker, but had remained silent on the journey, and it was still Katie that had given Dave the odd word of encouragement and support as he desperately tried not to show how much he was suffering.

"I think there's one at the other end of the street. This bit's all furniture shops and cafés." I kept to myself that the reason I knew it so well was that Chloe had dragged me up here to choose pretty much all our furniture, wanting something a little more personal than what the huge warehouses in the Milton Keynes shopping centre had to offer. Another pang of loneliness and heartache stabbed inside, and I hoped that there would be a time when I felt safe and secure enough to allow some time for all the grief inside to come out and then allow me to keep her close inside. I needed it, and I felt I was cheating Chloe by not getting rid of some of the pain so I could then work on savouring our memories and committing them to a safe place in my mind. Surely that's what the grieving process was supposed to be about. Not this shutting out of everything, just to try and keep my head clear.

For the moment, I kept my head down, and avoided looking in the windows of the shops we passed, holders of invisible snapshots of my previous life, focussing instead on the weight of the gun and the pack on my back while I stared at the cobbles.

"Hey, look at that white van!"

Jane trotted up past me and ran a few steps ahead before I could slow her down by grabbing at her sweatshirt sleeve with my free hand. "Hey, no running ahead. What van?"

"Over there! Look!" I followed the excited pointing finger that bounced up and down as she jumped with the kind of energy that only a child could have after everything we'd been through in the past twenty-four hours. "Look!"

It was white, but it wasn't a van. It was a minibus parked outside the little parade where the chemist was, and it only took a second or two for all of us to catch on to what Jane had seen that had sent her bouncing. The engine was running, the sound coming over the silent air towards us in a steady thrum, and from the exhaust a grey mist pumped out into the haze of rain. The deadness in my legs lifted as they instinctively picked up the pace.

"There's people." Turning around, I grinned at George and the others behind me. "There's people in a shop up there! Come on!"

The straps of the rucksack dug painfully into my shoulders as I jogged, but that wasn't going to stop me from running. Just the idea of other people alive out there sent a shockwave of anticipation through my system. I don't think I'd have slowed down even if I'd accidentally fired the shotgun, which I was waving around in a cavalier fashion, trying to manage its length and weight and not succeeding. As George caught up with me, I almost felt a pang of envy at his grace, the weapon tilted into his shoulder. Even for a tired old man, he was managing a whole lot better than me. I could hear Nigel puffing somewhere behind my ears. It didn't surprise me that he'd abandoned Dave in order to keep up with the guns. Maybe that made him more of a natural survivor than the rest of us, but I'd take my chances as I was.

"What if they're not friendly?"

George sent a disparaging look over his shoulder. "As long as they've only got two legs, they'll be fine by me."

By the time we'd trotted the couple of hundred yards up the slight incline, the minibus slowly getting larger and larger, all our eyes focussed on it, no longer any thought for what might leap out at us from the recessed doorways or windows around us. My breath was hot as it raced in and out of my lungs. My face glowing, I stopped and almost leaned my gun against the wall before realising how stupid that was. Nigel was beside me, way more out of breath than I was, and looking behind me, I could see that George had slowed down to wait with Katie and John, who between them were trying to keep up and support Dave's weight.

"There's no one in here." Disappointment flattened Jane's voice as she peered on tiptoes into the slightly tinted windows. The green letters on the side read MEADOWBANK SCHOOL, and I figured by looking at the painted flower that it was a primary or middle school. My heart ached for Jane, suddenly aware of just how lonely she must be. No other children to play with, to share her fears with without being patronised or smothered in platitudes.

I stepped back and stared into the face of each of the shops. "Hello? Is anyone there?"

There was a dry cleaner, an off-licence two doors further up, a small co-op and the chemist we'd been looking for. The only one that didn't look broken into was the dry cleaners and that didn't come as much surprise.

"Hello?" I called out again. John echoed my call with his own, but there was no answer, and my heart started to sink. Maybe we were too late. Maybe there were widows lurking inside that had killed whoever had left the engine running out here. I stepped forward and was about to try searching in the co-op when a voice startled me.

"About bloody time! Are you the cavalry?"

Peering out of the off-licence doorway, an arm waved in our direction, a bottle of beer gripped in one hand. Attached to the arm was a middle-aged man, his face hidden behind an overgrown, curly silver-grey beard, his body tall and lanky, thin apart from a small paunch jutting out under his cable-knit sweater. Great. Another born survivor. Where were all the Arnold Schwarzeneggers when you really needed them?

Grinning, he made his way towards us, and we met him halfway. He held out his hand, his skin slightly leathery from what I imagined were too many Spanish holidays, and a thick gold chain bracelet shone conspicuously on his wrist. Twinkling, his bloodshot eyes were blue at the centre, and despite the slight drunken sway in his stance as he pulled himself straight, I found myself warming to this stranger.

"Oliver Maine. Nice to meet you." His rough-edged voice had an upper class accent that oozed private schooling, a contrast with the bottle of Carling Special Brew by his side. Despite his age, there was something of the teenager about him. "Now can anyone bloody tell me what's been going on? Where the hell is everybody?"

"Don't you know?" Katie was incredulous. After all we'd seen and been through, it was hard to believe that there was someone alive who wasn't all too aware of the widows.

He shook his head, helping himself to a cigarette as I opened my pack to take one for myself. I lit it for him, cupping the light to protect it from the wet, and he took a long drag, shaking his head.

"What is it? Some kind of chemical warfare? A plague?" He stared at our blank expressions and shrugged. "I'd had a bit of a drink. I thought it'd help me get rid of the blasted headache I'd had for a day, which I'm pleased to say seems to have disappeared, and I remember being in the pub, and I vaguely remember leaving, but after that it's a blank. Woke up a couple of hours ago in my flat. I'd slept a whole day and night. Anyway, I decided a hair of the dog was required and when I came out, it seemed to me that every other bugger had disappeared off somewhere. So where the hell are they all?"

Watching the slight shake in his hand, I knew that a hair of the dog was probably the way that most of Oliver Maine's days started. The shake wasn't the only thing that gave his drinking problem away. It was his choice of drink. Carling Special Brew was lethal. A bottle of that would knock my socks off, and our new friend was drinking it first thing in the morning.

"It's a long story."

He grinned again, refreshingly undisturbed by the lack of human company. "Well, if it's a long one, it'd better be bloody interesting. Is that your bus?" He laughed, a bubbly warm sound. "Not exactly army regulation, is it?"

John frowned, the rim of his baseball cap darker where the constant rain had slowly soaked it. "It's not ours. Our cars got wrecked. I thought it was yours."

"No, nothing to do with me. I only live round the corner. I walked."

I turned round to look into the other shops, Nigel and John doing the same. If the van wasn't Maine's, then who the hell had driven it down here? The question was momentarily forgotten as Dave, leaning against the bus, threw up, clear liquid spewing down the front of his clothes.

"We've got to get him some medicine." Katie nodded in the direction of the chemist.

She was right. Dave's medicine was what we'd come here for in the first place. "John, why don't you and Jane go in the co-op and get some supplies. Put them in the minibus. If the driver doesn't turn up, we may as well take it." No one argued with me. We were like scavengers now—the morality of taking what wasn't ours no longer applied. A lot of things no longer applied. "Nigel, you keep your eyes open out here with George."

His eyes narrowed. "Do I get a gun?"

No fucking way, you whining selfish fucker, was what I wanted to say to him, but I bit my tongue. "No, George has got his, and John can take the other one. He's got Jane with him." The slight black look that

Nigel sent in the direction of the despondent child may have been missed by some, but I definitely saw it. Turning away, I pushed open the broken door into the chemist. "Come on, Dave. Let's get that arm seen to."

Oliver Maine hadn't needed asking to help Dave through the door, and he watched with concern as Katie started to carefully peel the bandage from the wounded arm. I'd stepped behind the counter and begun rummaging through the various books and medical catalogues, desperate to find some kind of information on all the boxes and bottles of pills that surrounded me in the pharmacist's area. I scanned for animal bites and blood-poisoning, or any all round antibiotic.

"What happened to him?" Maine's question was directed at Katie, an indication of how bad Dave's condition had got. His pale face was sweating badly, and his eyes shook slightly, glazing over as if they were unable to focus.

"He got bit by a widow." Katie didn't look up, gently unwinding the layers of bandage.

"What the bloody hell's a widow?"

"That's part of the long story. Here, take the bandage. I want to get the dressing off." Her voice was soft, the kind of softness that could never be found in a man's voice, and it made my heart squeeze. The surprised, sharp breath that followed made me stop my search and turn.

"Shit." She exclaimed. "Shit. Oh, *shit*."

"What the hell is that?" There was no hint of joviality in our new comrade now, and keeping hold of the packet of antibiotics designed to treat fuck only knew what that I'd found, I came quickly round to join them.

"What? What's happened?" No one spoke and I followed their eyes to the uncovered wound.

I stared down in disbelief and more than a small amount of disgust, not sure I knew what I was seeing, my mind scanning its memory banks to see if there were any images locked away that were even vaguely similar. It drew a blank.

His arm was red, an angry crimson spreading out from the injury. There were deep cuts in his skin where the mandibles had clamped down on him, the rivers of poison blaring out against the pale inner arm, but that I could deal with. That I could understand. What was new, what was so alien, was the *stuff* that oozed from the bite, the white, thin, stringy substance that erupted outwards, coming from *within his arm,* that spread, winding its way along the limb and under his wrist, reaching down to his fingers and stretching up towards his elbow. I felt escaping air catch in my throat as my eyes slowly crept up to look into Dave's sweaty face.

A weak smile attempted to take hold of his lips, his own voice wet and breathless. "If you try and tell me that's normal, I'll punch your face in."

Katie ripped open the box of pills and pressed some into his mouth. "These look pretty strong." She tried to smile, but her attempt wasn't as good as Dave's. "At least the packet says you can't drink with them, so I'll take that as a sign they're good for you." Her patient took them and swallowed, his grimace betraying how they stuck dryly in his throat, and Oliver pulled a Lucozade from the shelf, opening it for him.

"No alcohol? That can never be good for you." He

passed the bottle of golden, sugary liquid. "Get that down you."

Scurrying off behind the counter, Katie scrabbled at bottles in a random panic. "Maybe if we can find some liquid antibiotic, something we can put straight into the wound, or some kind of bleach or antiseptic, maybe that could stop it. Maybe if we—"

"Stop it." Dave's tired voice cut her off, his calm the antithesis of her manic rambling. "Just stop it, Katie."

Despite his words, she continued to peer into the shelves around her for a few moments until her movements slowly wound down like a clock and finally she stopped and turned to face him, leaning across the counter and resting her face in her hands.

Dave coughed two or three times, a too-wet, phlegmy sound coming from deep in his chest, and then breathed raggedly before speaking.

"That's not going to work, and we all know it." His eyes shook slightly with fever, but behind them his clear mind was apparent.

Slowly, Katie straightened up and came back round, leaning next to me against the counter. "But there's got to be something we can do. There must be." Her voice sounded more like Jane's, the hopelessness and fear making her quiet words sound childlike. The seconds ticked by in silence, and I stared at the walls, the shelves of shampoo and baby lotions, anywhere rather than at Dave or at the others.

Finally Dave let out a long sigh. "There is something you can do. It is the only thing you can do." He stared at Katie and then at me. "You can cut my arm off."

His quiet words took a couple of seconds to sink into my tired brain.

"No fucking way." My head shook. "No fucking way. There must be something else."

"Look at my arm, Matt. Look at it."

I did, and a wave of revulsion again washed over me as I stared at the white strands that I was sure wriggled slightly with life as they twisted around his limb. "If you don't amputate, this is going to kill me. I know it, and you know it."

His shoulders slumped forward, shrinking inward in the plastic chair, as if his body had got smaller since the bite, smaller with the awful acknowledgement of the truth that he'd come to before the rest of us.

I wasn't sure the counter could take the weight of my body and soul, but it stood up to the task, and leaning against it, I rubbed my face, feeling the itch of unshaven stubble, my hand resting across my mouth for a moment.

"Where are we going to do it? How?" I looked at Kate and Oliver. "The hospital's miles away, and I don't think small town doctor's surgeries have the equipment we need."

"I don't really fucking care, I just want you to cut it off." The monotone and tiredness that oozed from Dave was scarier than if he were screaming. "I need to get it *out of me*."

Oliver waved one of his gangly arms at the cigarette pack sticking out of my jeans pocket and I opened it. We all took one and ceremoniously passed the lighter round. It was our new friend that broke the silence.

"There's a vet's at the other end of Willow Grove." Using the glowing end of the cigarette, he pointed out towards somewhere through the left wall. "It's about a mile or so out that way. I used to have a dog." He smiled slightly and shrugged sheepishly. "I loved that dog. Border collie. Anyway, he got sick." Cigarette smoke was thickening the air, but the sting of it almost felt good. "They were good to him up there. They've got a hospital out back where they do operations. That could be a good place."

Glancing first at the sky outside and then at my watch, I stood upright. "Well, if we're going to do it today, then we'd better do it soon. It's midday already, and we need to get to Hanstone by the time it gets dark." None of us wanted to spend another night like the one before. Hanstone Park seemed like a haven in my mind, a place where we would be safe, and I imagine it was the same for the others.

"Tell me, Oliver." Dave pulled on his cigarette, his hand trembling, his tone light. "This dog of yours. When it got sick and you took it to this vet's ..."

"Yep?" Maine hooked his hand in one of Dave's armpits and pulled him up.

"Did it live?" The rattling in his chest forced his words out in a wheeze.

"Nope. But it was a bloody old bugger. And anyway, he had a vet operating on him. You've got us." Cigarette clamped between his teeth, he smiled. "Which makes about a million to one chance of us doing it right and you surviving."

"Oh, good." Dave grimaced slightly as Katie rewrapped his damaged arm. "I feel so much better now."

Maine chortled out loud, slapping the injured man heartily on his back. "Oh, but you should. Don't you watch the films? The million to one shots always come in."

The door behind then flew open and Jane erupted in, all excitement and energy. "We've found who was driving the minibus! It's a woman!" Her shining eyes shot round each of us, unaware of the surreal madness that had been taking place only moments ago. Our silence obviously frustrated her.

"Well, come on!" She huffed impatiently, before turning on her heel and heading back outside.

Dave was still trembling a little as Katie safety-pinned the bandage, hiding the monstrosity that was spreading underneath. "It's time we got going, anyway. Matt's right. We need to get this done quickly. So let's go." Oliver helped him to his feet and Katie filled a carrier bag with a selection of pills and liquids that she must have felt we would need.

Pushing away from the counter, I followed Jane and led the others out, unable to match the child's enthusiasm, the knowledge of what we had to do shortly turning my stomach, preventing me from feeling any kind of joy at a new survivor, instead only a grim anger at what this new world was throwing at us, at *me*.

The rain was still warm and thick, but coming down slightly slower than earlier, small patches of sky clearing above. Standing by the front of the minibus, John twisted and smiled at us. The slim dark-haired figure next to him didn't, but continued leaning forward on the bonnet, writing on a small notepad. Jane tugged at my sleeve.

"I think she's deaf." She smiled, pleased with herself. "I figured it out. No one else."

Gently drawing the girl's attention to us, John took the notepad and held it up. "This is Rebecca." The name was written in beautifully shaped, even letters across the plain paper. The author smiled nervously, her full features and dark eyes complemented by the olive skin. Although she was slim, there was something athletic in her build and she looked strong in her jeans, tight-fitting maroon polo neck and leather jacket. A deaf girl. A beautiful deaf girl. There was no doubt about that, all cool tall elegance.

My head suddenly filled with her beauty and Dave's wound, images of that living whiteness cutting through her skin as it strangled her face, and then her face turned into Katie's elfin one, the strands eating into that, and I wondered if perhaps loneliness may not be the worst thing about all of this. Maybe the worst bit was having people to care about, to fear the loss off, especially now, when human company was so rare and precious.

When I spoke, the harshness in my voice surprised all of us. Apart from Rebecca, of course, although she could probably "hear" it in the faces of the others. "That's great, but we've got to get going. Everyone on the bus. Sit in the front with me, Oliver. I need you to direct me to the vet's."

A flash of something like annoyance seemed to surface in Rebecca's eyes as I pulled open the door and got in behind the wheel. I guess she still saw it as her car, but this was a brave new world, and if someone was going to drive us then I wanted it to be someone that could react quickly to any kind of warning. I didn't look at her again as I adjusted the seat, but she must have figured that it wasn't that big of a deal, not worth being left behind alone for at any rate. The door at the back slid shut and I pulled away, the heavy slow chug of the minibus miles away from the smooth ease of the Mitsubishi.

"The vet's?" Nigel was in the seat directly behind mine, and even the rustle of his ridiculous suit was irritating. "Why are we going to the vet's? I thought we were going straight to Hanstone. That's where we need to be going. We need to be going there right now." His index finger jabbed at the back of my shoulder blade, as if to add emphasis to his words in case I chose to ignore them. "There'll be people there. Proper people that can sort all this out."

Staring forward and ignoring him, it was only my grip on the steering wheel that stopped me from turning round and punching him in the face.

An uneventful twenty minutes later and we stood in a nervous huddle in the centre of the reception area of the small practice. Even Nigel had stayed silent since Dave had explained just why we needed our little diversion. The air smelled damp from the warm water that had quietly soaked us outside, hiding in the fibres of our sweatshirts and jumpers.

"So, who's going to do it then?" Dave opened the clinical white door that should lead into the small consulting rooms and the hospital, if the sign above was to be believed. Nigel hovered at the back of our small bunch, as if trying to make himself invisible, but his efforts were unnecessary. I would have guessed that Dave would rather have chewed his own arm off rather than let Nigel anywhere near him.

George caught my eye, and we nodded to each other, my heart sinking. If George was our leader, then I seemed to have become his general, and I wasn't sure if it was a responsibility I was ever going to learn to enjoy.

"That'll be me and George, then." The smile I tried to give Dave must have looked more like a death mask stretched tight across my skull, but it was the best I could do while trying to quell the rush of fear that sent a hot flush racing out of every pore of my skin.

"The rest of you might as well get a bit of a rest." George was right behind me. "John, you keep that gun. Come with us to the operating room, just in case, and then come back and keep an eye out. Katie can look after the other gun. If there's any trouble, shout, but I've got to warn you, depending on how we're getting on in there, it's unlikely that we're going to be able to come out and help." His words were greeted with a round of silent nods, apart from Rebecca, who had been trying to communicate something to John, and finally resorted to scribbling on the small damp notepad she'd used outside. She held the sheet up firmly in my face, her expression fiercely determined to be heard.

I have some medical training. I am a nurse for the handicapped. I can help.

My heart raced slightly. "So you know about amputation?" The pen scribbled furiously again.

No, I'm not a doctor. But I know a bit about drugs. He'll need painkillers. And something to knock him out.

I stared at her words for a second or two before shrugging. "Well, I suppose that's better than nothing. As long as you think you can handle it."

Tucking her pad into the back pocket of her jeans, her dark eyes glared at me with disdain. I didn't know why I felt the need to somehow be angry with her; maybe even then I sensed that she was different from me, Katie, Jane and the rest of us, that she was somehow outside of this nightmare. Whatever it was, I was out of patience and good feeling and she was the easiest person to take it out on.

187

With enough of a nudge for me to feel her annoyance, Rebecca took Dave's arm and smiled gently at him before following John through the doorway.

Bringing up the rear, I flicked on the wall switch and banks of strip lighting hummed into life above us. Leaving the others, I consciously avoided glancing back into their wide eyes, not even Katie's, not wanting to see their dread at what we were about to do. I followed John as he cautiously checked each room we passed, shouldering his responsibility well for such a young man. I wondered wryly if some of it were for Rebecca's benefit. I wasn't the only red-blooded male left alive, that was for sure.

Well, I thought as I watched them both moving ahead of me, I'd give him ten out of ten for trying, but I'd guess he was a little young for the cool-headed Rebecca.

We turned to the left, where the corridor thinned slightly, a bank of empty cages running down one side, and my mind drifted back to the dead cats at the farm; I wondered for an awful moment if all the pets in England had gone the same way. *All the pets across the world.* We certainly hadn't seen any strays since yesterday, and I couldn't remember hearing any barking. My heart constricted with the thought, and I tried to retain some optimism. The birds had survived. And so had we. Maybe some of our four-legged friends had made it through, too. Only time would tell.

"This must be it."

At the end of the corridor, next to a small bathroom, a kitchen and a room with a narrow set of bunks probably for when vets or nurses needed to stay over, we found a room not dissimilar to the smaller consulting rooms, but with a much larger examining table and adjustable lights above it. Taking her leather jacket off, Rebecca made a pillow for Dave and helped him to lie down, keeping one of her hands wrapped round his in support. Her naturally olive skin had paled, and for the first time I allowed myself some sympathy for her. She hadn't needed to volunteer her assistance; there was no way in hell we'd ever have known she was a nurse, and God only knew that changing a few bedpans and dressings on ulcers wouldn't compare with what we were going to do now. Despite myself, I had to admit she had some bollocks. Metaphorically, at least.

John left us to go back to the others, and I shut the door as George and Rebecca rummaged through the equipment and medication. Rebecca found something that she obviously recognised and filled a syringe, flicking the end professionally before squeezing out the bubbles of air. Smiling at him in the way only a professional could in this situation, she slapped his good arm until a vein rose. The needle slipped in easily.

"Will it put him out?"

She shook her head.

"But it'll stop the pain?"

She nodded, but it was more hesitant than I would have liked.

Dave grabbed my hand. "From the shoulder, Matt." His bloodshot eyes were desperate. "Take it all off. Not just from the elbow. No chances." His head lolled back, his pupils dilated. "No chances." The words came out in a rush of breath and spittle, and despite his head rolling away from me, his grip stayed firm.

I returned the squeeze. "Okay, mate. Try and relax. That's what we'll do." Slowly, as the seconds ticked by, George pulling open cupboards and doors behind me, I felt his sweaty palm reluctantly relinquish mine as he drifted off into a semiconscious state.

"What was that?" I tugged on Rebecca's sleeve so that she could read my lips. "Morphine?"

She shook her head and held up the bottle. Ketamin. It meant nothing to me.

It works on animals. I'm hoping for the same with Dave. Not sure on dosage though. Guesswork.

The paper was tilted just in case Dave could read it. It didn't read too promising for him.

"This should do us." George pulled a small surgical saw from a drawer on the far side of the room. As he pressed the button on the side, the small blade buzzed into life, rotating faster than I could see, like a baby circular saw, all high-pitched noise and tinny action.

George's face had greyed close to the colour of his hair, and looking at the gleam on his wrinkled forehead, I knew I wasn't the only one breaking out into a cold sweat.

"We're going to have to heat this up somehow. To cauterise the wound. Otherwise he'll bleed to death. The wound's going to need sealing as we cut."

"Well, how the hell are we supposed to do that?" I looked around me in frustration, as if expecting a blow torch to appear miraculously on the sterile benches running around the white walls.

"I don't know, Matt. We need to think."

Rebecca started to cut away the arm of Dave's jumper and even the short sleeve of the T-shirt beneath, not bothering to unbandage the wound. For a brief moment I wondered how we would keep his arm warm afterwards, now that she had damaged his clothes, wrecked them; then came the surreal sickness of reality, the dawning thought that we would not be taking Dave's arm with us when we left. It would lie here and rot. Another piece of debris from a demised world. Depending of course on whether that stuff inside it would let it rot. Or maybe it would sprout eight legs and come after us for revenge. In the new world in which we lived that didn't sound so ridiculous, and the revulsion of the thought cleared my mind.

"The kitchen. There's a kitchen just outside. There was a cooker. You can heat it up there."

"Good thinking. I'll go. Get everything ready. I'll heat it till it's blue, but I don't know how long the metal will keep the temperature." George smiled, but there was no joy in it, and he pulled a handkerchief out of his pocket and wiped his forehead with a trembling hand, staring at the saw in his other. "I mean, Jesus Christ, what am I saying? I don't know anything. What the hell are we trying to do? Why couldn't someone else do it?"

"We're the best chance he's got, George." I grabbed his arm, forcing the old man to look at me, lowering my voice, just in case Dave could hear beyond the spaced out delirium he seemed to have drifted into. "And if it was me laying there, I'd be very glad I had *you* panicking about how best to do this. And you know why? Because I didn't even think about cauterising the fucking wound. If I'd been on my own doing this, Dave'd be fucking dead by now."

He nodded at me, his eyes glittering slightly, but that moment of mild hysteria seemed to have passed. By the time he'd taken a couple of deep breaths his shaking had calmed down.

"I'll go and get this hot. Have some bandages ready.

And something to stitch him up with. We'll have to try and leave some skin to cover it."

Rebecca must have been watching us speak, because she held up a box to catch our attention. Sutures.

"Good girl." George's smile was genuine as he left us.

The few minutes that he was gone passed too quickly, and suddenly the moment had arrived, Rebecca standing by to seal up the stump, George with his glowing, buzzing saw, and me holding Dave's arm slightly out from his body. I could feel sweat on the inside of the tight latex gloves, and as George lowered the metal to Dave's skin, I squeezed my eyes shut. I couldn't help myself. What the hell were we doing? This was crazy. This was more than crazy. The world spun in those next minutes, spun around me, dragging me into it, forcing my eyes open for fear I'd otherwise fall over.

I'm not sure what was the worst part of it. It was all terrible. Etched indelibly in my mind where it'll stay until the day I die. It could have been the sound of the saw, inhuman and relentless, or the feel of that infected arm vibrating in my hands as George wielded our so-called operating equipment, sending it crunching through Dave's flesh and bones. And then there was the thin high-pitched scream he let out as the blade started its job, too late for Rebecca to add to his medication, his chest rising up from the table in sheer agony, just before he blissfully passed out. And finally there was the awful thump as the arm hit the table, no longer attached, no longer a part of Dave Randall.

I let go as quickly as I could, wanting to rip off the gloves and disinfect myself, decontaminate my body and soul from the whole experience. I fought the urge and as George moved away and dropped the saw in the sink, I used all my strength to pick up the heavy, lifeless limb and deposit it in the tall bin in the corner.

Rebecca took over after that, tight determination on her face as she stitched his arm back up, stretching the untidy loose flap of skin George had managed to leave over the burned raw flesh and antiseptic cream she'd covered the crisp wound with. I didn't watch for long, instead going out to the small bathroom where I splashed cold water over my face and then threw up violently in the sink, my legs threatening to crumple under me, hot sweat erupting out of every pore. I didn't take much pride in the fact that I remained standing. Not when I thought about George and Rebecca and the more gruesome parts they'd played in this operation.

I wet my face again, needing the coolness to soak and calm me, and then straightened up, taking a few long shaky breaths. Looking at my face staring back at me, haggard but at least sane, I let myself off the hook. This was serious shit, and I was getting my fair share to handle, but at least I wasn't cracking up. Not in anyway that I, or anyone else, could notice. Not like our friend Phelps out there at any rate. Running my wet fingers through my hair, I let the water drip down my tired, pale forehead and into my bloodshot eyes. And then I retched again. And again. And this time I allowed myself to slide down the wall and rest against the cool tiles as my head spun. In the quiet outside, I could hear that someone was doing pretty much the same thing in a much more gentle way in the kitchen next door. Perhaps Rebecca wasn't so tough after all. As my sides ached with heaving, I found that I warmed to her with that realisation.

* * *

We let Dave rest for an hour before moving him, but that was as long as we could allow. Rebecca had injected him with more God knows what, and it calmed him down, knocking him out for small periods of time, but every fifteen minutes or so he'd gasp into consciousness and cry out, the agony clear for all to hear, and then he'd sob, long, soulful sounds, worse than the cries of pain, and then Rebecca would soothe him and he'd quiet down. She packed a bag of dressings, lotions and drugs, and eventually, the time came for Dave to be half-carried, half-dragged out to the van, his good arm slung over my shoulder, his whole body weight leaning into me. He screamed a lot then, and all I could do was grit my teeth and ignore it, George up ahead, opening the doors and sending the rest out to open up the bus, Rebecca following behind with her bag and a couple of blankets designed for use with injured animals.

Outside the weather had changed again, a far more tropical feel hovering about us. For the moment all was quiet. There was thunder in the air, but no rain, and for now all we were beaten with was a hot wind more suited to the plains of Africa than the southern English countryside.

My shoulder straining, I carried Dave out to the van, where John and Oliver helped lift him awkwardly inside. Thankfully, he'd passed out again somewhere along the way, his body a blood-soaked wreck.

"Will he be all right?" Katie took my hand as I stepped back onto the pavement, but it didn't bring me much comfort. Not after all that.

I didn't look at her, but stared ahead at everything and nothing, not wanting to see her beauty just now.

"I don't know. He lost blood and we couldn't give him any more. And then there's the possibility of infection."

And then there's the bite. The words screamed silently in the quiet of my own head. I didn't share them. I didn't think any of us needed to hear them out loud.

PART II

CHAPTER FIFTEEN

By the time we arrived at Hanstone Park it was late afternoon, and although the sky had darkened overhead, as yet the rain had stayed off. Pulling up the heavy handbrake of the minibus, I felt the muscles across my back and shoulders scream slightly, tight with the tension that had been building up through the day and the slow drive from Woburn. Although the trip had been uneventful, I had been certain every time we came through a tight blind bend there would be a barricade of angry, hissing, all-knowing widows waiting for us.

Help me ... please ... I shuddered just thinking about it.

While driving, I'd shared my experience of the widow taunting me in the farmhouse and it seemed that no one, not even Nigel, could come up with a different theory than mine—that the widows were somehow telepathic, or shared some other kind of collective consciousness. It wasn't a comforting thought as we drove through the silent towns and hedged fields, eyes peeled for signs of life. We had seen a couple of people as we'd driven through a small village, but they ran away as we stopped. We didn't go and look for them, but instead Katie shouted out the window that we were going to Hanstone Park, and that it would be safer for them to try and get there, too. They didn't come out, and after a few minutes we drove away. Their survival plan was their business.

Katie and Rebecca had kept Dave dosed up with painkillers on the journey and tried to keep him as comfortable as possible, but he'd been coming round for the last twenty minutes or so, and as I slid open the door to the back I could see that he was conscious.

"Stay there till we get inside, mate."

He nodded slightly, his face grey and in obvious pain. George was already out from the passenger side, and John, Oliver, Jane and Katie climbed down from the back, followed by a very crumple-suited Nigel. Rebecca stayed inside with Dave.

I lit four cigarettes and passed them round, inhaling my own hard. God, that tasted good. We hadn't smoked in the bus, not wanting to add any more chance of infection to Dave's already poor odds.

"It may seem like a stupid question, but just how are we supposed to get in?"

Nigel stared at me with a blend of disgust, amusement and sheer victorious hatred shining in his eyes. I wondered if he'd rather we all died out there if it meant that he could make me feel that I'd got it all wrong. It was as if he blamed me for the whole stupid mess the world had become. Because that would make sense. Maybe it did in Nigel's mad, mad world. I tried to hide my tired irritation by turning my back to him and taking a long look at our situation.

The worst part was that as we'd driven round the perimeter I'd had the same thoughts. The whole complex was surrounded by high metal fencing of at least fifteen feet and topped with barbed wire, and large signs painted onto the grey surface at regular intervals declared it electrified. We could only assume it still was, and even if it wasn't, we hadn't brought a ladder and a leg up wasn't going to get us over this one.

"Easy." George said, lighting his freshly filled pipe. "Someone will let us in. Look up there."

Above us, on either side of the solid gates, two security cameras peered down. George walked over to where I was standing, and then back to where he'd been leaning against the bus. The silent dark eye followed him, whirring and clicking as it did so. The one on the other side stayed trained on John, who was carrying one of the shotguns across his shoulder.

"That movement's not automatic. Someone's controlling them. I suggest you put that gun down, John, if we're ever going to get an invitation inside."

John did as he was told, laying the gun on the floor.

"We've got a sick man here!" Oliver called up to the camera, gesticulating into the back of the bus. "Let us in!"

I doubted the camera could pick up sound, but Oliver's gesturing would either make whoever was on the other side think we were all insane or they'd be coming down to let us in.

John had climbed inside the bus, and emerged with Rebecca and an unsteady Dave, placing them firmly in the sight of the camera. "Let us in! For fuck's sake, let us in!"

Katie stood with Jane in the sightline of the second camera, waving frantically at it. All our hopes were caught up in getting into Hanstone, and if that didn't happen, then I'm not sure how much strength we'd have to carry on. It would be the end of Dave, that was pretty much for sure. My own anxiety rising, I joined my waving and shouting at the cameras with the others. If nobody let us in now, then they could burn in hell. For a few tense moments nothing happened, then finally the mechanics burst into life and the two large gates started to slide open, freezing after a couple of feet. Whoever was inside wasn't taking any chances, either. The space was big enough for us, but the minibus was going to be staying outside.

"Thank Christ for that." Oliver ushered Jane and Katie in first, before coming back and helping John and I quickly grab our few bags from the van. By the time George followed carrying the guns, everyone was on the other side and the fence was quickly closing behind us.

"Well, we made it. I always wondered what it looked like in here." George's words were quiet as we took a couple of steps forwards and huddled together, uncertain of where to go or what to do next. About a hundred yards ahead of us there were two red and white striped car barriers with a central security box in the middle of the wide road; beyond that the wide tarmac led into the compound, the road occasionally splitting to the left and right but also maintaining the straight thick path into the distance beyond.

From outside, the vastness of the facility hadn't been obvious, but now that we were inside, it was clear that it must have been at least a square mile. Far beyond some buildings and lawns on our left, I could just make out the tips of aerials and the towering top of some kind of pylon.

"I feel like we're at Langley or something." John was staring at the serious looking grey buildings that were almost hidden by neatly trimmed trees and plants.

"What's Langley?" Jane peered out from behind Katie.

"An American place. Where all the spies work."

"Cool."

"Yeah. I wouldn't mind being at Langley now, but this'll do."

From what seemed to be between some bushes a little way ahead on our right, a man darted into the road, waving an arm in our direction as he ran towards us awkwardly, like someone who didn't run often, arms and legs all slightly uncoordinated and trying to head off in their own directions.

"This must be our host." Still carrying both guns, George started to walk towards the figure, Jane running ahead, and we all followed, John allowing himself to be a human walking stick for Dave, with Rebecca alongside. Oliver, Katie and I managed the bags, while Nigel dragged behind, all sulky schoolboy. We must have looked like a bedraggled bunch, a far cry from the ordered group that had loaded up the wrecked four-by-fours not that long ago.

We met just beyond the barriers, the gangly man grinning and saluting.

"Dr. Chris Whitehead. Good to meet you." Panting, he put his hands on his hips and sucked in hard, getting his breath back. "I was beginning to think we were all alone in here." His eyes were tiny and dark as they darted around the group before coming to rest on me. I held out my hand.

"Likewise. I'm Matthew Edge. And this is George Leicester." The old man tilted his pipe in a gesture of hello and then introduced the rest of the group, finishing with Nigel, who still hung back slightly, oozing with suspicion as well as sweat and gel.

"Are you saying no one else has thought to come here?"

Still breathing heavily, Whitehead took a bag from me as I spoke and slung it over his shoulder.

"No, you're the first. We were hoping for more but…well…we'll see. Let's get you inside. Come on." Turning on his heel, he began to stride back the way he came. He may not have been much of a runner, but he exuded nervous energy, his grin twitching slightly in his boyish freckled face beneath the short cropped brown hair that hinted at a wave as unruly as his limbs. He was younger than me, twenty-six at most, but his checked shirt tucked into high-waisted jeans suggested that he didn't have time for fashion even before the past couple of days. I followed him onto the lawn, walking hard to keep up, needing to ask him more questions.

"We? You're not alone here then?"

"Oh no. This place is manned twenty-four hours, although the staff had started to thin out quite dramatically in the past few weeks. The women had been laid off a while ago, after all this started to come to the surface, although of course we kept tabs on them." His arms gesticulated unnecessarily as he spoke, as if only to release some of that excess energy he seemed to carry. "Still, we could count the daily staff and army at a hundred and fifty. The soldiers left last week to get back to wherever. We haven't heard from them since. Most of the rest left the day before yesterday. Those with families wanted to get back to them." He ducked beneath some trees and we followed. "I told them it was probably pointless, but you know…emotions take over. Most went. They said they'd come back, but so far none have."

A small path appeared behind the trees and we stepped onto it.

"But some did stay?"

He nodded, but his face darkened, a little tic twitching at the corner of his mouth. "Yes, eight of us stayed. I don't have a family, not to speak of anyway," he tried to smile, "and I'd been called in here a month or so ago because of all this. I'm a geneticist, you see." Listening to him, I felt as if I must have been sleeping all this time. *Just what the hell had really been going on here while Chloe had been getting fatter? And why the hell hadn't they told us?* I fought my anger. There was no point anymore. Whatever they'd been up to, we were all in the same boat now.

"So, I really had nowhere else to go." Whitehead was still talking, his words like his movement, quick and almost stuttery. "Nowhere safer than Hanstone, at any rate. Unfortunately, some of those that stayed found it all too much. Three of them killed themselves this morning. When we got confirmation of what was happening. The scale of it…" He shook his head slightly with the memory, and then pointed towards a long level building, his fast mind veering off at a momentary tangent.

"That's the dormitory. I'll get you settled in there.

Basic, but pleasant. Anyway, I found them at lunch-time when I was checking the perimeters." He paused, his step almost slowing. "I think I knew. I knew what they were going to do. They had that look." For a moment, his manic body almost stopped completely, but he shook himself out of it. "Still, they're gone. We're here. Since then, I've closed off some areas, but we've still got all we need. And the generators are working, so as soon as the electricity stops, I'll fire them up." He pulled open the door to the sleeping block.

I stepped into the cool interior. "What makes you think the electric is going to stop?"

He dropped the rucksack on one of the single beds that ran down one side of the wall. "Because it has in London. And it's bound to eventually, isn't it?"

A thousand questions leapt into my mouth, but Whitehead was already scurrying away. "Get your-selves settled in here and I'll be back in about half an hour. The showers are at the far end, and there are a couple of private bedrooms beside them if you want to fight over them. I'll let the others know we've got guests and see if we've got anything in our medical supplies to help your friend."

He'd disappeared before Dave had even made it into the building.

"Well, if you boys don't mind, I think Rebecca, Jane and I will be taking those solo rooms." Katie heaved her rucksack back on her shoulder and headed off with the other two in search of their bedrooms. John had opened up one of the regulation wardrobes beside each bed.

"Hey, look. Clean clothes. Cool."

The other cupboards revealed similar finds, even the

underwear drawers holding socks and pants. Pulling out a bland jumper and trousers, Oliver Maine held them up against him. "Bit short for me, these. Anyone got anything longer?" George tossed him a pair of jeans. "Try these."

Having yanked out most of the contents of the small wardrobe and chucked them on the bed, John grinned. "I'm not seeing much in the way of sharp suits here, Nigel. You may have to just get scruffy like the rest of us."

Nigel said nothing, and I couldn't help letting out a laugh along with Oliver. There was nothing I liked about Phelps and I was tired of pretending to, especially now that we had reached our destination and were at least relatively protected from the outside. It was about time the crazy bastard faced up to that. He wasn't liked and it was him that needed to work on that, not the rest of us.

By the time Whitehead got back almost an hour had passed, but no one minded. The showers were hot and powerful and I'd stayed under mine for thirty minutes, only reluctantly leaving the soothing jets to rub myself down and get dressed in a vanished man's clothes. Getting dry wasn't much of an issue. The air was getting hotter as night fell, but it was a dry heat, not like the humidity of earlier.

Pulling my trainers back on, I wondered how the rest of the world was faring. If it was this hot here, just what the hell was it like in the deserts of Africa? And perhaps, more worryingly, what was happening to the polar ice caps? Were great icebergs melting and breaking away, sending huge tsunamis towards us? It wasn't impossible. Not if this new English weather was anything to go by.

Standing up and stretching, trying to shift the deep-seated muscle tension running down my back, I could almost hear Chloe wryly laughing at me for my eternal pessimism. It hurt my soul and I was glad when the hut door flew open and Whitehead stepped inside.

"Sorry I'm late. Got into a bit of a discussion." His grin was less confident than earlier, and with a slight sink in my stomach I guessed that the discussion had perhaps been more of an argument, and probably focussed on us.

"Still, all sorted now. Dinner's just about ready. Time for a quick tour of the necessary first."

The girls came out of their little annex of rooms, baggy trousers pulled in tight with belts, men's shirts hanging loose over the top. The only one with her original jeans on was Jane. No belt was ever going to make men's trousers wearable on her, although she could have worn a T-shirt on its own as a dress without being at all indecent. Still, it had to be said, none of us were looking at Jane for long. The two on either side of her, their hair still damp, were too much of a distraction.

For a moment, no one said anything. There was something about a woman in a man's shirt that was truly sexy, and Rebecca and Katie weren't exactly unattractive at the worst of times. Katie's slight, elfin features and tiny build seemed more fragile, and although Rebecca was probably the more beautiful of the two, my attraction to Katie wasn't fading, however much I wished it might.

Her eyebrow raised. "Feel free to stare."

Whitehead, who seemed the only one amongst us oblivious to their femininity, laughed. A short, almost comic sound.

"So sorry. I should have said. We do have some women's clothes, but they're in the other dorm across the site. We haven't been using it, and I didn't think. I'm sure we can sort something out in the morning. Now, come along."

"What about Dave?" Rebecca had started to scribble the words, but George got them out first. "Should we just leave him here?"

Dave's bed was at the back of the room, nearest the toilets and showers. Rebecca had changed his dressings and he was asleep or unconscious—had been for at least twenty minutes. If it hadn't been for the odd moan and twitch I would have thought he was dead. His temperature was raging, though, and without knowing my arse from my elbow medically, I knew no doctor would disagree that this night was going to be critical for him.

"Oh, yes. I almost completely forgot." He pulled a tipped syringe from his shirt pocket. "This is morphine and a strong antibiotic. It should help him." He scurried over to the bed and muttered to himself as he searched for a vein. "It'll knock him out for a few hours, so he'll be perfectly safe while we're gone."

I was pleased to see Rebecca watching carefully as Whitehead pinched off the tip and injected Dave. I wasn't too sure that I'd want that bundle of nervous energy sticking a needle in me.

"There we go." He turned to the rest of us as he straightened up. "Now, there's a few things I want to show you before dinner. Won't take long."

Following him out into the warm night, I was amazed by how light it was. The whole complex was covered in a series of powerful floodlights, making the grounds far brighter than they had been in the hazy grey light that mother nature had provided; but as I looked over to my left, it seemed that that half of the area was in relative darkness, only an occasional pool of light visible.

"Why is it so dark over there?"

"This morning we decided that it was uneconomical keeping all the systems running all over the site. We've got the two generators and plenty of fuel for them in the underground tank, but it seems a shame to waste it. We're keeping ourselves on this side mainly. The canteen and food store are here and one of the comm centres, so we're keeping that all on full power, and of course all the cameras are running, but they pick up movement with infrared, so the floodlights aren't necessary in all areas, and we've upped the voltage on the fences." He peered over his shoulder to make sure we were all listening, especially Jane. "Don't feel tempted to touch those, not at any time of the day or night. You'll be fried alive. Obviously there's a barrier before the fence, just in case, but still…be careful."

Slightly ahead to our right, a large pond shone in the reflected light.

"That's pretty." Janie's eyes were wide with it all.

"Yes. Yes, nice to sit next to during your lunch hour. When the weather's good, of course." That tic in his mouth twitched again. "Not that bad weather seems likely. At least, not cold weather at any rate. And lunch hours are pretty much a thing of the past. How fast things change."

Sticking to the path, we skirted round the pond and

came back to where we'd walked when we arrived. A severe grey stone building sat cloaked by trees. From where we stood, I could see the barriers a couple of hundred yards away, and the imposing fence further beyond. Thank God we'd got inside. I didn't know what would have happened to us by now if we hadn't. Despite the heat, I shivered.

"This way."

Whitehead led us up a small flight of stairs on the side of the building and pushed open the heavy door. "This is the communications centre." The room was full of machinery and computer screens, some with lights flashing, others dead. Compared with the brightness of outside, the yellow light in the windowless room seemed dingy. "Most of this we're not using. It won't work, or we don't know how to work it."

I followed him carefully down a slim aisle between the desks, not wanting to knock or damage any of the equipment, whether it worked or not. The whole inside of the place looked like it belonged in some kind of spy film or TV series.

"That's Daniel at the control desk."

Ahead of us, an unshaven man of about thirty-five in a black hooded sweatshirt raised his hand, but kept the set of large headphones on his head. His eyes moved past me and George, stopping at the women, his expression darkening slightly. He didn't say anything, but at least smiled slightly. Maybe that was the cause of the "discussion" that Whitehead had mentioned. Maybe the other residents weren't so keen on being joined by women. I didn't let it get me down. They were going to have to get used to it. And I was sure they would. They were men, after all, and the whole of our sorry history showed men being suckers for women. Besides, if worst came to worst, we would outnumber them.

"Daniel's our expert at this, really. Most of the hi-tech stuff has stopped working, but the morse is getting through, and so is the voice equivalent, whatever they call that." He grinned again, more relaxed. "I deal in living cells, not electronics, so this is all alien to me. But it is relatively simple to work. You'll get some training in the morning when we work out a rota."

Listening to him, I felt that George had met his match in this highly strung scientist. Between the two of them, I figured they'd probably think of just about everything.

In front of Daniel was a bank of monitors. "Those feed back from the cameras. It was on those two," he indicated the last two in the middle row, "that I saw you earlier." Now all I could make out in them was darkness and the vague outline of our abandoned minibus.

George had come alongside and peered closely into one of the monitors. "Where is this camera?"

"Along the back perimeter. There's a small wood on the other side of the fence and then it backs onto fields."

He leaned in even closer, his old eyes sharply focussed. "There's something moving, isn't there? That's what these red flashes of light that keep coming up are. Am I right?"

Daniel pulled his headphones down so they sat around his neck. "You're right. There's some of those things out there. In the trees." His voice was deep and had a rougher accent than I'd expected from someone working in a place like this. I guess I just thought they'd all talk like something out of a British World

War Two film. I watched the red outlines as they dipped in and out of the screen, or maybe bits of the creatures were just being shielded by branches or dense leaves.

"What are they doing?"

Daniel stared with George into the monitor. "I think they're trying to figure out what to do next. A few got fried on the fence last night trying to get in. We counted about ten, in fact. These ones turned up about twenty minutes ago, but so far they haven't touched the metal. They're coming close, but not close enough." The distaste and hate in his voice was like a low hum buzzing under every word.

"They won't."

The finality in my words made Daniel's head snap round. "What makes you sure?"

"They'll have learnt from the mistakes of the others. Even if they weren't here last night. They'll know."

Help me…pleeease…

Those hissed words were never going to leave me, just as the first time I heard them would stay etched in my brain.

"Trust me. We've learned a little bit about these things on our way here."

Whitehead shuffled behind me. "It sounds like we've got plenty to share with each other over dinner. Daniel'll stay out here. We're aiming to keep this room manned twenty-four/seven, and now that you're all here that should be easier."

We turned to follow him out of the slightly claustrophobic, sweaty building, but George stayed staring at the screen for a moment or two before squeezing Daniel's shoulder.

"Widows. That's what we call them. It seemed right given what they came from."

The other man nodded at him before pulling the headphones back up and staring at the monitors, where silent red shapes moved amongst the trees.

CHAPTER SIXTEEN

I don't know what I was expecting to be served up, but sizzling chicken fajitas and a Mexican beer weren't on top of the list. They were, however, just what was needed, and within minutes of the dishes being served, I had juice dribbling down my chin, never having been very good at wrapping the damned things.

The canteen was cosy, the long tables and benches made of pine, creating a less austere regulation atmosphere. It felt more like we were eating in a school than a government facility. The chef for the night, Michael, came out of the kitchen and joined us, but took his seat at the far end of the table opposite Nigel. He was older than Whitehead and Daniel, easily in his fifties, and I noticed with a glance down that he had a wedding ring on. For a second I considered telling him that it really would have made no difference if he'd left the safety of the compound and gone home, but I figured that was for him to work out by himself. He smiled and seemed friendly enough, but didn't really make any effort to join in the conversation.

"I thought you said there were five of you left?" John swilled his messy mouthful of food down with a long swig of beer. "Where are the other two?"

Unlike the rest of us, Chris rolled his tortilla with precision, not a drop of juice or sour cream escaping. "They're out doing a patrol. Checking the perimeters. Obviously the cameras keep a pretty good overview of things, but it doesn't hurt to be safe."

George nodded. "It seems you've got it all pretty well sorted out, given the situation. Remember, we've got those two guns with us if you need some weaponry on patrol. We've taken on a couple of the widows. You'd need something."

Whitehead smiled. "Don't worry, we've got guns. This is a government place after all, and until a couple of days ago we had a pretty large contingent of army chaps here." He left his beer untouched, sipping water instead. "We have our own armoury, and a few grenades and equally delightful toys the boys in green left behind in case we needed to defend ourselves."

Most of the meal was taken up with the retelling of our trip to Hanstone, and how we'd all met. I left out the detail of Katie and the widow in the pub, how it hadn't attacked us. With everything else that had happened, it didn't seem important anymore. I said a little bit about what happened to Chloe, and I noticed Michael listening pretty intently to that. Rebecca shared a bit, slowly answering questions on paper, or with nods and mimes if it was quicker.

She lived in a flat annexed to the home where she worked for handicapped children—Meadowbank. That was where she'd got the bus from. The children weren't deaf, but had severe difficulties, mainly a combination of physical and mental handicaps that made it difficult to do anything for themselves. She spent most of her time trying different light therapies and vibrations with them, as well as the ordinary day-to-day nursing things like bathing and feeding them.

She hadn't really noticed anything wrong around her. Most of her days were so involved in just taking care of the children that she didn't have time to see if nurses were off sick, and it was the kind of place where people did have time off. It was stressful work, and if you weren't at your best it was no good coming in. She did notice that a few had put on weight, though, but she hadn't mentioned it. A flicker of tired humour had crossed her face as she'd scribbled, *Women don't mention putting on weight. Only losing it. Not to each other's faces, anyway.* And then she'd got gastric flu and been really sick. Sicker than she'd ever been in her life. If you were sick at Meadowbank you had to stay off until you were completely better or you'd risk infecting the children, and so by the time she was well enough to go back in it was all over.

She paused, put her biro down and took a long drink from her beer, taking almost half the bottle down in one go. The rest of us stayed silent, just staring at her as she shut us all out for a moment, and for the first time since I'd met her, I saw the true depths of her soul in those dark eyes. I wasn't the only one to see it. She was a special person. A *good* person. I wondered how many were left amongst us. I felt ashamed for how I'd treated her when we first met. I should have seen her properly then. Not been so caught up in all my own crap.

Unlike the rest of us, she hadn't tried the radio and phones, and her first real knowledge that something was very, very wrong was when she'd stepped into the main building of Meadowbank that morning. Like Oliver Maine, she'd missed day one of the new world completely, lying in her bed feeling sorry for herself.

The reception area was covered in the white stuff. Huge ropes and strands spread across the surfaces along with some foul smelling slime. When she went upstairs, she found the children all dead. Not cocooned, not being eaten, just dead. There were pillows on the floor that maybe hinted at suffocation. She didn't know what had happened. She didn't really want to know.

As she recounted this part of her story, her face had tightened and her scribbling became more frantic. She wanted this bit of the story to be over quickly; you didn't have to be a body language expert to tell that.

There were three of the widows in the building that she came across. Two were eating their way through the cocooned bodies of Nurse Harold and Nurse Garner in the small playroom. The third dropped from the ceiling in front of her as she ran back down the stairs. It stared at her, it's jaws working and then leapt over her, leaving her free to run. And run she did. It wasn't long after that she found the rest of us. She'd been going to head for London.

"I wonder why it didn't attack you?" While the stories were being told, Katie had gone and made coffee, and George spooned three sugars into his mug.

Rebecca shrugged. Katie gave me a stern warning glare, but I didn't feel the need to share our experience at The Plough with the rest. If it meant anything, we'd figure it out when the time came. I poured myself some coffee and lit a cigarette. I figured that the severe NO SMOKING signs plastered to every wall were no longer relevant and if anyone tried to enforce them then I'd tell them where to shove it. Not particularly liking my newfound aggression, I inhaled and asked the question I'd been waiting to get to all evening.

"So, what's the cause of all this, Chris? You're the doctor, the geneticist. You must have some idea."

He leaned forward, his elbows resting on the table. "Genetically modified food. That's where the smart money is. They, or I suppose I should say *we*, let it get out of control."

"GM foods? But we've been eating those for years and never had any problems." Nigel sneered from behind his beer, and it was nice to see even our friendly mad scientist send him an irritated glance.

"That's a fool's argument. I think we can definitely say we've got some problems now. Just because the results aren't immediately apparent, it doesn't mean that things aren't definitely going on beneath the surface. Remember Thalydomide?"

George stuffed his pipe, and I hoped he'd remembered to pick up a couple of packs of that tobacco when we'd been in Woburn. He lit it before speaking. "But how? How could they mess with the genes of crops to this extreme? It sounds crazy, even for our government."

Whitehead raised an eyebrow. "That's if it was our lot that did it. As far as I can see, it's a mixture of everybodies mistakes."

"Oh, good. The one time we all work together and we leave the world screwed. That's just great." Katie seemed less than surprised despite her sarcasm.

"No, they didn't work together, but a lot of people messed with a lot of genes. And then the cross-pollination started, creating new genetic hybrids. But the worst were the modifications that weren't advertised to the public. I know that we started to play with hormones in plants *and animals*. To make them more productive, larger, tastier." He was becoming agitated and excitable now that he was in his own field. "Some of that work was made public, but not all of it. The ordinary man on the street definitely didn't know just how much tampering was going on.

"And there was a Scottish research centre that started to think about how they could make plants repellent to insect life, so farmers could cut down on insecticides. They had problems with protesters. News of their research leaked, as it invariably does." He shrugged. "Can you see where it's all going? A little bit of the experiment floats away on the wind, meets up with a little bit of another experiment and then who knows what could happen."

George frowned. "So, you think that's the cause?"

I felt my own anger rising. "So you guys fuck about with nature without having a fucking clue what you're doing and the world pays the bill. Jesus fucking Christ, don't your lot ever think?" My cigarette jabbed at the air in front of him as I levelled my accusations directly at him, our sole remaining perpetrator of crimes against humanity.

"No, we don't. Not really." He met my gaze and his frank honesty deflated me. "We're too busy with *wanting to know* rather than thinking about the consequences. That's how we end up with nuclear bombs as well as radiation therapy. If we thought about how it was all going to end up we'd never be brave enough to try anything. We're a bunch of selfish bastards. Too focussed on the curiosity. We forget it killed the cat and cats have nine lives, ergo curiosity must be pretty fucking dangerous."

Hearing that kind of language in his neat delivery was almost comical, and John snorted in his beer. He held out his bottle. "Well, cheers mate. Just don't do it again."

Whitehead smiled sheepishly and chinked his mug against the glass. "I think the lessons have been learned. No more research for me."

"Although of course we are going to need some kind of pesticide to kill these things with, so I wouldn't make a statement like that in a hurry." George's comment may have been made with a touch of tongue in cheek, but there was truth in it. "We still haven't figured out how the widows intend to reproduce, but I'm banking on them not obliging us by dying out all by themselves."

"You're right." Whitehead was nervously earnest again. "But there are facilities working on that. I came up here from one in north London. They loaned me out, as it were. It was a top research centre with better defences than this place, and an army presence. They'll be working twenty-four/seven to come up with something. As soon as they realised there might be a problem they started working on it. We haven't got hold of them with the radios yet, but they probably don't have such basic communication equipment. That's not their primary function, after all."

Jane, who had been almost dozing against her sister, sat up. "You really think they're going to find a way out of this?"

"I don't see why not. If there's one thing that scientists are good at, it's producing dangerous chemicals."

Jane and John looked convinced, but I wasn't so sure. "But you haven't heard from these guys in the past couple of days?"

"No, but there are people out there. People like us that are surviving. We've made contact with them, and eventually the army will come. I'm sure of it. We are only two days in, remember."

His enthusiasm was hard to fight, and when we'd finished our coffees, we only had time to say a brief, tired hello to the two men who'd been out checking the perimeters before heading back to the dormitory, Whitehead with us. I was glad to see he was finally wilting, too. There was something a little too super-human about all that energy.

Dave was still sleeping, and without turning the main lights on, we all undressed, leaving on enough to be decent, and slipped beneath the duvets of our single bunks. Nigel had taken a bed at the end by the door, as far from the rest of us as he could get, and from what Dr. Whitehead had said, that was where the rest of his team also slept. That was fine by me, and bad luck to them. I couldn't imagine that they'd like Nigel any more than the rest of us, even if they hadn't been exactly welcoming themselves.

I waited until the others had finished and then slipped along to the washroom to brush my teeth. The strong taste of fajita still lingered and it was good to shake it off with a quick scrub, rushing the hard bristles over my gums, enjoying the burn of peppermint.

Idly, I wondered how long our supply of toothpaste would last. It was funny the things that suddenly became matters of concern, ideas popping into my head out of nowhere. What would we do when it ran out? There were probably several lifetimes of toothpaste for each of us out there in the untapped shelves of supermarkets around the world, but I wasn't too keen to get back out there and retrieve it. Not today, at any rate.

"I like a man who takes care of his teeth."

Despite the softness of her voice, I almost leapt out of my skin. "Jesus, Katie!" Spitting the foam out, I rinsed with water from the tap. "You made me jump."

She giggled. "I could tell." Holding up her own toothbrush, she nudged me out of the way with her hip. The unexpected contact sent shivers through me, and I was suddenly aware of how close to naked we both were, in just T-shirts and underwear. And it had to be said hers was slightly more revealing than mine was, hinting at the curves of her small breasts beneath the black cotton, her nipples pressing against the cloth as she brushed. She'd taken her bra off, that much was obvious.

Swallowing, I looked away, feeling my own heat rising, uncomfortable and awkward, trying not to think about how closely we'd spent the night before, and how warm and good she'd felt sleeping in my arms. If she tried that tonight, dressed as she was, I didn't think I could be trusted to keep my hands to myself. Not wanting my thoughts to be too evident, I decided it was time to retreat.

"Anyway, good night." Stepping backwards, I felt as if I might trip over my own feet, and having dropped my eyes from her breasts, all I could see now were her slim, toned legs, disappearing at the thigh under her shirt.

I turned to leave, my heart beating fast in my chest, but she called me back. "Wait."

"What is it?" I peered through the doorway, as if the wall between us would provide some kind of protection—for her or for me, I wasn't sure which.

"Jane's sleeping in with Rebecca." Her skin looked paler in this light, smooth as marble under her loose somewhere between auburn and brown curls. She took a step closer to me, her voice dropping. "She's Jane's new best friend." There was a hint of something a little like jealousy that made her mouth turn down for a split second, and then she smiled again as she came another foot nearer. I could feel blood racing to all parts of my body, and I knew that if she came much closer she'd be able to see it, too. There was no way I was going to be able to hide my desire in just Calvin Klein underwear and a T-shirt.

"Anyway," shrugging, she leaned into the doorframe, "that leaves me alone in my room." The green in those hazel eyes shone as she stared at me, waiting for some kind of response. Despite her attempts at adult seduction she chewed on her bottom lip, slightly giving away her nervousness. Her twenty-one years didn't seem so very old as she stood there, leaning into me so that I could almost feel her body heat. I don't know what she would have thought if I'd told her it was that chewing that tilted the balance.

I didn't move away. Maybe I should have. Maybe I should have felt an overwhelming sense of grief for Chloe, said *Thanks but no thanks* and then like a gentleman taken my frustrated body back to bed to toss and turn sleeplessly. Maybe I should have done those things. And maybe if Katie had been more like Chloe, like Rebecca was, darker and more sophisticated, a curvy woman of the world, any man's match, *then* maybe I would have stood back. Maybe it would have been too much. Maybe the guilt or the memories would have forced me to turn away. Maybe. And that's what the small part of my brain that was rationalising was telling me as I stood there, my body shaking slightly.

But if I'm honest, and I've got to try to be, because, shit, this may be the last thing I ever leave to the world, and if anyone is around to read it I sure as fuck want it to be the truth, because otherwise what the hell is the point, *if I'm honest,* then I think none of that would have made a difference. Standing there in that bathroom, after two days of living in pretty much constant terror, I felt safer than I had since I ran from my house, I felt more alive than I had in a long, long time, and there was a beautiful young woman, maybe one of the last few in the entire world, wanting me to have sex with her. Asking me. So was it guilt I felt? No. Somewhere deep inside maybe it lingered, but the world had changed too much for that. Life had become shorter and harder. And that's what I responded to.

I ached to lose myself in sex, in the most natural act two people could share, the closest thing a man could get to being joined with another person, if only for a little while, and aside from all that animal lust that raced angrily in my veins, I wanted to feel close to someone, really close and warm and safe, in a way that I hadn't for a long time, since maybe that morning with which I started this sorry tale. I guess this must read like I'm making excuses, and maybe I am, because I know of at least one dark eyebrow that'll raise slightly on reading this, but baby, I've got to tell it like it is. And this is how it was.

I was too tired to play the game, and watching her watching me, I felt my own urgency rising. Without speaking, I slipped one arm around her tiny waist and tugged her in close to me, my mouth on hers, my tongue exploring hers, meeting and probing, testing each other, tasting each other. The feel of her thighs touching mine made me groan with the tingling shock of surprise, and she grinned slightly, pulling back a little, enjoying her moment of power in that way that women do when they realise that our thinking brain has shut down for the night, and all male focus is on possession and passion, the animal in us alive and kicking, humanity put aside.

Dropping my toothbrush, letting it clatter to the ground to be retrieved later, I slid my free hand around the back of her neck and pulled her firmly back into me, back into kissing me, needing to feel her rapidly moving chest as her breath raced in and out of her. I held her tightly as my other hand dropped from her waist, seeking entry under her shirt. I had never felt this aggression in the sexual act before. Maybe it was the need to be the *man,* to be in control after everything that had happened. Maybe this was my way of once again dominating the female species on behalf of all my fallen comrades. Whatever the reason, behind my eyes I could only see red and my body burned just to take her. This wasn't making love. This was pure, human, animal sex.

My hand rose upwards and I found her smooth buttocks. Squeezing tightly I pressed myself into her, letting her feel the effect she was having on me. She moaned, the tables turned, me again in control if only because of my physical dominance. Releasing my grip slightly, I spun her round so that she faced away from me, and the fingers of one hand pushed upwards to twist the nipple of her small breasts. I bit and kissed her neck, my other hand sliding up her flat, quivering belly and then into the top of the G-string that separated us. Our breathing was laboured, hers quick and full of small whimpers of almost words, mine loud, the air pumping through me almost as quickly as my blood.

Too eager to tease, I slid over her soft pubic hair, a tiny triangle in that soft mound, and reached for the delicate, swollen bud protruding a little from her lips. My middle finger pausing to work it slightly, feeling the final brick in her wall of resistance fall away as she leaned into me for support, her head falling back onto my shoulder, I pushed further down, my fingers reaching into her. She opened her legs, no invitation needed, and I groaned as I dipped into her soaking wetness, pushing first one and then two fingers deep inside.

"Oh Jesus..." Her words were barely audible as I paused for a moment, concentrating on teasing the one breast that I could touch, enjoying her squirming in my hand, letting me know just how much she needed me.

"Fuck me, Matt." Her eyes rolled sideways, blurry and unfocused. "Take me to bed and fuck me."

My cock was ready to explode, but I wasn't ready for the bedroom yet. This animal urge needed to be satisfied somewhere away from there, away from the conformities of our old society. I pulled my fingers out and slid them upwards, rubbing up against her soaking clitoris, before sliding them down again, slowly but surely penetrating her before repeating it again. It took only three or four strokes before she was fucking my hand, hard and fast, fighting the restraining arm that held her in place, her own need to come overwhelming.

Her body sucked at my hand, and it seemed that while my fingers were in her, she wanted them rubbing her and when they were rubbing her she wanted them inside her, but fighting my own urge to let go, I carried on, steadily stroking in and out of her, until eventually she was moaning so loudly that I had to take my hand from her breast and cover her mouth. Finally, not long after that, she squealed behind my palm, her teeth biting into me, a shudder convulsing her as she came, all her energy draining away.

Blood rushing in my ears, I took my hand away from her mouth, her body limp against mine, and pushed her forwards over the sink, tugging her pants down, her firm arse up in the air as she sunk her arms and head into the bowl for support. Pulling myself free from my underpants, I thrust into her, hard and fast, with no thought for her comfort, only for my own pleasure. Her vagina was deliciously tight despite the hot wetness that was soaking her, and gripping her buttocks so intensely that I could feel my fingernails digging into her skin, I fucked her, pounded into her as deeply as I could go, her feet slipping with the pressure, only my hands and cock keeping her in place.

Within seconds I could feel my orgasm rising, my toes curling, clinging to the tiles, and as she tried to stand up a little, to escape from the pressure, she lifted her head, shifting the angle of penetration. Without slowing my thrust, I pushed her head back down with one hand, holding her there. The moment of domination was too much and the orgasm ripped through me, my jaw clenching as every muscle in me tightened to the breaking point, the waves of pleasure exploding in every cell and synapse, before I collapsed over her, sweating and panting. For a few moments, neither of us spoke, and then eventually, as she pushed back slightly to wriggle free of the taps, she peered over her shoulder at me, lucidity back in those pupils. Her breath was still coming fast. "Okay, so you've fucked me." She smiled. "Now take me to bed and fuck me."

And I did.

CHAPTER SEVENTEEN

The next few days passed like halcyon days where we almost convinced ourselves that all was going to be okay, and that we could stay forever cocooned in our retreat behind the electric fences, ignoring, or at least pretending to ignore, the comings and goings of the widows on the other side.

Things inside Hanstone Park were pretty good going, all things considered. Whitehead had given us a pretty thorough induction, making sure we all knew the full state of affairs. The slightly paranoid element of my personality thought that maybe a couple of the other men hadn't been so keen to share all their stocks and supplies, or at least the *knowledge* of their stocks and supplies, but I still figured they'd realise they could trust us in the end.

True to Whitehead's word, the electricity had gone off, but we had plenty of petrol for the generators and the food stores were overflowing. It appeared that our civil servants really were fat cats, or aspiring to be, at least. Several chest freezers were packed neatly with a variety of cuts of meat, and the chillers held vacuum-packed cheeses and bacon, as well as two vast store-rooms filled with catering-sized tins of everything you could imagine.

The only thing that constantly reminded us of our new world was the weather. The thermometers attached to the outside of a couple of the huts confirmed our suspicions that the daytime air was getting hotter, averaging about thirty-four degrees centigrade and creeping up by half a degree per day, and our nights were full of torrential rain and loud claps of thunder. We could only hope that it would level out soon, otherwise the widows would be the least of our problems. Whitehead couldn't explain it, nor could anyone else. As far as he could tell, the plants weren't giving out any new elements that could cause a climate change, and no one could see a link between what happened to the women and the weather. Unless they were controlling it, and that wasn't something I wanted to give much thought to. Just how much power could they have? There was always the bland possibility that it was just a little freak of nature, a hot spell, *one of those things*. And it had to be said, bland was sometimes appealing. Unlikely, but appealing.

Due to the floods of rainwater, it seemed that after only a few days the plant life was becoming more lush and green, leaves and shoots growing larger and springing up almost out of control. Even in the compound we had seen it, and it hadn't been long before Chris was out on the riding lawnmower trying to rein it back in under our control. No one complained about the use of petrol, not even Nigel. It was good for things to look as we considered normal, even if they weren't.

I'd got the hang of the basics in the comms room,

Daniel being a patient teacher, if not the friendliest of men, and I enjoyed my shifts there. At least there was the possibility of new contact and the knowledge that we weren't on our own. We'd had contact with a group of men holed up in London, in Paddington Green High Security Police Station, and they in turn had contact with a couple of groups elsewhere, although we hadn't been able to get through on their frequencies; but we all kept in touch one way or another.

Although we hadn't yet heard from the facility that Whitehead had come up from, there were a small group of scientists in a centre under the Tower of London of all places. They sounded a little more scared than those in the police station, and my heart would sink when I'd hear them calling through the headphones. We needed positive stuff, not all that negative shit, especially from the kind of people that had caused it all anyway.

From what the London boys in the police station had said, I was glad we hadn't headed in that direction. The capital's streets were teeming with widows, and although they'd managed some foraging parties dressed in full riot gear, they'd lost three of their group. They *had*, however, discovered that mace worked pretty much like an acid on the widows, but the problem was getting close enough to deliver it. They were working on that. I figured that we'd have lasted about a day if we were lucky, if we'd just bowled up in our minibus.

Our contacts for the day had been made by the time I'd gone on shift, and although I'd religiously scanned the dials, it had all remained just quiet static for hours. There was a rumour that there was some kind of colony of children in Scotland, but we hadn't had any confirmation of it, and it sounded too weird for me to buy into. If we found it hard to survive, then I couldn't see how a bunch of kids could.

I only had an hour or so left to go and boredom was quietly settling in when Dave pushed the door open. I grinned and waved, watching him keep the door open with one foot as he bent to pick up the two mugs he'd put down in order to get inside, carrying them both with the one hand. The door swung shut behind him, and he came forward, putting the drinks down and then picking his own up. I did the same. Despite the heat, the tea was strong and refreshing and just what I needed.

There was no denying that Dave had thinned since his ordeal, but colour was back in his face and his flushed cheeks were covered with a thin film of sweat. Leaning against the desk, he rested his mug against his chest.

"I've just finished my first patrol of this place. Big, isn't it?"

I nodded. "Who did you go with?"

He raised an eyebrow. "Jeff. Not exactly talkative, is he?"

I shook my head. The sense of them and us had remained even though we'd been here nearly a week, and I couldn't figure it out. I don't know why they resented us, but they did. Maybe it was to do with the women, but they didn't seem to treat the men any better, although it had surprised me to see Nigel engaged in the occasional quiet conversation with them in the dorm or canteen.

"None of them are, really. Apart from Whitehead. Not that he could shut up if he tried." We both smiled.

Dave sighed. "He's a crazy man, no doubt about that."

The scientist's manic enthusiasm for our situation hadn't calmed down, and his new big idea was wanting us to go out and get him a widow to experiment on. A live one. One thing that all of the residents were unified on was that none of us were quite ready to figure out how to do that yet. There were too many widows congregating at night, and getting one on its own wasn't going to be easy. The other thing we agreed on was that if, and it was a big *if,* we did decide to fetch one in, then it would be a dead one.

I watched Dave, the unnecessary arm of his shirt pulled tight and safety pinned to the opposite side, as he drained his tea. It was amazing to see him up and about and looking so well. He'd had a couple of days after we'd arrived that had been touch and go, and then he'd finally turned the corner and woken up starving, fever-free and lucid. His eyes had even cleared that awful yellowy bloodshot colour and from then he'd gone from strength to strength, and it looked like he was going to be fine. Catching my gaze, he stared back quizzically. "What?"

"Nothing. It's just good to see you back on form. We were a bit worried about you for a while there." Picking up the pack of Bensons, I took one for myself and then held it out for him. Grinning, both of us ignoring Rebecca and Jane's clucking and mothering advice against his engagement with the evil weed, he took one and then leaned forward for a light.

"Thanks." He exhaled with the pleasure of a long-time smoker. "I was a bit worried myself. Especially knowing it was you lot that were my only hope. Seeing your pale and panicking mug holding onto me didn't really fill me with confidence." He winked before his expression darkened slightly as he looked into the monitors above my head, even though there was no sign of activity showing up in the silent trees.

"I'm not sure how long I'd last one-armed if I had to go out there." His voice softened. "But I'll worry about that when it comes."

"We'll be there for you, mate. We haven't come through all this to leave you at the last. One for all and all that shit."

He smiled, but I wasn't sure how much he believed me. "It's funny—only a month or so ago if I'd had to face the prospect of losing an arm, I'd have been a mass of self-pity. Today, I'm just buzzing with the joy of being alive." He drew in on his cigarette. "Speaking of the joys of being alive, even I couldn't help but notice that you and Katie seem to have got a little closer. What's the story?"

I shrugged. "Not sure there is a story. Not yet at least. Time will tell."

I wasn't avoiding talking to him out of embarrassment, I just really wasn't sure what the hell was going on with Katie and me. The first couple of days had been brilliant. We'd spent pretty much every minute we could together, and although it wasn't love, it was a pretty good feeling. There was a sense that maybe it could develop into love, given time and nurturing. But then all of a sudden she'd gone quiet on me, withdrawn into herself, and then the previous night I'd found myself back in the dormitory with the other men. She'd said she wanted some time to herself, to think things over and let the reality of what had happened to us all sink in, but I wasn't buying that. I guessed that maybe she'd just gone off me.

At first I'd thought she might just be jealous of Jane's new attachment to Rebecca. The girl seemed fascinated by the woman's deafness with that open honesty only children have, and I thought perhaps Katie didn't like that and had kicked me out of her room in order to get Jane to sleep back in with her, but it sounded pretty lame, even in the confines of my own head. I'd tried to talk to her at breakfast, but she'd kept herself pretty busy in conversation with George and I knew what signals I was getting. If I'd said I wasn't hurt and frustrated then I'd have been lying, but there was nothing I could do about it. And maybe that's what pissed me off the most.

Dave stubbed his butt out in the ashtray, which had been nearly empty when I'd started my shift but was now looking respectably full. It was amazing how quickly you could get back into the habit again.

He nodded at the radio. "Any more news?"

"No. Not since this morning. I've been trying to get hold of that bloke in Manchester, but I'm not getting any comeback. London hasn't heard from him, either."

"London" was how we referred to the men in Paddington Green police station and the ones in the Tower of London were simply called "Science." Not exactly code names, but it made it easier to talk about them, and on a darker note it also stopped us from getting too personal. What if we stopped hearing from them? This way that possible outcome would hopefully be less painful. Or less scary for those of us left.

As it was, I had a hollow feeling inside as I stared at the machinery. Manchester hadn't been heard from for over a day, and as he was a one man band, I didn't think any of us held out much hope for his survival.

"How much longer are you on here for?"

I stretched, leaning back against the seat, and looked at my watch. "Not long. About thirty minutes or so, and then Chris takes over." I grinned and thought about the long nap I was going to take before my stint on the perimeter and dinner. It seemed that sleep was pretty high on my list of priorities these days. It was for all of us. John had slept twelve hours the first day we'd arrived. They say that shock makes you sleep, and so far that little medical fact was standing up. Although, it had to be said, very few of my sleeps were dreamless. I looked up to see Dave staring back at the screens.

"What are we going to do, Matt?"

"What do you mean?"

"In the long run. What will we do? We can't exactly stay here forever, can we? We'll use everything up. Especially the gas. We'll either run out of supplies or they'll get in. And what then?"

It was a question that I hadn't wanted to think about, but that had loitered in the back of my mind waiting for this moment ever since we'd arrived. It was great here. Really good, but it wasn't any more than a stopgap measure and anyone that thought otherwise was just kidding themselves.

CHAPTER EIGHTEEN

The peaceful spell could never have lasted, and it was only two days later that it started to break, the inevitable no longer needing delay. I woke up suddenly in the night, not sure if it was thunder outside or maybe the sound of the door clicking shut that had forced my eyes open from my deep sleep. My heart thumping slightly, I lay there in the dark and listened for anything unusual, but the only noise outside was that of the rain hammering down on the roof of the building. That wasn't enough to wake me. We'd all got used to that steady noise over the past few days.

Frustrated at finding myself wide awake, I peered at the glowing hands of my watch. It was three o'clock in the morning. The only shift working would be in the comms hut. The final perimeter patrols were always done by midnight, and the next one wouldn't go out until five. So who could have been going outside? No one. It must have just been some fragment of a dream that woke me. Not that I could remember dreaming anything at all. I lay there for a moment or two, listen-

ing to the torrent of nature outside, and the soft
breathing and snoring of those around me. My sheet
was soaked with sweat, but at least the air didn't seem
any hotter than the night before, which was a good
thing. Unless, of course, I was just getting used to
the heat.

Sighing, I quietly got up and padded out into the
corridor and then into the bathroom, needing to
splash some water on my face. I didn't bother with the
lights, not wanting to disturb anyone else's sleep. I
headed straight for the sinks, their pale sheen glowing
slightly in the gloom. Turning the taps on, it was good
to feel the coolness of the liquid rubbing into my skin.
At least the floor was cool. Maybe if I could get my
temperature somewhere back down near normal, I'd
have half a chance of getting back to sleep. Turning
round, I leaned against the enamel sink, trying very
hard to ignore the memories of what Katie and I had
done in that room not so very many nights before, and
enjoyed the sensation of the water drying on my skin
before heading back to bed. Out in the small hallway,
my eyes couldn't help but stray towards Katie's room.
I paused as I stared. The door was open. That wasn't
like Katie at all. Creeping closer, thinking I would just
pull it shut if she were sleeping, but secretly hoping
that she was awake and maybe ready to talk to me, I
reached for the handle.

"Katie?" I whispered the word in the doorway before peering in. The bed was crumpled, but empty.
Stepping inside, I whispered her name again, but it
was obvious she wasn't there. So where the hell was
she? Feeling more perplexed than alarmed, I turned to
the other private room. The door was ajar. Surely
there wouldn't be room for all three of them in the tiny

single bedroom? I pushed the door open slightly. Jane was there curled up in her makeshift bed, the covers kicked off, and Rebecca's long, slim body was stretched out beside her in a vest top and pants, the sheet pushed to the bottom of the mattress. Her vulnerability made her look even more beautiful, and despite wondering where Katie was, I stood and watched her sleeping for a moment before stopping myself, feeling slightly embarrassed at my invasion of her privacy.

Returning to the dorm, I sat on the edge of my bed. Katie had been on the last patrol of the night, so she should have been in bed by half-twelve at the latest. My eyes having adjusted to the darkness, I studied the beds around me, looking for one that was empty, but the only flat mattress I could pick out was Oliver Maine's, and he was on comms duty. So whoever had been on patrol with Katie was sleeping. So where was she?

Muttering angrily under my breath about how it was none of my business and why the hell did I care, I dressed quickly in jeans and T-shirt and slipped out, pulling the door shut behind me. I grimaced as the water hit me, the hot rain no longer shocking, but no less unpleasant than it had been that first night. The floodlights were thrusting brightness into the night, but whichever direction I stared, I couldn't see Katie, so I jogged over to the comms building. Maybe she couldn't sleep either and had gone to have a chat with Maine. It was plausible, but it didn't ring true. Katie had been too moody recently for me to believe she'd go in search of company. Or maybe it was just my company that she was avoiding; that was a pretty likely possibility.

As I stepped into the hut, Oliver Maine waved his

gangly arm at me in such an overenthusiastic way that it could only prove without a doubt that he had been fast asleep only moments before.

"What are you doing up? Is everything okay?" He shuffled some bits of paper around on his desk as I approached, probably more to remind his dazed and awake self of where he was and what he was supposed to be doing than to look efficient, and I noticed the overflowing ashtray and the small bottle of whiskey placed almost hidden by the far leg of the desk. No doubt some of that had been added to the strong black coffee in the pot. Well, this was no time to pull Maine on his drinking. I figured he'd cut down hugely since all this started and I'd rather have him like this than shaking and shivering and wondering when his next drink would be coming. Whatever Maine had been in his previous life, in this one he was trying to make good, and the odd Irish coffee wasn't going to make much of a difference.

I shrugged. "I don't know." I was feeling more and more unsettled now that Katie was missing from here, too. "Katie's not in her room. Have you seen her?"

"No." Lighting a cigarette, he smiled sheepishly, rubbing his beard. "I think I dropped off for half an hour or so, but I'd have woken up if she'd come in here."

"Well, if she's not here, and she's not in the dorm, then she must be out there." My agitation was now turning into concern. Where the hell was she?

"Jesus." Maine was wide awake now and a flash of self-disgust at his napping shot through his eyes. "Why would she want to go out in this weather? Is she a sleepwalker?"

"No." Although the truth of the matter was that I didn't know. Maybe she was.

"Well, if she's out there somewhere, we should be able to pick her up on the monitors."

We scanned the screens, looking for the flashes of red that signalled heat and movement.

"There!" Maine pointed, the gold watch and bracelet jangling together on his leathery, tanned wrist. She was moving through the trees towards the back of the compound, far into the half that went without flood-lighting. She wasn't running, but moving fast, *determined*, heading God only knew where. Glancing at the surrounding monitors, there were no signs of any widows on the other side of the perimeter fences, and I did a double-take before I could believe it. They'd maintained a steady vigil every night, so their absence should have been a cause for some kind of alert, but that would have banked on Maine being awake. Great.

"Where the hell is she going, Matt?" There was a note of uncertainty in Oliver's voice that unsettled me. He sounded nervous of her. And if Maine found her behaviour disturbing, then what Nigel and some of the others would make of it, I didn't want to find out.

"I don't know, but I'm going to go out there and get her. Let's keep this to ourselves, shall we? She's probably just sleepwalking like you said." I nodded at him, hoping he read between the lines of what I was saying, and he winked back. A serious gesture of trust, rather than his normal gregarious twinkle, and I knew he was onboard.

Going outside, I jogged down past the pond and back to the wide main road that divided the compound into two halves. The weather had become worse since I'd got up and the wind whipped the heavy rain into me, forcing my eyes into a squint as I peered into the darkness ahead, getting my bearings. The idea of travelling into that pitch blackness wasn't appealing to me, even though logic dictated that there was nothing hidden in there apart from Katie, and that if there had been any breach of the perimeters the alarms would have been raised. Still, I felt like an astronaut about to venture alone onto the dark side of the moon.

"Shit." The word tumbled out of me as a fork of lightning broke the sky in two; only a couple of seconds later, thunder groaned, trying to keep up. Great. The weather was going to be getting worse before it got better, but then that had been the pattern of the week, so I shouldn't have been surprised.

Having prevaricated enough, I crossed the road, heading out on a diagonal path. The monitors divided the enclosed area into a grid system, and I knew from where we'd spotted Katie that she was heading for the fence where there was the least amount of trees and shrubs on our side. What if she was sleepwalking and she touched the fencing? There was nothing people-friendly about the electric charge that was running through the thick wires. She'd be dead by the time she let go, if the power hadn't thrown her back to the dorm. Neither image was particularly pleasant. I passed the eerie shapes of abandoned buildings that we'd chosen to leave unused in darkness—they seemed to stare at me accusingly and I pushed my legs into a run, annoyed at my own imagination for making me so jittery.

My legs were burning by the time I'd done about four hundred metres and I slowed to a jog as I started to pass by the overhanging trees. There was no path out this way, and I could only imagine that these wooded areas served not only to make the work surroundings more pleasant but also to keep out prying eyes. A little ahead and over to my left I could make out the looming tower of the radio pylons as the lightning gave me a moment of light. The pylons only had a bank of hedges between them and the high fences, so I knew I must be getting near to where Katie was.

Finally, I came into the clearing and stopped, the sweat and rain combining to stick my thin T-shirt to my skin. The fencing here was three deep but had no solidity, mainly a mesh of crisscross wire, and I could make out the trees on the other side, hulking dark shapes menacing us, the branches seeming to reach out greedily. I stared, my focus coming a little further forward. Katie stood only a foot away from the first fence, her back to me, hair slick against her face, the heavy water having straightened it, making it even longer down her back. Her sweatshirt and joggers sagged, waterlogged, and I wondered briefly how heavy they must be to wear soaking. What on earth had made her dress like that to come out here? But then what on earth had made her come out here in the first place?

She must have heard me coming up behind her, but she hadn't moved.

"Katie?" I kept my voice low as I came alongside her. She didn't respond, but kept staring at the fence, her brow furrowed with concentration.

"Katie?"

"Shhh!" One slim finger flew to her lips. "Shhh. Listen."

Pausing for a second, I tried to pick up whatever she

was listening to, but there was only the rain and my own heavy breathing. This was ridiculous.

"*What?*" I couldn't keep the edge of frustration out.

"Can't you hear them?" She sounded incredulous. "Can't you hear them? They woke me up." For the first time her eyes flashed in my direction, and I could see that she was crying. "Can't you see them, Matt? They're out there."

My stomach tightening, I followed her eyes into the gloom while wrapping one arm round her shoulders and firmly pulling her back a few steps from the fence. I didn't need to ask who *they* were. She didn't resist, but kept staring, chewing on the nails of one hand. It took me about thirty seconds or so until I finally picked out the first sheen of that awful translucent skin followed by a bank of glowing red eyes.

"Jesus." Suddenly they were everywhere, creeping out of the camouflage of the trees and bushes, some in the branches, some wrapped round the trunks of the trees. How could I have missed them? My skin crawled and I dragged us back further. I could feel Katie trembling next to me as the widows hissed and prowled angrily in front of us, their annoyance at being held back by the electricity obvious.

"They're waiting." She whispered into the wet air. "They're waiting for something. Can't you tell? Can't you feel it? They're waiting for something." The desperation in her voice chilled my heart. I didn't understand what she was talking about, but what she said was enough to scare me.

She let me lead her back to the comms room, her head on my shoulder, her sobbing adding to the moans of the storm around us. But despite our physical closeness, there was no real sense of contact. Something had come between us, something to do with the widows, and that made fear eat at my insides. I figured it probably terrified her, too. At least her body felt slim and firm beneath her clothes. Surely she would be fine. She had to be.

Things haven't finished settling down yet. We're still in the beginning. John's words echoed in my head. They'd never really left since he'd spoken them outside the scout hut. Who the hell knew what could happen next? And something had happened to Katie tonight, there was no arguing that.

I was glad to get back to the bright side of the compound and relieved to see George sipping coffee alongside Maine.

Oliver stood up, freeing a chair for Katie. "I didn't wake him. He came in just after you left." He was obviously concerned that I might think he'd broken our trust.

"That's okay, mate." George was different from the others. I couldn't imagine keeping anything from him.

"I woke up when you left the dorm, and it was too damned hot to get back to sleep." George Leicester was refilling his coffee mug and slipping a large measure of Maine's whiskey into it. "And then my old man's curiosity just got the better of me." He put the cup into Katie's hand and wrapped her fingers round it, ensuring it was gripped before he let go. "There you go, love. Get that inside you and you'll feel better."

Maine handed me a mug and I sipped the steaming, heady liquid, standing in silence for a few moments while Katie's sobbing slowed down to just the occasional hitch in her breathing.

"What happened, Katie?" George pulled his chair close so he was facing her on the same level. "What made you go outside in the middle of the night? What upset you?"

Her tears were drying quickly, but she chewed on her bottom lip. "There was something...something buzzing in my head." Pausing, she took another mouthful of the coffee. "It woke me up." Her voice was getting stronger. "At least I think it woke me up. I'm not really sure."

"Why aren't you sure? Was there something else that might have woken you up?"

"No. No, I don't mean that." Frustrated, she put the mug down on the table and stood up. "It's gone from my head. It's *going* from my head. I remember being outside, but I don't remember getting there. And I don't know what I was thinking when I was out there. Or how long I was out there." The slightly high pitch in her tone showed her fear. "It's all getting confused in my mind, like a dream." She stared at me and then at George, as if he was a better bet for answers. "How can that be? How can memories from only minutes ago have vanished?"

For once it was George that paused and I cut in, taking inspiration from Oliver's suggestion of earlier. "Maybe you were sleepwalking."

She stared at me incredulously. "Sleepwalking? But that's crazy!"

"Is it? You just said that you can't really remember waking up or being outside. Sounds like sleepwalking to me."

George's wise old eyes narrowed and I knew he didn't believe it any more than Maine on the other side of the room, but I figured he knew what I was doing. There was no need for Katie to be any more disturbed by this ordeal than necessary.

"But I don't sleepwalk. I've never done it." Although her words were denying the possibility, there was hesitation in her voice. She *wanted* to believe it, and no one could blame her for that.

I shrugged. "Well, this isn't exactly a normal situation, is it? It's likely we'll all react differently than normal."

"But I went out there and there were widows there. Lots of them, waiting for me." Her eyes flickered as she desperately sought a memory she could trust. "Weren't there?"

Taking a quiet, deep breath I shook my head. "You said there were. In fact, you insisted there were. But I didn't see anything out there." I looked over to Maine and the rows of mercifully dark computer screens. "You were watching out for us. Did you see anything?" My voice was measured, but I hoped he was picking up what I was expecting from him.

"Nope. Just you two staring out at the fence. There was no activity at that end of the compound at all."

Good man. I could forgive him the occasional drink on duty for the smoothness of that lie.

Katie's eyes widened. "Are you sure? Are you sure there was nothing out there?"

We both nodded.

"So you see, sleepwalking is the only thing that makes sense." I smiled gently at her, and eventually she nodded.

"Yes, I guess you must be right." She sniffed, wiping her nose on the oversized soaking sweatshirt.

Standing up, George yawned. "What do you say we all go and try some sleeping again? I know my old bones could do with a couple more hours."

"Yes, me too. Let's leave Oliver to the radio and get back to our beds."

Katie followed us meekly as we crept back into the dark of the dormitory, and we stayed silent until we'd reached the girls' rooms at the back. She said good night without turning to face us, and before I could even get embarrassed by her casual dismissal of me, the door clicked quietly shut. George and I exchanged a concerned look, but before we could vocalise our concerns in whispers, the door opposite opened. Jane and Rebecca were both awake, the small bedside light on.

Rebecca's hands flew into a series of precise actions, her dark eyes focused on George. When she stopped he started, and he must have conveyed the events of the past hour pretty well, because she frowned slightly before continuing their silent conversation with elegant gesturing fingers.

I watched amazed before interrupting George's flow with a nudge in the ribs. "When did you learn to sign?"

A small pinch of pain crossed his face and he shrugged. "My grandson was deaf." For a moment his pain passed into me. He'd used the past tense. I guess George had decided it was time to come to terms with the probable fate of his daughter's family.

Rebecca's hands burst into life again and this time George smiled.

"What's so funny?" Despite Rebecca being the one with the disability, I suddenly felt very left out.

"She says you'd better learn, because she doesn't intend to write everything down forever."

"Yes, ma'am," I responded, aiming my words and raised eyebrows at the dark girl sitting cross-legged on the bed. She grinned at me, and once again I got the impression that I'd very much underestimated this woman.

"Is everything okay?" Jane sounded more curious than concerned.

"Sure it is." I paused. "Why don't you sleep in with your sister tonight, Jane? I'm sure she'd like it. I should imagine she's been missing you over the past few days." Ever since she kicked me out at any rate, I almost added.

The little girl shook her head adamantly.

"Why not, honey? Have you two had a row?"

"No, nothing like that." Her expression was fixed and stubborn.

"So what is it? What's the problem?" I perched on the side of the bed, and Jane glanced sideways up at me.

She wanted to tell me something, that was for sure. "Try me."

She took a deep breath and blew her fringe up. "She smells funny. Bad funny."

I looked at Rebecca, but she shrugged. What Jane said obviously didn't surprise her, but she didn't seem to share the little girl's opinion.

"I didn't notice anything. Are you sure you're not just imagining it?" I wasn't lying to make her feel better. I'd held Katie close to me coming back from the fence and sat close to her in the comms room, and she'd just smelled warm, sweet and feminine to me.

"I'm not lying. I knew you'd think I was making it up. I just can't stand how she started to smell." Her bottom lip stuck out slightly and trembled, making her look very much like a child. "I wish I could change the way it makes me feel. I really do." She tucked her

knees under her chin, hugging them closely, and her
next words were so quietly sad I could barely hear
them. "But she just smells so bad."

Tears started to tumble down her cheeks and Rebecca stroked her hair.

"Hey, that's okay. You don't have to go. Stay here
with Rebecca if you want to." I hated myself for upset-
ting her, and wished I hadn't said anything at all.
"Katie'll probably just go straight to sleep, anyway.
You stay here."

She didn't look up from her knees. "Rebecca smells
nice. She smells normal."

George tugged me gently back, and nodding a good
night at Rebecca, we closed the door, leaving the
woman to comfort Jane.

The gloom of the unlit dorm washed over us again.

"What do you make of that?" I could barely make
out George's face, even though he was whispering
close to me.

"I don't know. I don't like the sound of that smell. I
guess we'll just have to wait and see." If I was honest,
the whole of the night's activities had left a twisted
knot in my stomach.

Our creeping was unnecessary since by the time I'd
reached my bed, it seemed that nearly all the dorm
were awake. John was sitting on the top step of the
open hut door, quietly smoking a cigarette, and Whitehead was perched nearby on the edge of Maine's
empty bed. For a couple of seconds, no one said a
word, the atmosphere charged with curiosity.

"So, what's going on?" It was Daniel that finally
spoke, his thick-set body merely a dark shadow at the
far side of the room, his naturally rough accent not allowing for any hint of concern.

"Nothing, really. Don't worry about it—just go back to sleep." I was too damn tired to talk about it now, and definitely not with Daniel. Our little group of survivors was quietly and slowly dividing itself into two, one group that listened mainly to George, and the other—surprisingly and rather worryingly—seemed to take its lead from Nigel. That crowd was pretty much Daniel, Michael and Jeff. Dean sat somewhere in the middle, and seemed to be pretty unimpressed with any of us. Whitehead said he'd always been a loner. The small ember of light from his bed showed that he was awake and smoking.

"It didn't seem like nothing." Jeff had sat up, and I didn't like the sullen accusatory tone that deadened his words. Ignoring him, I went over to the door and sat down alongside John, lighting a cigarette of my own. The rain had eased a little but was still coming down in a steady stream, and lit by the brightness of the floodlights it was a little hypnotic to watch, like staring into the flames of an open fire.

George's mattress creaked as he climbed back under the sheets. "Well, it was something that turned out to be nothing, let's put it that way. Katie just went sleepwalking and Matt got worried." He yawned, and I wasn't sure how much that was for effect or for real. "But everyone's back in bed now, and no harm done."

"*Katie* went sleepwalking?" The emphasis in Nigel's voice made it perfectly clear that he was unhappy about it being one of the girls rather than one of us.

"Yes, Nigel, that's what I said. Now why don't we all get back to sleep before our chattering wakes Dave up?"

Dave was snoring steadily and I figured it would take more than one tense conversation to raise him, but Nigel grunted and laid down. "We should keep an eye on her. She hasn't been acting normal lately. I don't want to wake up and find her trying to eat me."

"Oh, shut up, Nigel." The words were out of my mouth before I realised I'd spoken my thoughts aloud, but the shock that someone as self-absorbed as Phelps had noticed Katie's change in behaviour had thrown me completely. But at least I wasn't the only one that was disgusted by his words.

"She's hardly fat, is she, so I don't think we've got too much to worry about there, do you?" Whitehead almost spat the words at Phelps.

"Well, you can't be too careful." Nigel lay back down, sulkily.

"I wouldn't worry too much if I was you, mate. You're just wishful thinking." John didn't turn round, but continued to stare out at the rain. "Katie's got too much good taste to eat you."

Chris Whitehead snorted boyishly at the barbed remark, and Nigel huffed beneath his covers.

"Well, we'll see who has the last laugh, won't we?" He hadn't lost any of his supercilious shit, and I bit my tongue to stop me from escalating this into a full scale row. It was as if he wanted Katie to turn into a widow just to prove himself right. What the hell kind of a person would think like that? A fucking crazy person, that was who, and the worst part was that he actually seemed to have found some people who would listen to him, so that must make them pretty crazy, too. Fucking great. I smoked with fury until the cigarette was finished and then lit another one, staring out into the hectic night. When I looked up, having finally calmed down slightly, I noticed that Whitehead had gone back to bed, and the room seemed to have lulled into a round of deep breathing, hinting at most people being asleep, or very nearly asleep.

John still sat beside me, smoking steadily. After about another twenty minutes, he ground a butt out on the step beside him.

"He's right, of course." His soft voice was low. "We will have to keep an eye on her. But I'm fucked if I'm going to let a crazy bastard like that know that he may have a point."

Standing up, he disappeared into the gloom behind me, and before long his steady breathing joined the others. Sitting there on the step, mesmerised by the rain and kept awake by my heavy heart, I felt very much like the last man alive. And in some ways I wished to fuck I was.

CHAPTER NINETEEN

"So, what shall we do? We can't just sit here staring at it all day."

Maine had been eager to let it in from the first moment Daniel had spotted it sitting down at the front gate twenty minutes previous. And maybe if there hadn't been at least fifteen widows prowling nearby I may have been more inclined to agree with him. But as it was, the idea of opening up our defences wasn't too appealing to me.

"Why aren't they attacking it?" Whitehead's scientific curiosity had forced his nose about four inches from the screen, as if he needed to be really close up to believe what he was seeing. What would he have done if our new arrival had appeared on one of the higher monitors? Climbed onto a chair to peer at it? Probably. I didn't put it past him.

Oliver was twitching, rubbing his hands against his rough silver beard, eager just to press the access button on the panel, showing the kind of anxiety I'd expect of him around booze. It was quite endearing, really. And it seemed these days that he'd got his drinking well and truly under control. Yin and yang. World goes mad, Oliver Maine quits drinking.

"What's going on?" Katie and Dave joined the throng around the screens that were our eyes to the outside world, Katie's voice still blurry with sleep. It was eleven A.M. and they'd both obviously just got up. Not that that was a surprise. Although Dave was getting back to health pretty quickly, he still got tired fast, and as for Katie, well, since that sleepwalking night three weeks previous, I'd caught her trying to leave the dorm each one. George and I were trying to keep a vigil up, but it was difficult, and the night before she'd been out the door before my subconscious dragged me awake.

Looking at her rubbing sleep out of her eyes, I felt almost envious. Whatever was disturbing her nights had pretty much ruined mine. The dry taste of sleep deprivation seemed to have taken up residence in my mouth, and for a moment I didn't know why I bothered. Part of me wondered if maybe I should just let Nigel find her outside in the rain. Why was I protecting her?

"Wow!" Her green eyes widened. "Hey, look at that, Matt!" Her eyes found mine and she grinned, all elfish excitement, melting my heart in two seconds. She worked on me. That's why I was exhausting myself to make sure she was all right without her even remembering in the mornings. I grinned back, suddenly once again putty in her hands. She'd done just enough over these past few weeks to keep me dangling on a string. We'd even had one more night together, but it hadn't compared to what had gone on before, and I was sad to find myself relieved to be back in my own bed. But I still cared for her. She was young and lovely and when in the right mood, could make me laugh with just a flash of her eyes and a sharp remark. Unfortunately, those moods were few and far between.

"Wow," she said again, this time staring straight at the screen.

"It's only a bloody dog." Nigel was leaning against the back wall, feigning disinterest. I think he was disgruntled because even Daniel and Mike had been livened up by its arrival, and so for the last fifteen minutes he'd avoided the sweaty throng around the monitors, putting himself in voluntary isolation at the back, making sure we could all sense his displeasure.

"Au contraire, Nigel." George lit his pipe. "It is not just a bloody dog. Firstly, it's very much alive, and I doubt I'm the only one that has noticed the distinct lack of livestock roaming around."

"Remember the fucking cats at the farm?"

Jane didn't blink at John's expletive, but bounced excitedly on Rebecca's lap. "They were all dead. All the animals were dead. All the ones we saw, anyway!"

"That's right, Jane." George winked at her. "So, firstly it's alive. Secondly, it's sitting outside this fence, as if it somehow knows we're inside, although how the hell a dog could tell a thing like that I don't understand. Thirdly, and most importantly, I think we'll all agree," he puffed steadily for a second or two, "it's surrounded by widows, who are keeping what seems to be a safe distance from it, with no apparent intentions to attack. And the dog doesn't even care that they're there." He paused. "So, let's leave the 'It's only a bloody dog' remarks for another time, and perhaps another dog."

Nigel may have abandoned the full suit look, but he

still wore stiff shirts and trousers with his polished slip-on shoes; as he pursed his lips he looked almost effeminate, the thin sheen of sweat that appeared on his receding hairline an obvious sign that George had got to him.

"Well, if you've got all the answers, then what do you suggest we do? Open the door to save *a bloody dog* and get ourselves killed?" He snorted with disgust.

George stared at him calmly for a few seconds before turning his attention back to the small screen. Although he was three people back, his height meant he could see the patient animal sitting on its haunches in the TV screen quite clearly.

"I'll tell you what I think we should do." He didn't look at us, but kept his eyes on the calmly still border collie and the platoon of widows that moved around it. "I think we should watch and wait. If it's still sitting there in a couple of hours without those things touching it, then I think it's worth the risk to get it in."

"And what if they attack it between now and then?" Maine waved his cigarette dangerously close to Rebecca's hair. He'd told us in Woburn that he used to have a dog, and it was obvious watching him now that he had a real soft spot for man's best friend.

"Well," George raised an eyebrow on his worn face, "if they attack and kill it, then at the end of the day, it's only a bloody dog. It's a new world we're living in, Oliver. You know that. We've got to be tough." He smiled kindly. "But somehow I get the strange feeling that this dog's going to be just fine." He turned away. "In the meantime, I think I'll do my duty taking a stroll around the perimeter. My joints could use it. You fancy joining me, Oliver? It'll make the time pass quicker."

Maine was hesitant, but George's almost parental tone was too persuasive. "Sure." Picking up his fags, he grinned. "Probably about time I did my bit to help the aged."

I noticed he still threw a quick glance over his shoulder before he left, though. That dog and its fate were going to be on his mind the whole way round.

As it was, the dog stayed on everyone's mind during those two hours. We decided to carry on as normal with our routines, but I figure each one of us peered into the comms room for a least one check during that time. John was on watch and his bladder must have been bursting, because no one had ever had so many cups of tea brought to them. And every person that popped in came out with the same silly grin and two words.

"Still there."

Having finished cooking up a shepherd's pie for dinner, I was mopping the floor when Jane and Rebecca came in. Her eyes shining, Jane grinned and planted her hands on her young hips.

"Time's up! Are we going to keep the dog? Are we? Do you think it's still out there? Do you?"

Rebecca smiled at me and I grinned back, neither of us needing sign language to share our warmth at the little girl's enthusiasm. Despite the problems with Katie and Jane's insistence that she smelled funny, it was great to see how Jane was coping. She'd buoyed up a bit after we'd heard the rumour about the camp of children up north, and although that sounded a touch too far-fetched to be true to me, her eyes had started to sparkle a little more with the hope that one day she might meet someone her own age. And children always cope better with change than adults do. They adapt much quicker than grown-ups, their imaginations allowing them to, their young minds not yet settled into the routines of a comfortable world. And Jane was living proof of that.

She humphed at me, expecting an answer. "Well, do you?"

I leaned the mop against the wall and trod carefully across the wet tiles to join them. "Yes, I do think he's still out there. If he wasn't, I'm sure John would have said something."

"Then come on!" She dragged me by one hand and Rebecca by the other across the grass and we stumbled giggling and laughing into the hut. Katie had crossed from the dorm and watched us from the top of the steps, her green eyes hard.

"How cosy." She whispered the words icily as I walked past, low enough so that Jane didn't hear. For the first time, I ignored her. She had no right to be bitter. Maybe it did hurt seeing Jane so wrapped up in other people, but it wasn't as if she were taking much interest in her little sister. From what I could make out, she hadn't even asked Jane to share a room with her. All Katie seemed interested in was sleeping and spending time by herself. And she sure as hell couldn't be jealous of Rebecca and I laughing together. She may have still been more my friend than she was anyone else's, but that really wasn't saying much these days. No, I figured she just didn't like to see us all happy for a moment without it having anything to do with her. And that was just bitchy.

Leaving her behind, I followed Rebecca and squeezed in close to where John was sitting by the controls. He was smiling and shaking his head slightly.

"The little bastard's just sat there the whole time. He hasn't moved. Amazing."

"What about the widows?" Whitehead was further back, having just joined the rest of us, and couldn't see the screen.

"They're still out there, but they've backed off. Look. They've pulled back about thirty yards. A couple have gone over the hedgerows on the other side of the road. They're still there, but not exactly looking like they're thinking of attacking. It's like they've gone back to normal sentry duty."

Sentry duty was what we had come to call the behaviour of the widows that we saw. It seemed that as we watched them, there was always a presence of ten to fifteen of them that watched us, as if reminding us that they knew we were here and were just keeping an eye on us while they wreaked havoc on the rest of the world. They weren't always the same widows, we were sure of that. As we did our share of duties, so the widows appeared and went in shifts.

"So, are we going to go and get it?" Maine looked like a man about to explode.

As usual, we all found ourselves turning to George for an answer.

"Yes. It would seem that we are."

Jane shrieked with excitement, rushing over to Maine and hugging him, completely overwhelming the older man before letting him breathe enough to hug her back.

Daniel took over at the desk ready to open the gates just a fraction, while John, Chris, George and I walked down to get the dog in. Dave had taken Jane to go and find some appropriate food for it, with strict instructions that my just-made shepherd's pie did not fit into that category. Nigel had stayed silent during the discussions and Jeff and Dean's loyalty to him became clearer when they disappeared with him to the dorm, obviously wanting no part in the excitement. Dean seemed more hesitant, but still went with them. To be honest, it was better without them. I wouldn't have wanted Nigel alongside me, and especially not armed.

We had upgraded our weaponry and had one proper flamethrower recovered from Hanstone's gardening lock-up, a shotgun and one of the semiautomatics left behind by the army, which I'd been elected to carry. John had the flamethrower, and grinned beside me. "Whatever you do, Matt, don't shoot the dog."

"Very funny. A little more respect for your elders, young man."

"Oh, no worries there. I've got plenty of respect. You're the one carrying the fucking machine gun."

"So I am." Not that I needed reminding of it as we trudged down the last few yards of the drive. My hands were sweating even though I was keeping my finger well away from the trigger. All I could see happening if I touched it was blowing my own toes away and then shooting everyone around me. The gun should have made me feel safer, but I felt like a walking hazard. Yes, we may have been mentally toughening up, but all those years as a mortgage advisor hadn't really given me the skills I needed for handing powerful weaponry. And over the previous few weeks while we'd been safe in Hanstone, the struggles we went through getting here had faded slightly.

We came to a halt at the gate, but my stomach continued to churn.

"Are we all ready?" George had the shotgun, still carrying it calmly over one shoulder. It was a last resort weapon, really. If the flamethrower and semi didn't do the job, then it was unlikely the shotgun was going to be that much help.

We nodded. It was Chris's job to pull the dog in and he got himself placed closest to where the gates would open and crouched down. John and I took our places standing above him and slightly on either side. George was a few feet back, the gun now pointing forward and straight.

"Matt," John removed the nozzle cap from his weapon.

"Yes?" Inexpertly releasing the safety, I let one finger rest very lightly on the trigger. My heart pounded in my ears with relief that nothing happened.

"Let's say the widows don't attack when the door opens. Shall we still let them fucking have it anyway? They're close enough to hit, and once the dog's in we've still got a few seconds firing time while the gates shut."

I mulled it over, while George raised his hand to the camera. Our signal to Daniel that we were ready. Why the hell not? And we sure as fuck needed the shooting practice.

"Sounds good to me."

Beneath us, Chris groaned. "Oh, that's great. Just great."

Buzzing into life, the thick metal squealed as it started to drag its doors apart for the first time in almost a month.

"Here we go." George called from behind us, and it took all my strength to stop from panicking and squeezing the trigger. I could only imagine all those widows clawing over each other to get to us. Which was ridiculous, I knew. If they were too close then Daniel wouldn't have opened the gates. Although on the other hand, it took the gates a few seconds to get themselves moving, during which time several widows could have come a whole lot closer. Great. Fucking great.

By the time I'd finished winding myself up into a full-scale terror, the metal was screeching and a small gap of daylight had appeared. Below me, I saw a black nose pushing and snuffling in, as if the dog could sense our urgency to get it inside. One inch became three and then four and then six and within twenty seconds the dog was wriggling its thin torso through the opening, tail wagging in its thick black fur, tongue licking Chris's face furiously, the weight of its body pushing the thin scientist tumbling backwards to the ground.

But twenty seconds was a long time, and when I looked up I could see that it wasn't going to be target practice after all. Four widows were closing in on us fast, and further back more were emerging from the hedgerows.

"Oh shit."

Without hesitation, John surged the flamethrower into life, sending a huge burst of flame out through the gap, his stance solid, no sign left of the hesitant teenager who had fought with me against the widow in the farmhouse. Through the shimmering heat and roar of the jet of fire, I could see that the widows were still coming. God, these fuckers were hard to kill. Shutting my eyes, I braced myself and pulled hard on the trigger, the gun thrusting back into my shoulder as it burst into aggressive life.

"Shut the fucking gate!" The noise of the gun blazed

in my ears, but now that my eyes were open I could see that we were at least keeping them back. One was up on its hind legs, still somehow coming forward, barely four feet away. The gate was closing, but too slowly for my liking.

"To the left!"

John pulled his flame round and I finally managed to aim my gunfire in a specific direction—straight at the bitch. The results were pretty satisfying, and as it jolted backwards, the power of the rapid-fire bullets and the flame too much for it to take, I heard it squeal in anger and pain. The grey of the gate finally closing off my vision, I gritted my teeth, suddenly surging with anger, and preferring it to fear I set it free, concentrating my aim on the eyes of another widow creeping in from the right.

It kept on coming and I kept on firing, sure I was damaging it, some of that bank of red bursting and oozing pus-like gel as the bullets hit home, but I seemed to have enraged the widow as much as it had enraged me, and shrieking, the strange sound still coming unnaturally from somewhere inside and outside the mandibles and suckers on its revolting body, it launched lithely at the gate just as the two sheets of metal clanged shut.

Self-preservation instinct forced the muzzle of the gun upwards so that the last few bullets went stray into the air as my brain tried to release the grip of my finger from the trigger.

Finally, the world was silent apart from the sound of our panting breath and the satisfying hisses and shrieks of frustration and pain from the other side of the thick metal.

"Stand back, boys. They'll be putting the electric back on."

The rest of the perimeter had stayed live, but this section had been shut down in case one of us made contact while getting the mutt. I wasn't sure what came first, the end of George's sentence or the soft crackle of live electricity humming along the gate. The widows must have been coming fast for them to get it going that quickly.

I took a safe step back before turning round. John nodded at me. "Good work, mate."

"You too."

"God, that gun is noisy. I thought my eardrums were going to burst." Whitehead was back on his feet, standing next to the dog, which seemed to have been sitting calmly throughout the small war raging in the ten inches of space that had been required to let him in.

George patted the sheepdog on his head. "Good boy." The dog looked up and licked his hand. "Now, let's see who you are, shall we?" Bending forward, he looked at both sides of the silver tag hanging from his leather collar. "There's no name. That's odd. There's just an address."

"Some people do that." John wiped a stream of sweat from his face. "So thieves can't call the dog and make it come. It's probably microchipped or something."

George paused and looked at the tag again. "Look at this address, Matt."

Pointing the gun away from us all, taking no chances, I pushed back the safety with more than a small sense of relief, and peered down to see what had puzzled George and read the address aloud.

"Nine Victoria Road, Chester." There was a telephone number, too, but I didn't bother to recite it. "Chester? Isn't that up near Manchester somewhere?"

George nodded. "How did he get all the way here from Chester? That's an awfully long way for a dog to travel by itself."

"Maybe his owners were down this way on holiday or something when all this shit started." John lit a cigarette and I hoped that the flamethrower wasn't leaking.

"I don't think so." Crouching, Whitehead examined the affectionate dog. "He's covered in little cuts and bruises, and he's pretty thin under this coat." He picked up one paw and looked at the pads. As he pressed into one, the animal let out a small yelp. "Yes, this boy's been on a long walk, that's pretty certain."

"But why would he have come all the way from Chester to here?" George sounded more bemused than concerned. I had to admit that the dog had me puzzled, too, but I doubted we were going to get any answers.

"Maybe that's what we should call him—Chester." I looked up to see if the others agreed, and John laughed.

"Yeah, I like it. Chester. That'll do." He whistled loudly at the dog. "Hey, Chester, come on."

The dog didn't even look up at the sound.

"He's very calm, isn't he? He didn't react to the gunfire at all." Chris followed his comment with a whistle of his own. Again there was no reaction. Whitehead checked the dog's underbelly. "Oh, yes. Definitely a he."

I smiled. "Lucky we had a scientist here to find that

out for us. Don't know what we'd have done without you."

"You're very funny."

We turned to walk back to the comms hut and Chester trotted alongside. John whistled again, but the dog's ears didn't even twitch. He tried again. Still nothing. He was intriguing me now.

"What's bugging you, mate?"

"I don't know. I'm not sure." He waved his hand slightly, causing a shadow of fingers to drift into the animal's sight range. The dog immediately lifted its head up, eager and alert.

"Look at that."

I looked at George and Chris to see if they had any more of a clue to what John was on about than I did. Neither of them seemed entirely sure of what it was that the teenager wanted us to look at. He stopped and we stopped alongside him, as did the dog, who looked obediently up at us.

"Sit." John looked right at the dog as he spoke. "Sit."

Chester stayed standing, tail half-wagging, decidedly unsure about why we'd stopped.

"Can we leave the training until later? I don't think you're exactly the Barbara Woodhouse type and I really don't want to carry this gun for any longer than I have to, safety on or not."

"Don't you get it, Matt?" John looked at me like I was stupid, and I was beginning to think he might be right. "It's not that he needs training. He's obviously fucking trained, he was walking to heel, stopping when we stopped. No, there's nothing wrong with his obedience."

"Get to the point, John." George was obviously equally confused.

The young man sighed and scratched Chester behind the ears. "Well, I'm just trying to figure out what the odds are that amongst our little group of survivors we'd end up with a deaf girl and a deaf dog."

"What?" Head tilted, Chris spoke for all of us.

"It's obvious. He doesn't respond to whistles and commands, and more than that, he wasn't at all freaked out by the racket from that gun. There's only one answer. Chester's deaf as a post."

Two hours of fussing and laughing later, my shepherd's pie was eaten, and it was agreed that John was spot on. Chester was a great dog, but he couldn't hear a thing. Just like Rebecca, he could pick up vibrations, but no actual sound. He was obviously clever, with a slightly mischievous edge that was to be expected in a dog bred for working, and although Chris couldn't put an age on him, after having a good look at his teeth he reckoned that he wasn't much more than three or four. I liked him straight away, stupid as that sounds, but at the centre of that coat flecked with brown there was a *good* dog. And it was good to have something perhaps saner than human company amongst us.

Jane and Oliver had made pretty strong bids to become Chester's favourite friend, mainly with overzealous hugging and food bribery, but it was Rebecca's chair that he gravitated towards when left to his own devices, nuzzling his black and white head under her hand so that she had no choice but to pet him. Perhaps he recognised that they were two of a kind, or perhaps he just recognised her kindness. Whatever it was, I figured Chester had made his choice.

"He's very affectionate, isn't he?" There was no animosity in Katie's voice now, and I wondered if she'd even noticed that the dog had studiously avoided her since he'd arrived. There was no growling or barking, he just evaded her touch. Maybe I was reading too much into it, but I kept thinking about what Jane had said. *She smells so bad.* Dogs had great senses and I wondered how much more acute Chester's remaining ones were to make up for his lack of hearing.

"I'm not surprised. He must be pretty pleased to find some friendly people. We've all had our share of shit getting here and it probably wasn't any different for him, poor thing. I bet he's had a rough time of it over the past few weeks."

I was surprised by Dave's sentimentality, but he had a point. After all, what had happened to the people that lived at 9 Victoria Road, Chester? Nothing good, I should imagine, and then Chester had been left to fend for himself. We'd doused some of his cuts and bruises with witch hazel and iodine, and there was plenty of evidence that his journey hadn't been any fun. It was a surprise he was still tame and not a nervous wreck.

The door opened and Jeff and Dean came in from patrolling, an awkward atmosphere instantly falling across the table. When we'd come back from the gate with Chester, Nigel had offered to take over on the radios, and Mike had stayed in there keeping him company. The other two had then gone out, changing the rota duty to take the patrol, and Daniel was checking out the petrol levels for the generator.

Dean had mumbled something about how we'd already done our bit for the day, but it was pretty obvious that they felt a loyalty to Nigel and would try to not make a fuss or pay any attention to the dog. I wondered if they realised how ridiculous that was. Maybe Dean did. He kept his eyes down as they took their dinner from the hot plate and sat at a bench a little away from us, occasionally talking quietly with each other. For his part, Chester had not shown any interest in them, either, and I was glad about that. If our group was going to divide into two factions then it seemed that the dog had decided which one he wanted to be part of. And that was ours.

Still the mood quieted down after that, and despite trying to chat to the other men about how the patrol had been, they weren't forthcoming with anything more than one word answers and we eventually gave up. After coffee I went for a walk with George in the warm heat, talking without ever saying anything important in that way that makes you feel good afterwards. Shooting the breeze, wasn't that what the Americans called it? Whatever it was, George was good at it, and I felt myself relaxing and feeling content in a way I hadn't since all this started. Maybe I was starting to appreciate the small things in life. Maybe Chester was bringing us good luck.

Deciding to turn in, when we made it back to the dorm the argument that had been brewing all afternoon was just starting.

"I don't see why he should sleep in here." Nigel had his pyjamas on and the ironed crease down the middle reminded me that he hadn't lost any of his uptight arrogance. However, he had gained something—a little extra confidence. Daniel's large figure was slouching behind him, his body backing up Nigel's words. "It's a dog. This is a bedroom. Dogs sleep outside. Are you all retarded?"

"Calm down, mate. Nothing wrong with a dog sleeping in here." Dave's voice sounded far from calm, the rage bubbling beneath the surface like a volcano in the first stages of eruption.

"It's a dirty animal and I don't want it in here! His fur stinks."

"Jesus fucking Christ! What is your fucking problem?" Dave finally exploded. "Why are you such a complete pompous shit? Who the fuck do you think you are?"

"You had to make it personal, didn't you?" Nigel sneered as he sucked air in, getting ready no doubt to start his own tirade against Dave and the rest of us, but George stepped in between them.

"What's all this shouting about? Chester?" His voice was calm but hard. He stared at Dave, then at the dog lying down with his head between his paws, brown eyes peering upwards, and then brought his own eyes round to rest on Nigel.

"The dog sleeps in here. It's not a safe world out there, so there is no way we're putting him outside. For a start, the weather's too stormy. He'd be soaked through in minutes. It's common sense that he sleeps with us."

Nigel snorted. "That's not much of a surprise. You were always going to take his side, weren't you?" His twisting face made him look mean and ugly as he pointed. "You lot haven't wanted me around since we first met, that much has been obvious! All you've done is talk behind my back and laugh at me. And I'm not going to put up with it anymore. Either the dog sleeps outside or we'll go and use the other dorm. I've had enough!"

For a moment there was silence as we all stood,

breathing hard, desperately trying to control our own tempers, so much pent up frustration with each other cutting into the air.

It was Katie, bless her, that broke the ice.

"See ya, then."

The cheeky lilt in her voice almost made me laugh out loud, as did Nigel's face. Did he really think we'd pick him over the dog? "Yeah, I hope it's nice over there." I couldn't help but add my sentiment to Katie's.

George, the grown-up amongst us, shrugged. "That's your choice, Nigel. Obviously, we'd rather you stayed here with us. It would be a shame not to all do our best to get along and work as a team, but if you feel you can't stay in here with a dog here, then the most sensible thing to do would be to try the other dorm."

"Screw you." Nigel muttered, coldly. "Screw all of you. You'll be sorry. You wait and see."

"Hey, there's no need for that kind of talk, we're all on the same side."

"Just shut up! Shut up, old man, no one's listening!" The shrillness of his words hinted at edges of madness, and Nigel must have heard it himself, because he stood still for a moment, hands on his hips, taking in deep breaths.

"I'm sorry. I'm sorry...I shouldn't have..." He sniffed. "I'll just get my things then. I take it that someone will unlock the other building?" The pomposity was edging back into his voice, and I just couldn't wait for him to be gone. The idea of a Nigel-free sleeping room was very appealing.

"I know where the keys are." Daniel was pulling his shirt back on. "I'll come with you. I think the others will, too."

There was no need to ask which *others* he meant.

The divide between us was becoming literal; the only one of the original Hanstone crew that would stay with us was Chris. That, however, seemed like a fair trade to me. We got the doctor and they got nutty Nigel. I only hoped tempers would have calmed down enough for everyone to carry on doing their shifts as usual by the morning. Our survival still very much depended on us being one unit, fatally fractured or not.

The door shut a little too loudly behind them as the men trudged out into the night in search of their new home.

"Good riddance to them," Dave muttered under his breath, and bent down to tickle Chester behind his ears. The dog chuffed an almost bark, as if in agreement, before laying himself down a few feet from the door and closing his eyes. And that's where he slept. We'd all expected him to go in with Rebecca, but he didn't show any inkling to do so, and with Jane on the floor already that would have been too tight a squeeze, so his chosen spot on the floorboards was probably a wise move.

That night, with Chester adding his snores to the collective, was the first in weeks that I wasn't woken from my hellish almost-sleep by Katie trying to leave the dorm. She slept soundly, and did so every night for the next week. It was bliss.

CHAPTER TWENTY

"You'd better come and take a look at this." Dean's normally impassive face was showing edges of concern as he came into the dorm, his hooded lids furrowing over his dark eyes.

"What is it?" I'd been on late patrol, and after crashing into bed I'd slept like a log, not even the sound of anyone else getting up stirring me, and when I'd opened my eyes it was past ten in the morning. Enjoying the rare peace of the empty sleeping quarters, I'd had a long, hot shower and was just pulling on my jeans when Dean had come in. I followed him out into the constant drizzle, heading towards the canteen.

"I'm not really sure. I was just cleaning up after breakfast when him and Katie came in late."

"Who?"

"Dave. He's not looking good."

My heart sank. Dave had been doing so well—what the hell could have gone wrong now when he was pretty much all healed up?

By the time we pulled the door open my T-shirt was

sodden and my hair, still damp from the shower, was dripping down my forehead. This rain was becoming ridiculous in a slightly scary way. If the weather didn't settle down soon, then it would seem that England was becoming a new tropical zone. Another sudden change that we had no control over.

"So, what's going on?"

Dave was sitting with his back to me, Katie beside him. George was there, too, as yet unshaven, and Nigel and Mike hung back slightly behind him. There was no sign of Rebecca, and I presumed she must be out walking Chester with Jane.

"What's happening to me, Matt?" Dave twisted round to face me, his eyes wide with dread, and I could see why Rebecca had got Jane quickly out of the way. "Good Lord, what's happening to me?"

I took a step closer. Jesus. *Jesus Christ.* What *was* happening to him? When we'd cut his arm off, we thought we'd taken all the infection away with it, but we'd been so, *so* wrong. My stomach twisted as I stared, the enormity of what I was looking at making me want to vomit. Trying to keep the horror from my face, I examined him. Had it been spreading from his shoulder all these weeks, slithering along his muscles and tendons, creeping into his veins, working its way through his organs? How could he not have felt it? Just how involved with him was it?

Dave sobbed slightly. "It's stopping me seeing properly. I can see it in the corner of my eyes. I can't concentrate on anything else."

The white strands that had characterised the widow's bite on his arm were working inwards from the corners of his eyes, appearing from within the socket, clinging to the slippery surface, twisted miniature versions of the thick coils that had been draped across the pub, each thread reaching out for another on the opposite side of his eyeball. I looked down to his nose, where more of the sticky strings oozed out of each nostril, weaving through his dark thick hairs as they emerged, creeping down towards his lips.

"It's okay, mate. It's okay." I squeezed his good shoulder reassuringly, although it was obvious that things were far from okay. "Have you seen this stuff anywhere else?" As I asked the question I noticed more erupting from his ear, the strands working both upwards into his hair and down towards his neck. I could only presume it was coming in equal volume from the ear on the other side of his head. How had it appeared so fast?

"Everywhere." His words were a whisper, and it seemed that this stuff that was seeping out of him was no barrier to tears, his eyes flooding. "Everywhere it can get out of me, it is. Look." He held up his hand. "It's even coming out between my cuticles and my fucking fingernails." He looked up at me in terror, the surface of his eyes looking like cracked ceramic where that stuff was covering them. "What's it doing to me, Matt? What's it going to do to me? What's it fucking doing to me *inside*?"

As he cried and sweated with fear, I thought I caught a vague whiff of something sickly and unpleasant coming from him, something that stopped me wanting to touch him or come too close. Was that what had driven Nigel and his groupies further back? Was that the same smell that Jane was talking about when she said that Katie smelled bad? It was a bad smell, that was for sure. There wasn't a better word to describe it.

I didn't like the way I could almost taste it as it invaded the air in my mouth and lungs.

Shaking the disgust off, I looked up at George. "What do you think?"

The old man shook his head, the grey stubble on his chin making him look tired and worn. "I don't know, Matt. I really don't."

I bit my lip, wishing that I could give Dave some comfort, but finding little inside to relinquish. "How are you feeling? Are you feeling ill at all?"

He shook his head, swallowing hard, trying to get his panic under control. "No, I feel okay. I feel fine. I think. Maybe a bit sick, but that might just be, you know, the shock."

"Good. That's got to be a good sign." I don't know who I was trying to convince, me or him. I don't think I was doing a very good job of either. "I'm going to go and try the radios. Maybe someone else has come across this as well."

Despite almost regular contact with the London boys and the scientists, as well as sporadic contact with some more intermittent survivors, we hadn't really shared much of our individual adventures unless they might be useful. We'd told about Chester, because there was definitely something interesting in the way the widows had ignored him, but I couldn't remember sharing the story of Dave's bite and amputation. I guess now was the time for that.

Taking over the controls and booting Jeff right out of the room, I brought the dial back to the frequency needed for contact with the men in Paddington. I hoped to hell that they were listening. Although in the beginning they'd manned the radio twenty-four/seven like we did, over the past couple of weeks it seemed that they'd reduced that a bit. It also seemed that a couple of voices were missing over the airwaves. We didn't ask, and whoever was left there wasn't volunteering the information, but I was pretty sure they weren't faring as well as we were. Hanstone Park was pretty well-defended, and more than that, pretty well-stocked. I imagined that for those holed up elsewhere the day-to-day issues of getting food and water were far more hazardous.

"Hello, London? Hello, London, are you there?" I figured the proper way was probably, *Are you receiving, over,* but who the hell cared any more about etiquette? It was communication that counted.

"Hello, mate." A tired voice with a south London drawl came back at me. Thank God there was someone there. "What's up?"

"We need some advice. Have any of your lot been bitten by a widow?"

"Why?" There was a moment of hesitancy before the word, and I wasn't reassured by it.

"Well, one of us sustained a bite over a month ago on our way here. Some white strands started to appear in the wound. We amputated his arm and he seemed to be getting better, but he got up this morning and that…" I searched for a word, "that shit is coming out of him everywhere. We don't know what to do about it. He doesn't feel ill, but this doesn't look good. Any advice, or should I try the scientists?"

The man at the other end laughed, but there was no humour in it. "The scientists won't know shit. They don't go out. Most of them are junkies now, anyway. Locked up with plenty of drugs and too much time on their hands—what else was going to happen?"

I wondered if the slight slur in his voice was tiredness or alcohol.

"Well, do you lot have any advice? Anything that might work on getting it to reduce?" *Or at least stop coming out of him.*

"Yeah, I've got some advice." He sighed so heavily into the radio that I could almost feel his breath. "Kill him."

The words were like a smack in the face. "What?"

"Kill him. Trust me, it'll be merciful. I've seen what's going to happen to him. He won't survive."

I couldn't bring myself to speak. How the hell had we reached the stage that we could calmly discuss executing one of our friends? What the fuck had been going on in London?

"I'm not sure we can do that." I couldn't keep the tremble out of my voice.

"Then your friend has my sympathy and my prayers. I think, though, that you'll change your mind pretty soon. When he starts screaming."

"Well, we'll see." I wanted this surreal conversation to be over.

"Get back to me on how it turns out. Good luck." His voice softened. "Look, sorry I didn't break that to you better. Things have been...tough here."

"No problem, mate. I understand." I didn't understand and I didn't want to understand. For a minute, as I sat there chewing my lip and regaining my composure before facing the others, I wondered who that man on the other end of the radio was. What had he been before this? A cabbie? An office worker? A fucking sandwich delivery boy? Who the hell knew? And who really cared anymore? He probably didn't recognise himself any more than the rest of us did. All those years I'd spent behind a desk selling mortgages seemed like a hazy dream now. Even Chloe was part of an old world. A dead world.

Hauling myself to my feet, I trudged back to the canteen. Someone had made tea, that old British favourite in times of crisis, and a mug had been left for me by where Dave and Katie were sitting.

I shook my head. "They don't know what it is. They haven't had anyone suffer a bite." There was only so far I could go with a lie, and this seemed the best option. I couldn't pretend that all was going to be fine, because I wasn't that good a liar.

"None of them have been bitten?" Dave obviously wasn't convinced.

I shrugged, finding it hard to meet his infected eyes. "That's what they said."

"So what the hell am I going to do?" He started to rock backwards and forwards. "Oh God, it's going to kill me, isn't it? It's going to kill me from the inside out."

I looked at George, wanting him to take over this nightmare scene, but it seemed he couldn't find any words. The problem was that we both believed what Dave was saying. This stuff was going to kill him, and there was nothing we could do about it but watch and wait.

It was Katie that broke the silence, calm and cool and unexpected.

"No. It's not going to kill you. We're not going to let that happen." He was keening beside her, and she stroked his arm. She was either unaware of the smell that was coming off him or she was ignoring it well. "Look at me, Dave."

The gentle command in her voice slowed down his movements and he brought his eyes up to meet hers.

"Now, you and me are going to go to the medical room and we are going to try every concoction of pills and lotions until we find the one that gets rid of this, okay? And I am going to stay right with you."

He nodded slowly. "But it won't work, it won't work...."

"You don't know that. These things evolved from humans. Something will kill this stuff. We just need to find it. Trust me. I won't let this kill you."

She was speaking so methodically that I almost believed her myself, despite what the man in London had said. How was she doing this? She'd gone from being royal pain in the ass to Florence Nightingale. Taking Dave's arm, she got him to his feet with a gentleness I'd never seen in her.

"Okay, guys, Dave and I have got some work to do." She smiled at me and then at Chris. "Can you let us into the infirmary? And let me at the drugs?"

Whitehead nodded. "I'll let you in, but you've got to know that messing around with drugs is dangerous. You might do him more harm than good."

She raised an eyebrow at the doctor, clearly stating that doing Dave more harm than good wasn't very likely given his current situation, and Chris shrugged.

"Okay, okay. But be careful. If you're not sure of something just ask."

"Don't worry. I'm not planning to empty the cabinet down his neck. I'm going to try lotions, potions and antibiotics first. Come and get us at lunchtime."

"Katie..." I wasn't sure exactly what I wanted to say to her, and she stopped by the door, looking over her shoulder at me and smiled.

"Don't worry, Matt. I know what I'm doing. Just let us get on with it, all right?"

I nodded and let her go.

A little before lunch, she popped her head into the dorm where I was lying down reading *The Kraken Wakes*. George had finally persuaded me to give it a go, and although given our present situation it was hardly light reading, it was pretty engaging stuff. I'd forgotten how therapeutic getting lost in someone else's world could be.

"You okay?"

She smiled, but it wasn't a victorious one, not that I expected it. All there was in the infirmary were the usual antiseptics and some antibiotics, and we'd tried Dave on those immediately after he'd been bitten. They hadn't stopped the stuff coming out of the first wound, so they weren't exactly going to make a difference now.

"Yeah, fine. Dave doesn't want to come over for lunch. I'm going to go and get us some food now and take it back, okay?"

"Sure, no problem. Has he got worse?"

"No, he just doesn't want anyone staring at him. It freaks him out, and you can't blame him."

"I understand."

She started to pull the door shut again. "So, you'll make sure no one disturbs us then?"

"Yeah, I'll tell the others."

"Thanks."

As it was, when I sat down with my plate on the long bench, I decided Dave probably had the right idea not wanting to come over for lunch. It was a depressed and quiet affair of cold ham and salad. We were all subdued, and even Chester didn't seem to care whether he got any scraps or not as he settled down in the gap between the girls chairs, sighing and snuffling, lying his head down between his paws. Even though I hadn't shared what had really been said on the radio, I don't think that if I had it would have made much difference. None of us believed that there was much hope for Dave, and as we sat there eating without any enthusiasm, it felt like we were on a death watch.

The ham felt slimy and tasteless as I forced myself to chew on it. *You'll change your minds soon enough. When he starts screaming.* I put my fork down and pushed my plate away. The silence was claustrophobic and the wet sounds of people methodically eating were making me feel nauseous.

"You all right?" George was a few seats away, his fork paused on its journey to his mouth.

"Just not very hungry. I've never been a salad man."

He stared at me for a moment, his eyes probing mine. "You know something we don't?"

"Nothing that's going to make a difference, George, let's just put it like that."

He continued to look at me before sighing heavily and putting his forkful of ham down untouched. "You know, salad's never really done it for me much, either. I think I'll sit this out till dinner." Pushing away from the table he stood up, leaving his plate where it was and walked slowly outside, filling his pipe as he did so.

Rebecca's brow furrowed and when I caught her eye, she signed slowly, *He okay?* I shrugged at her, not needing to put my pidgin ham-fisted efforts into practice to reply. I think my face was probably speaking pretty clearly for me. Were any of us okay? Sure as hell not Dave, and if we were honest, then all we were doing was sitting around and waiting for the screaming to start.

Not wanting any company, I gave George a head start before I stepped out into the temporarily dry air and lit up a cigarette. I had a funny feeling that if anything was likely to kill me early, it wasn't going to be fucking fags.

The howling started at four-thirty, making me drop my book and leap up from my bed as the sound filled the air. It was loud and full of pain, but it wasn't Dave, it was Chester. What the fuck was making the dog howl like that? My heart thumping, I raced out of the dorm without putting my shoes on and ran towards where I thought the noise was coming from. Had a widow got into the compound somehow? Had it bitten Chester? What the hell was making him howl like that, what the hell was it?

As I ran through the overhanging branches of the trees, I saw him sitting in the clearing by the comms hut, his head thrown back letting out the heart-wrenching sound. John was coming equally fast from the direction of the canteen, and over in the distance even Nigel and Mike were jogging over from their new home in the other hut. The teenager reached him first, a few feet ahead of me.

"What is it? What's the matter with him?"

"I don't know. What the fuck is it, boy?" Between us we searched his fur for any sign of injury as the others gathered in a crowd.

"Has something hurt Chester? Is he okay?" Jane was almost crying herself as she fell to her knees on the grass, hugging the dog's neck and making our examination more difficult.

I stood up, perplexed. "No, I don't think so, honey.

He doesn't seem to be hurt. You found anything, John?"

"No. Nothing." He stroked the dog's head, and the howl lessened into a pitiful mewl. "There, there, boy. It's okay. You're okay."

"Something freaked him, though." What could it have been?

"Did you ever see that film, *The Thing*? The one with Kurt Russell?" I stared at Nigel, waiting for him to make whatever shit point he was heading towards, and when it came, he didn't disappoint.

"Well, maybe the widows are going to start erupting from him now. Maybe that's what's pissing him off." He laughed slightly at his own poor attempt at humour, and if Whitehead hadn't turned up I think I'd have stopped stroking the trembling animal and beaten the life out of the pompous shit, no matter who tried to stop me. Sometimes I dream of that day and wish I had. I really do. As it was, I didn't and Whitehead stumbled over to us, his eyes wide.

"You'd better come." He swallowed hard, the action almost comical, one arm waving absently behind him. "You'd better come and see…in the infirmary…." He turned on his heel and started back the way he came, pulling on George's sleeve, dragging him back with him. The rest of us trotted after him, apart from Jane and John, still soothing the anxious dog. It seemed that Chester had no desire to follow Chris Whitehead, and I wondered if whatever had disturbed the doctor was what had set the dog off. The infirmary. Dave. What the hell had happened to him now?

As I tumbled through the doorway, a pace or two behind George, my feet seized up, my legs incapable of taking me further forward until my brain could translate what my eyes were seeing into some kind of rational meaning. I stood swaying and staring, mouth open. *I won't let it kill you.* Wasn't that what she'd said? *Just let us get on with it, all right?*

I fought the urge to gag, and my leaden legs finally found the strength to step forward and come alongside George. I could feel his body shaking next to mine, his breath coming quickly. "Oh, no. Oh, Lord no."

Dave lay on the infirmary bed, his arm hanging down the side, his eyes shut. Beside him was a packet of sleeping pills and an empty glass. On the table was an empty bottle of wine that Katie must have snuck out of the canteen, and two plates with the remnants of smoked salmon and what looked like fine pate and toast on them. The condemned man's last supper. The tips of his fingers were blue where the blood was settling, and a small amount of dry puke had crusted at the edges of his mouth as if something inside him had desperately tried to get the sleeping pills out.

My gaze moved round to the tableaux at the other end of the room, pulse quickening, not wanting to accept what I saw there. Not ready to accept it.

Why she hadn't taken the sleeping pills as well, I don't know. Maybe she thought they wouldn't work on her. Maybe she wanted a fail-safe, no shit method. Whatever the reason, she'd done what she'd set out to do. Her small lifeless body hung from the makeshift noose tied round the metal curtain pole, the stool kicked away, sideways on the ground. Thankfully, her head was lolling forwards. I wasn't sure I could take the sight of her bulging eyes and thick tongue, her elfin beauty destroyed by strangulation. There wouldn't have been enough weight to break her neck, and a thick sob squeezed out of me with the unwanted image of her kicking and struggling as she slowly lost her breath.

It took a moment before I realised she'd pinned a note to her jumper, and I shuffled forward, needing to read it. It said one word. One word was all that was needed.

FAT.

Oh Jesus.

Whitehead was stammering behind me. "She must have planned it...she must have...they must have talked about it this morning...."

Staring at her, my heart aching, I wondered if she'd held Dave's hand and soothed his brow as he drifted away. I wondered if they'd talked and laughed over their last meal, reliving precious memories. I almost felt a pang of jealousy at that shared experience. Why hadn't she talked to me? Why hadn't she told me?

Needing to know, I reached forward and lifted her jumper, wanting to see her skin beneath. My breath stopped in my throat. *FAT.* One word that said so much. She was still slim, not big like Chloe got, but beneath that smooth surface, unnatural lumps and bumps protruded like bags of loose fat under her skin. *Oh Jesus, Katie.* I was barely aware I was crying, the tears blurring my vision and burning my eyes, and George pulled me back, slowly taking my shoulders.

"She must have been so scared, George. She must have been so scared."

"Yes, son. She must have. Now let's get her down from there, shall we?"

My brain thudded painfully, a headache raging into life. This had happened much more quickly than it did with Chloe. Only a few days ago, Katie had been strolling around in vest tops. There was no way she could have been hiding any of those unnatural excesses of flesh from us, so how could it have happened so fast? How could it have done this to her so quickly? And why didn't she say something? I remembered the way the widows hadn't attacked her in the pub. Could they sense the change in her even then? Christ, I hated them, and I hated the scientist who had allowed them to happen.

"Come on, Matt. You've got to be stronger than this."

George squeezed my shoulder, and the surprise of his touch made me slam my gaping mouth closed, biting down hard on my tongue, bursting the flesh and filling my mouth with the sickly taste of blood. Pain gripped me and as I cursed the shock of the scene around me lost its grip slightly, the added brightness created by my hot mind dimming slightly back to normal light.

Without speaking I wrapped my arms round her still-warm body, trying not to feel the too-familiar lumps beneath her clothes, as George reset the chair and untied her, letting her slump over my shoulder in a fireman's lift. Her slight frame seemed too heavy and my arms shook as I slid her onto the narrow examining table in the far corner. Vessels burst, sending rays of red toward her pupils; her too-wide eyes stared at me from above the thick purple lips that I could remember kissing not so many weeks before, when they were slim, pink and hot with human desire.

It was Katie, but not Katie; a distorted interpretation of what she had once been, and staring at her and then at Dave behind me, tears rolled down my face and I couldn't stop my sobbing, their faces blurring with those locked in my head forever that I would never see again. Too many to mourn, even Chloe just one of thousands or millions, a tiny speck in this tragedy.

"Holy fucking shit." Nigel must have followed us inside and through my tears I turned to see him standing in the doorway, hands on his hips, taking it all in. "Holy fucking shit." His eyes rested on Katie, and I saw a flare of victory in them. "I knew it. I fucking knew it. She had one of those things growing inside her, didn't she?" He stared at me, and then George. "I told you we shouldn't trust those women, but oh no, you wouldn't have any of it. Well, now look." He pointed at Katie as if what he was saying would shed new light on the situation, as if she were going to sit up and agree with him and his pompous prick attitude. "And there's two more back there." His voice was rising with angry indignation. "What are we going to do about them?"

My shoulders slumped. I didn't have the energy to shout back, or to even get mad. Phelps would never *see* things the way we did, the way any decent person would. Shouting would only serve to make him more fucking self-righteous. I let out a long sigh and almost laughed.

"She killed herself, Nigel."

"So?" His ever-sweaty brow furrowed, not seeing how the method of her death could have any bearing on what he had to say.

"Yes, she had a widow growing inside her. Do you think she wanted that? Do you think she did it on purpose? She killed herself, for fuck's sake. And she did it for us as well as for herself. She wanted to kill the widow, and to do that she had to kill herself, and you want to talk about trust?" My voice was tired, low and even and maybe that gave it more power, because when I met Nigel's eyes there was real hate trembling in them. His mouth worked to get the words out.

"We might not be so lucky with the other two. They'll turn next, I fucking promise you."

Where did he get so much loathing from? After all that had happened in the world around us, surely those of us that had survived should learn to trust and respect each other. His negativity drained the remains of my energy.

"Nigel, Jane is a little girl who has been through enough already, and now we've got to go and tell her that her big sister is dead, and all you can think about is the vague possibility that she might turn into one of these things one day. You're a father. Surely you feel more than all this suspicion and hate. What if it was your little girl?" I stared at him. *And what the hell happened to her, anyway?* "What if it was Emma that had made it and I was suggesting that she had no hope? How would you feel then?"

His jaw gritted for a moment and I got the feeling that he was fighting the urge to strangle the life out of me with his bare hands, and I couldn't understand why. He stood like that, frozen, his fingers twitching, for a full ten seconds letting out a long sigh, and leaning against the wall behind him, shutting his eyes. I could almost see the shudder of emotion rippling through his middle-aged body.

"You're right. Of course you're right. I'm sorry." He covered his face, rubbing at his eyes. "I don't know what comes over me sometimes. It's just all too much to bear."

Now it was my turn to be lost for words. I hadn't actually thought what I'd said would have any effect on Nigel at all, but it seemed that my quiet tirade had hit home.

His shoulders shook slightly, almost as if he were crying, but his hands were shielding most of his face and I couldn't see for sure.

"I think that's what the problem is. I think when I look at Jane and Katie, I think of my poor Emma and I can't handle it." He looked up, eyes slightly damp. "I'm sorry, Matt. I really am. That girl killed herself to protect us all and that must have been a terrible decision to make. I can see that now."

He was still wearing a suit shirt, and sweat stains stretched in huge crescents from his armpits, darkening the blue. The sight of it turned my stomach, and I wondered how much he meant what he was saying. It was a bit of a turnaround for him, but then I doubted I would ever really understand this man. I knew that I would never really like him, and I wondered if that was making me suspicious of his change of heart. The thought made me feel guilty.

"Don't worry about it, mate." My words sounded hollow even to me. "This shit affects us all differently."

He shook his head vehemently. "No. No, it doesn't. It shouldn't." I didn't know how to deal with this new contrite Nigel and just stared at him as his words blubbered out. "I've got to change the way I look at things. I've got to give that little girl some support. As if she were my Emma." With that real tears oozed over the rims of his eyes and he cried openly.

For a second, I thought about going and putting an arm around him, but I couldn't quite bring myself to do it.

"Speaking of which," Whitehead was standing by Dave's body, his composure a little recovered, "someone better go and break this news to Jane before she comes wandering in here looking for her sister."

My heart sank with the prospect, but George took the burden from me. "I'll go. By my age, you've had a little experience of handling these things." The expression on his face, however, told a completely different story.

"I'll come with you."

I stared at Phelps, not sure that I'd heard right. "I'm not sure that's such a good idea. I mean, she doesn't know you that well and—"

"Please. I need to start somewhere. I need to do this. I was a father, after all, of a girl the same age."

Was. The past tense. It unsettled me, but George nodded.

"Okay. But let me do the talking." He didn't sound like he wanted Phelps along at all, but I guess he decided that this new truce was too delicately in the balance to risk cutting Nigel out. I doubted it was going to make too much difference who told Jane. You couldn't make something like that less painful. It was going to destroy her. I was sure of it.

"And I'll start preparing the autopsies."

"Jesus, Whitehead." I turned my disgust on him. "Can't you give it at least an hour?"

He shrugged. "Sorry. I didn't mean to sound so bad taste. Not thinking straight." His eyes were sad, and with him I felt none of the anger that I would associate with Phelps's crassness. There was nothing intentional about Chris.

I nodded back, my eyes still filled with tears that I

was desperately holding within the red rims of my sockets, and then coughed, trying to clear my voice.

"I'll go and get on the radio again while you two speak to Jane. I said I'd let them know how things had turned out, and I may as well do it now."

Leaving Whitehead there amongst our dead, I went back out into the sticky air and, feeling as if I could cry forever, let the tears loose for a few private moments before reaching the hut.

CHAPTER TWENTY-ONE

It took me an hour or so of numbed transmitting to get a response from London, my brain slowly adjusting to the horror of what Dave and Katie had done as I sat there, repeating words without listening into the microphone on the desk. If I'd waited much longer I think I would have been in an almost semi-vegetative state, the constant repetition working like a mantra. When the same voice came back through the headset that I'd heard this morning, my whole body shook as reality took hold again.

The man at the other end still sounded tired or drunk or whichever. It was difficult to tell. I wondered if he thought the same hearing me.

"Our man killed himself. With one of the women. She was getting fatter." The words felt heavy just leaving my mouth. "I guess they figured that it was better to go out together and in control than wait for whatever was going to happen to them." All I could see as I spoke was Katie's death mask, and I wondered if I would ever be able to remember her as she had been alive. I doubted it. It was hard to picture Chloe before she started getting fat. I could do it, but it took concentration, and I figured my memories of Katie would be damaged in the same way.

"It was probably for the best." There was little sympathy in the words, but then I hadn't really expected it. The world was hardly full of hope these days, and so Katie and Dave really hadn't stood a chance of any miracle recovery. He continued to slur slowly into my ears.

"Have you seen any black widows at your end? Smaller than the normal ones?"

"No." My stomach tightened slightly. Were they evolving again? "Why? Have you?"

"No, but I caught the end of a broadcast from somewhere in Wales. It didn't really make sense, it was just some bloke laughing very loudly and talking about these black spiders. He didn't seem to be transmitting to anyone in particular, just randomly. I tried to get a fix on him from some of the others, but it seems that less and less people are out there on the airwaves."

He didn't need to spell it out. If they weren't on the airwaves, then it was likely that they were gone, dead, over and out. More Katie's and Dave's. The precious remnants of humanity slowly being wiped out.

"I was planning on contacting you this evening, actually. I've seen something that might interest you. Something fucking positive for once."

"Oh really?" God, I needed something good, but I didn't think there was much that was going to cheer me up today.

"Yeah, I've been outside today. Didn't really have a fucking choice—no food or water. Anyway, there's some activity out there. Human activity."

"Like what?"

"It's the army. Well, more like small squads of mercenaries in scruffy army clothing, but they seem pretty organised, so I can only reckon that they're something to do with whatever's left of the central government. I've seen three lots of them out there today, and they're all doing the same thing."

"Which is?"

"Spraying the widows with blood. They're going into buildings and attacking them. I saw them get one of the bitches out on Pall Mall. They squirted the blood at them and it worked like fucking acid. The thing was dead in seconds. It was fucking amazing to watch."

Great as it sounded, it was too confusing. "That can't be right. The widows eat people. How can they do that if our blood is poisonous to them?"

"I don't know. I don't even know if it's human blood, or even if it's blood at all. Maybe it's blood they've tampered with." He paused, as if his few moments of animation had exhausted him. "Whatever it is, it smells like blood. The streets are covered with it, and there's much less widow activity out there. I've decided that next time I hear them pass, I'm going to try and join them. It's better than sitting here and doing nothing but trying to survive and fighting a losing battle."

The desperation was clear in his voice, and I got the impression that he was the last of that band of survivors to still be with us. It was probably the best thing for him to do, but my heart ached with the thought of losing more contact. As each day passed, it seemed that we were alone in safety in the whole of England. I knew that couldn't be the case, but that was sure as hell how it felt, especially on days like these.

"Well, good luck mate. If you do go, make sure you let whoever's out there know that we're here."

"I will. And good luck to you lot, too."

I'd only just signed off when Rebecca came into the hut, her dark eyes sad and damp. Without trying to communicate, she sat on my lap and hugged me tight, maybe as much for herself as for my comfort, and for a split second I couldn't help but wonder what was growing inside her taut olive skin. Still, she smelled good and as we quietly cried together, her fingers running through my hair, I let all my emotions out.

Jane sat quietly picking at her food at dinner, her eyes alive but dulled. Rebecca had left me to join her, Chester's head resting on her lap as he sat between them. The little girl seemed isolated, a little of her closeness with Rebecca gone, as if she didn't trust the older woman to always be there, and I couldn't blame her for that. Everyone she had known when this had started was gone, leaving her in the same boat as the rest of us, but so, so much younger. On top of that, she and Rebecca had to deal with the fear. The fear that what had happened to Katie was going to happen to them. It made me feel guilty for my moments of self-pity earlier.

Nigel sat opposite them, dishing out big smiles of sympathy and trying to make conversation with John. It seemed that his new sense of camaraderie had spread to the others, as earlier they had all traipsed back with their belongings to rejoin us in the original dorm. Something about that had made my heart sink, but I figured it had to be for the best. I might never learn to like Phelps, but we were going to have to learn to rub along. John didn't look too comfortable about it either, sitting there talking to Nigel, but then he'd have to learn, too. Beggars couldn't be choosers, and the world was getting slim on people.

George took the seat opposite me, his eyes glancing over to where the girls were. I swallowed my food.

"How did she take it?"

"It depends how you look at it. She cried, but she wasn't surprised. She just kept saying that she knew because of the smell. Something tells me she'd come to terms with Katie's loss before today." He took a mouthful of food and chewed it without enthusiasm. "Still, she's a very disturbed little girl now. She's going to need lots of love and attention."

Across from us, Jane yawned long and hard.

"She must be in shock. A long sleep will do her good."

I was nodding in agreement when the door opened and Whitehead came in. Not bothering to get himself any dinner, he came and sat down. His face was on the green edge of pale and covered in a slick sheen of sweat. He may have been a scientist, but pathology wasn't for the fainthearted. I hadn't really thought about that when he said he was going to do the post-mortems, but now, looking at him, I could see that he'd really been through it.

I put my own fork down. "What did you find?"

His bright eyes shook as he leaned forward. "Well, that white stuff was all the way through Dave. Some strands were getting thicker, too. I can only think that it cocoons you from the inside out. I guess eventually it would have completely covered him. A bit like the original victims were cocooned."

The thought was repellent. "So, even if you get bitten, kill the bitch and get away, the bite ensures that you're still food for another one?"

"That's about the size of it."

"Jesus." I seemed to be calling out to God quite a lot recently, but I figured there wasn't fuck he'd be able to do about this shit. He'd given us our free will and this was what we'd done with it. I guess it was our turn to sort it out.

"What about Katie?" George asked the question that I'd avoided.

"Well," Chris blew into the air at an invisible fringe, "it wasn't what I'd expected, but it explains the weird lumps of fat."

"What does?"

"In a human the baby gestates in the womb, starts small and grows from there, right?" Now that he was talking science, some of that sickly look had faded from his face.

"Yes, even we know that much, Chris."

"Not with the widows, though." He paused, ensuring he had our full attention. "It seems that small parts of them develop in different areas, mutating from the host's original organs, and then each of those sections make their way to the womb, where they finally come together." He shrugged. "Or so I think. The widow growing in Katie was only just starting to form, so there was nothing in her womb but a few strands of white stuff linking all the other bits together. I guess those contract at some point to pull it into the womb before it comes out."

We all stared at each other for a moment, George and I trying to take in the complete alien nature of these creatures.

An image crept into my head, sending a shiver down my tired spine. "It's definitely dead though?" The idea of that thing continuing to grow in Katie's corpse revolted as well as terrified me.

Whitehead didn't look so confident. "As far as I can tell, yes. But then again, I don't know shit. I took some precautions with her body and, needless to say, I locked the door behind me."

I didn't want to know what he'd done to Katie to make sure that thing was dead, but I comforted myself with the idea that she would have wanted anything done to stop the thing inside her from surviving.

"What about the blood thing the guy in London told me about? What do you make of that?"

"Who knows? I tried some samples on a section of the widow that had been growing inside Katie, but no reaction. I'll try again tomorrow. Maybe take some from Chester to see if animal blood is any different." He looked tired. "Maybe whatever it is only works on live widows."

We'd kept our voices low so that Jane wouldn't hear, but I doubt she was listening, anyway. When I turned to check on her, she was staring into space, leaning her head against Rebecca. It wasn't long before she was being carried out by Nigel, fast asleep, and by ten o'clock most of the rest of us had joined her.

Someone's leg banging hard into the bottom of my bed woke me, along with curses and low voices telling someone to be fucking quiet. By the time I'd dragged my brain awake and sat up, I wasn't alone, George reaching for the light switch to dispel the grey gloom of dawn. My vision still hazy, I saw John falling out of his bed and a booted foot kicking him hard in his naked stomach as the leg passed. Swearing and wheezing, he curled round on himself, sucking in his breath, obviously in pain and unable to move. What the fuck was going on? It was all happening too quickly for my sleepy eyes to take in. Slowly adjusting to the light, the figures spread around the room became clear to me and as I realised what I was seeing my blood chilled.

Down by the door, Nigel had Jane held close to him, her young eyes wide over the thick barrier of his arm, and a couple of steps closer to my end of the dorm Michael had Rebecca held in the same way. It must have been his leg that banged into my bed as he passed, and I stared at the mild-mannered, middle-aged man that had barely spoken two words to me since we'd arrived. What the fuck was he doing and why?

Only when he swayed slightly did I catch the glint of metal against Rebecca's slim throat as her hands pulled at his arm with no hope of getting it off her. He couldn't meet my horrified gaze and turned a little, dragging Rebecca with him despite her attempts at resistance, to where Daniel stood, pulling open the door.

"Jesus, Nigel. You're not really going to do it, are you?" Jeff was on the far side of the room, staring in disbelief. Very slowly, I reached down and pulled on my jeans, not wanting to provoke any kind of reaction that could result in the girls getting hurt. My heart pounded hard against my chest.

Across from me, George had helped John onto his bed, where the kid was wheezing. The old man already had his trousers on, but his thin chest with loose skin and only a few white hairs made him look weak and vulnerable.

"Do what, Nigel?" His voice was calm and strong, though. "What are you going to do?"

"We're going to give them what they want." Nigel was grinning and insanity shone in the sweat on his face. "We're going to give them what they want and then maybe they'll leave us alone."

Outside I could hear desperate barking. Chester? It had to be. Michael had gone for a walk with him earlier and must have tied him up somewhere. All the pieces of this awful deception were slowly slotting into place. God, we'd been fools to believe that Nigel had changed. The dog's bark pierced the hut. At least he hadn't been harmed. He sounded full of life and anger from here, and I wouldn't want to be Nigel or the others if he broke free.

"What do you mean?" I asked. Nigel's words echoed meaningless in my dulled head, and the other man stared at me, his face very much animated and alive.

"These two belong with the widows. Any sane man would know that. They've probably got them growing inside them right now." Jane whimpered, tears leaking over Nigel, but the man took no notice. "They'll turn. Just like the other one. Just like all the others. Like my wife, your girlfriend, and just like my Emma would have turned. We should never have brought them with us."

"So what are you going to do?" George was trying to move closer, but Nigel brought his knife a little nearer to Jane's neck, forcing a sob from her and freezing the old man where he stood.

"We're going to give them to the widows. Right now. Maybe then they'll leave us alone. They don't want us, we're too much work for them. There's plenty of food out there. It's the women they're waiting for."

Despite the awfulness of it all, a laugh burst out of me. "You can't believe that, surely?"

Daniel glared. "Either way, the girls have got to go. I'm not sitting around waiting for them to change while they use up our supplies."

So that's what it was about, for him at least. Saving resources. Saving himself for a little longer. Who would he come for next? George for being old? John for being young? Disgust heaved at my belly.

"Now come on." Nodding at Nigel and protecting his route through, Daniel looked more like a thug than a civil servant. "And if the rest of you have any sense, you'll stay in here."

Still grinning, Nigel yanked the girl down the steps past Daniel's hulking shape, and Michael followed with the struggling Rebecca, who threw me a desperate look over her shoulder. Daniel lingered, glaring at us, and it was when he turned that John and Oliver Maine launched themselves past me, taking him tumbling down the outside stairs in a flurry of obscenities and aggression.

Galvanised into action, George and I ran past them, the three now a bundle of flying fists, and I wondered if our two were hitting each other more than Daniel, but at least they were pinning him down and keeping him out of the way. Jeff and Chris followed after us, and I grabbed the scientist's arm. George disappeared behind the dorm in the direction of the barking, I presumed to find the dog and release him. We needed all the help we could get now, and I figured Chester would be a pretty good weapon if it came to defending the girls.

"We need guns!"

Chris shook his head. "Can't get to them. It takes two keys. I've got one and Nigel's got the other." Once again I cursed Phelps. When we'd had the split in the camp, he'd suggested that the arms were in the hands of only one group. Dividing the two keys was the best solution we could come up with at the time.

"Fuck!"

Jeff shook his head. "I've got one." In his hand he held a small pistol. "I took it when you were arming up to let the dog in. I wasn't sure how all this was going to pan out then, so I thought this might be a good precaution. I should have kept it under my fucking pillow instead of in my drawer. I couldn't get to it back there." His eyes were desperate. "I just didn't think he was going to fucking do it."

There was no time for guilt and I grabbed the gun from him. "Dean's on the gate. You go and stop him activating it. We'll go after the others." Slapping him hard on the shoulder, I pushed him away, and turned to run towards the gate, Chris alongside me. Without the burden of dragging unwilling hostages, we covered the ground more quickly than the struggling figures we were so desperate to catch, and within a few minutes I could make out their outlines under the floodlights only a hundred yards or so ahead of us.

"Matt!" A breathless voice called from behind us, and not stopping moving I peered over my shoulder to see Maine catching us up. One gangly arm signalled behind him. "Left John with Daniel. He's not going anywhere. Oh shit, the gate..."

The rumbling sound was instantly recognisable, but Jeff must have dealt with Dean one way or another, because almost as soon as it started to squeal open, the gate started shutting again. Thank God he hadn't barricaded himself into the comms room, and the thought instantly begged the question of why he hadn't. I guessed, as the air burned my hot lungs as it raced in and out, that as the time to put their stupid plan into action had approached, Jeff wasn't the only one to get slightly cold feet. I figured that Dean had been quietly hoping that someone would come and stop him.

"Oh shit!" My legs pounded harder into the concrete road, desperate to move quicker. Ahead of us, through the closing gap in the gate, three widows appeared, leaping into the compound, hissing and snarling, the red eyes glowing in their translucent skin around the bulbous area that could only loosely be described as a head. I was close enough to see the desperate plea all over Jane's face as Nigel launched her forward, his own expression one of manic glee.

The next few moments passed in slow motion. Jane tumbling through the space in front of her, hair floating around her, the thin T-shirt she wore as a nightshirt rising up around her young legs as she tried in vain to propel herself backwards. The widow that was furthest forward reared up to embrace her, the suckers on its underbelly pulsing as its thin legs danced out in front, almost luring her into its reach.

Feeling the shout rising from my stomach, desperate to get to her, to stop what was happening, my own body lurched forwards as my feet betrayed me, stumbling over some outcrop of stone in the ground, the scream vanishing as my breath was knocked out of my chest with the impact.

Still clinging to the gun, I dragged myself up on my knees in time to see the little girl disappear into the deadly female embrace, two legs wrapping round her, hugging her tightly into the suckers underneath, the rest of the body dropping down, keeping the creature's catch safely hidden away.

Screeching with delight, its red eyes dared us to try

and take her back. The widow's front mandibles clacked and through the gaps in its remaining legs, I could see Jane struggling from within the bloated sheen of thorax, her hair dangling down, her wide terrified pain-filled eyes visible for a brief moment before strands of white appeared, securing her to the widow's belly. Where was that awful stuff coming from? The suckers? It must have been. If I didn't have the awful knowledge that made me understand better, I would have said that she was being held in a protective maternal embrace, the web and suckers looking after her, rather than eating into her. Oh God, how could this be happening? How could Nigel do something like this?

While I knelt there staring impotently at the widow, Maine rushed past me screaming like a banshee and threw himself at the creature, pulling at its body, trying to reach the crying child lost beneath, ignoring the way the creature snapped at him, biting his arms, penetrating him with its death-laden saliva.

Finally hauling myself to my feet, I raised the gun to shoot the monster but with my inexperienced eye didn't trust my shaking hand to hit the target, although I wondered whether maybe I should just shoot Maine instead, or the trapped shape of Jane. Both were lost to us, that much I could tell. I tried to aim, but my eyes were a blur, and frustrated and moaning I lowered the gun.

Within seconds my inactivity didn't matter. The second widow pounced lithely and swiftly onto Oliver, its legs grabbing him firmly around the middle, the pull almost folding the surprised man in two, sucking him back with it over the fence, disappearing in seconds. He was gone without a murmur or scream. All those years of life, vanished. Jesus. Jesus Christ.

All hell was breaking loose in front of me. With a shriek of anger, seeing the widow encapsulate Jane, Rebecca wrenched herself free of Michael, his knife slashing her arm, a spray of blood flying out from the deep cut. Behind her, the third widow scuttled towards the terrified Nigel, who looked like he'd suddenly lost faith in his own hype about the widows leaving us alone. Mewling, he cowered backwards as it approached, but there was nowhere for him to go. He wasn't quick enough to outrun it, and his own disbelief stopped him from trying. Teasing him, the widow took a quick step forward, close enough to touch, but not doing so, almost enjoying the middle-aged man's pitiful wail of fear as it danced around him. Frantically trying to keep out of its way, he jerked awkwardly, yelping and squealing like a terrified pig.

"Help me! Help me!" His eyes finally found mine as he whined, and I stared at him uncomprehending for a second before once again lifting the gun, but the widow was too fast. Bored with its game, it jumped towards him, mandibles closing round his leg and bringing him down on the grass.

"Get it off me! Get it off me!"

And from out of nowhere, Phelps's prayers were answered. Chester flew like the bullet I should have fired out from behind one of the buildings, barking as he pounced on the sobbing figure, pinning him to the ground. Lifting his head, the fur on the back of his neck rising up, he snarled at the widow, who hissed, but let go, blood dripping from it, creating strange pink tracks running down its disgusting skin.

The two creatures stared at each other over the injured man for a few seconds, as if sizing each other up, and then a screech of true agony distracted us all, drawing our attention back in the direction of the gate and holding it there. What the hell was going on? It looked at first as if Rebecca were being attacked, her blood covering the widow, but then I realised that it was the widow that was crying out in awful agony as Rebecca smeared her blood on it, her face full of wonder as the monster burned on contact. Grabbing its leg with one hand, she held it firm, her injured arm raised above its bank of eyes, dripping into them and dissolving them as if it were acid falling. Desperate to break free, it twisted and turned, but she kept hold as it weakened, until finally it crumpled to the ground, resigned to its fate.

Behind her, Michael stared, and I should imagine that my face had the same strange expression of awe on it, but without the hatred that somehow was mixed in with his. Like a robot on autopilot, he lifted the knife that hung at his side and strode towards her. At first I presumed that he was going to finish the widow off, to claim some glory from this miracle that she was producing, but as he got closer, his eyes were glowing with rage and they were focused on Rebecca.

"You fucking bitch! What makes you so fucking special, you freak?" He screamed at her as he broke into a trot, but the words were lost in her silent world, as was the sound of the shot when I calmly put a bullet in his chest. He crumpled instantly, dead and surprised, his part in this nightmare suddenly very over.

When I pulled my eyes back up from his oozing chest, everything was quiet. Nigel sobbed quietly on the ground, but the third widow had gone, probably escaping over the fence, not wanting to take Chester on. My head pounded. Would Chester's blood have the same effect as Rebecca's? Was it because of their deafness that this happened? Could it be as simple as that?

Chris jogged past me and knelt down by Michael, checking for a pulse. I could have told him not to bother, but I guessed we needed to go through these routines.

"He's gone."

I nodded, ignoring the dead man, and headed over to the injured one. John and George had appeared, maybe they had been there during those mad few minutes, but I didn't know. John took his T-shirt off, wrapping it round Rebecca's arm before they, too, headed towards Nigel.

He was pale and sweating, sitting up now, staring at the gaping wound in his leg.

"Oh, God, it hurts. Oh, God." He looked up at us, his eyes wide. "We need to wash it quickly, get the stuff out. Don't we? It'll be all right, won't it? Won't it?"

I looked down at his ripped calf again and then at the grass, thinking about Dave and all that stuff that oozed out of him. That stuff that filled his insides. No, it wasn't going to be all right for Nigel. Not at all.

"What are we going to do?" George's voice was quiet and calm, but full of dread. He knew as well as I did what had to be done.

"I'll do it." John took the gun out of my limp hand, but before he could even lift it, Chester growled, stepping in front of the sobbing man. What the fuck was he doing?

"Get the fuck out of the way, dog."

Rebecca stepped forward, taking her place alongside Chester, blocking any chance of a shot. Shaking her head angrily, she lifted her arm, and wincing with pain signed at George, her fingers trembling as she worked through the words, he occasionally signalling to her to slow down, or repeat something. The colour on his own face drained as she finished.

"They're right. We can't shoot him." Behind them, Nigel's breathing was heavy with relief and tears.

"Why the hell not? That thing bit him. It's the fucking humane thing to do."

George stared at him. "I know."

John wasn't the only one that was confused. I was too tired for this. Jane was gone. So was Oliver Maine. There was too much to take in.

"So what's the problem? What was Rebecca saying to you?" My signing was getting better, but there was no way I was up to conversations and translating her at full speed.

George and Rebecca stared at each other for a moment before he stepped away from Nigel a few feet, signalling for us to follow him. Phelps wasn't going anywhere. Despite his injury, he was probably capable of walking, but the shock had drained him. I doubted he would have been listening even if George spoke to us right next to him.

The old man tapped his top pocket and sighed, finding no pipe there. "God, I could use a smoke right now." He looked at John and Chris and then his eyes rested on mine.

"I think it's got something to do with that collective consciousness thing that the widows have. When Rebecca grabbed that thing's leg and it was dying, she could see images from it. Maybe because it was dying it was sending them out stronger, you know, like life flashing before your eyes, and maybe because it was here with us it sent out the images that it did."

I was tired of being surprised by the widows and what they could do. "And what did it send? What did she see?"

George's eyes drifted away slightly, as if he were seeing it all for himself instead of through Rebecca's signing. "It was about Nigel. What happened in his house."

"And?" John sounded like he wanted to hear, but didn't. I felt the same way.

"I think it was pretty similar to what happened to you, Matt. She had him frozen against the wall of the house, just like he said she did, and there was the moment of release, when the widow came out of her, just like he said there was."

"So? What's the problem?"

"Emma was there, too." He didn't look at our shocked expressions, but stared at the crying man on the grass not so far away from where we were standing.

"She'd come home from school and she'd been in the house when it all started, that power slamming them into the wall and holding them there. She was beside Nigel, trapped and terrified, unable to move or speak for all those hours, and then had to endure seeing that thing slither out of her mother, killing what was left of her with its birth."

Watching George swallow, I could feel the dryness in my own throat. What I had been through was awful and terrifying, but I was at least a grown-up. And although I'd had to see our child dead on the kitchen floor, I hadn't had to suffer seeing the widow come out of her. I knew my Chloe had let me go before then. How the hell had it been for Emma?

Coughing slightly, George continued softy. "And in that few seconds after it had come out, while it adjusted to the world and itself, the grip let go of them. But they were both too stiff and numb to run away. You commented on that, Matt, when Nigel first told us his story. You said how lucky he was to have been able to run straight away because you could barely stand. He bit your head off. Do you remember?"

I nodded, feeling my stomach churning. I could sense where this story was going but I needed to hear it for myself. We all did.

"Nigel had pins and needles that slowed him down as he stood up, and Emma was numb with cold and cramp. She was crying for him to pick her up and so he did. By this time the widow was up on its legs, I should imagine showing none of the clumsy awkwardness that young farm animals do, and it hissed at them, coming forward. Nigel tried to step backwards, but his legs just wouldn't move, they wouldn't coordinate, especially with the girl in his arms, and the thing was coming closer and closer, and then he did it. He threw his daughter at it, and as she screamed while the widow began to devour her, he fell to his knees and crawled out of the house. All the time with her shrieking out for him to save her."

"Just like what he did with Jane." I could barely squeeze the words out.

"Uh-huh. And Rebecca, and, crazy as it sounds, Chester, are right. That's why we can't shoot him."

What did he mean we couldn't shoot him? He had no chance of surviving, that much we did know. Surely it would be better.... The thought stopped suddenly as my throat tightened with the realisation of what they meant. I stared at John, his face a reflection of my own shaking acknowledgment, and then I looked away. Chris had already turned to face Nigel.

"I agree."

Jesus. Would this be justice? Not to put him out of his misery, but to let him suffer in agony as that stuff took hold? The coldness of our new life washed over me with the memory of Jane and Oliver Maine and all the damage this man had caused. Yes, maybe this would be justice for them. Or at least a little payback. Staring at George and Rebecca, her dark eyes hard, I felt horror at ourselves and what we were about to do, but also horror at what had happened, at what he had done to his own child.

"Let's get on with it, then."

Chris turned and met my eye. "I know where we can put him."

John and I hauled the sweating man to his feet, draping his arms around our shoulders for support and letting his legs drag as we walked.

"Are you going to amputate my leg?" he spoke breathily within his sobs, but I couldn't look at him. "Maybe it'll work better because we'll catch it quickly. Is that what we're going to do?" I could feel his warm breath against my cheek as he sought out some response from someone, anyone.

Dawn was past now and the temperature rose in the muggy air. I wanted to get in the shower and wash the feel of him off me. I wanted to wash it all away. When no one answered him, Nigel started to cry again, his sobs getting louder as we turned away from where the infirmary was.

Finally, we came to an outhouse about a hundred yards behind the dorm. It was obviously part of the original buildings and it was made of stone with a thick wooden door that needed a shove to open it, even after it was unlocked. Nigel was making a mewling sound and I was sure there were words mixed up with it, but I didn't want to hear them. His sweat smelled sharp with fear, and although I felt that this was the right thing for us to do, I just wanted it to be over.

The air inside was musty and dark, but there was a single bed in the corner and a toilet and a sink.

"What is this place?" John whispered the question as we ushered the dead weight inside, setting him down on the bed. He didn't try and move or get out, but dropped his head, his shoulders shaking as he cried.

"It's the closest thing we have here to a prison cell." The normality in Whitehead's voice chilled me. "It's not been used in years. I don't really know why it's still here. We can bring him some food and water down to see him through."

"How long do you think it will take?" George looked at me, asking the question, all of us talking as if Nigel weren't really there. It was easier that way.

"Who knows? Maybe fetch enough supplies for a couple of weeks." I hoped to hell it wouldn't take that long, for our sakes if not for his.

We all waited there silently for Chris to return with a rucksack full of supplies, none of us wanting to make anyone else be the last one there, to alone have to go back in with the food and water and then lock the door behind them. Even Rebecca, pale and still bleeding, waited, leaning against the wall, Chester by her side. We'd all reached the conclusion that this was what had to be done, and we needed to see it through together. A new order had taken hold and our old laws no longer applied. I think this was the first day that we accepted that. Maybe we were slower than the survivors in the rest of the country, but then maybe at Hanstone we'd had it easier than them.

We waited there until Chris had placed the bag on the floor in front of the bed, and then without a word we turned, walked out and locked the door. I never saw Nigel Phelps again.

CHAPTER TWENTY-TWO

It all happened much more quickly than it had with Dave, probably because this time we didn't even try to get rid of the stuff or stop it spreading. It was only four days before Nigel started to scream, and then he screamed for a further three. Until then, he had shouted occasionally, full of anger and obscenities before breaking down into cries and sobs, but the screaming was something else, cutting through the heavy air and scratching on the inside of our skulls.

We'd found a CD player and took to playing The Rolling Stones loudly, concentrating hard on listening and singing emptily along, and although it gave us temporary relief in the dorm, everywhere else there was no escape. We kept ourselves occupied with the mundane occupation of survival in a quiet haze, no energy for any real communication, not while Nigel was so busy dying so loudly.

Dean proved no problem to us. He'd been relieved when Jeff had come in and taken over the gate, and Daniel was pretty bashed up with broken ribs and nose. I don't think it was just his bones that were broken. That angry fire had gone out in his eyes, and whatever spirit was left in them faded with each of Nigel's tortured outbursts, slowly becoming more muffled, but no less disturbing as the hours ticked by. We stayed out of his way, and he out of ours, and that arrangement seemed to suit. After all that had happened it was difficult to maintain levels of hate and there was no more real animosity between us. None of us had the energy for it.

Chris kept himself busy with blood samples from Rebecca and Chester and found that both worked like acid on the widows. It seemed that the simple genetic defect that had probably been a curse to them throughout their lives up to this point was now what made them the envy of every other survivor on the planet. Was that what the army had discovered? Was that the blood that they had been spraying the streets of London with? We could only guess. Maybe there were others as well whose blood worked in the same fashion. I hoped so for all our sakes.

Working long hours, his face a mask of concentration, maybe the only one of us who could block out those awful wails from time to time, Chris tried various dilutions of it to see how effective it could be. If we were going to use it as any kind of weapon, the supply wasn't endless and there was only so much it was safe for either of them to give up at any time.

It was on day two of the screaming that I ended up in Rebecca's bed, holding her tight, and on the morning of day three we made love for the first time, slowly and naturally curled up under the sheets together. It had none of the animal urgency of that time in the bathroom with Katie, but it was pure and sweet and felt right.

When the screaming finally stopped nobody mentioned it. Neither did anyone volunteer to go in and bring his cocooned body out. But we did decide that justice had been done and it was time to remember our dead.

We stood in the rain, and quietly, with a gravitas that only he amongst us had, George spoke about them all, each in turn, ensuring we protect them in our memories for however long we had left ourselves. He talked of Jane's bravery and Katie's quick tongue and impish looks. He talked of Dave's solidity and strength and the childlike good humour of Maine that disguised his own courage, the courage that had led him so fearlessly into his own death. We would remember them all, and carry them with us through whatever the future held for us that were left behind. It was a sober, quiet afternoon, but we did what was needed and it was time, after that, to let them rest. It was either that or go mad hankering after the past, after what was over and done with, untouchable and out of reach.

The man in London had gone, and although we still tried occasionally, we didn't really hope to hear any more of him. I liked to think that he had found the army boys and was busy with them purging the streets of widows like some mad Rambo character from a bad eighties movie, but who knew? I liked that thought better than him screaming like Nigel, and so I clung to it.

We weren't manning the radios twenty-four/seven ourselves anymore; our enthusiasm had dwindled with our numbers and the airwaves were depressingly quiet except for the odd crackly reception of a broadcast that there was a colony of children near Edinburgh.

Whoever was transmitting it wasn't receiving, only sending, and for all we knew it was just an old recording playing on a loop.

Our quiet safety had been broken, and there was a sense that we were just stagnating, waiting to eke out whatever existence we had left, the feeling already making me come round to the idea that I couldn't stay, when two things happened to secure the thought in my head.

The first was that Rebecca discovered she was pregnant, and happy as we both were, we decided to keep that news to ourselves for a while. The second wasn't so good.

It was only about nine-thirty, but we were going to bed earlier and earlier then, or at least relaxing in the dorm whiling away our time, trying to avoid the empty ticking of the hours of our lives by hiding in the cosiest of our rooms. In many ways, I imagined that this is what prisoners of war had felt like way back in the forties, loads of routines filling up their days, but no real sense of anything gained. Rebecca was reading a book in our room and I was losing badly at chess to Chris when John came in from outside and called me over to the far side of the room. Dean and Daniel were already asleep. They didn't talk much even to each other by then, and I wondered how they could sleep at all with the memory of their involvement in what happened to Jane and Oliver Maine.

Leaving Chris to contemplate his next killer move, I padded quietly over to where John waited. As I got closer I could see that he was pale and shaking, sucking on his cigarette hard. "Matt, I need you to come and look at something."

"What?"

"Come in here. I don't want to show you in front of everyone."

Lighting a cigarette of my own, I followed him into the clinical whiteness of the large bathroom. "So, what's up mate?"

"This." His eyes wide with dread, he lifted up his T-shirt. "Tell me what the fuck that is."

His thin chest had three large lumps in it and a variety of smaller ones close by. As I stood there staring, I was sure that I saw one move slightly, or grow bigger. My stomach ripped its way to my throat. What now? What the fuck now?

"I'm not liking the look on your face, mate. Not one fucking bit." Smoking hard, John moved slightly from foot to foot, his anxiety stopping him from standing still.

Using the excuse of dragging on my own cigarette to squint and therefore not meet his gaze, I dropped my view back to his exposed midriff. Reaching out, not wanting to touch but really needing to know how it felt, I gently pressed against the largest of the irregular boils, which stretched the skin thin over his pale torso. Something unpleasant gave slightly under my fingers, but I could feel gristle in it, and maybe liquid. Something not nice. John winced and I pulled my hand away.

"That hurt?"

"Hurt's not really how I'd describe it. It's more like just fucking weird. Like something tugging at me. What the fuck is it?" Despite the coarseness of his language, his voice wavered with fear.

Not answering, I stared at it. This wasn't like the string stuff that had come out of Dave. This was more like Chloe and Katie. But how could that be?

John wasn't a girl, and looking at him, it wasn't like he was getting fat, it was just the lumps. But these lumps were harder, more defined than that female change had been.

"We've got to tell the others, John. This isn't normal."

"I knew it." He rolled his eyes. "I fucking knew it. I'm gonna fucking die, aren't I?"

Opening my mouth to say something reassuring, I found that the words wouldn't come out. I tugged his shirt down over his naked chest. "Come on, let's see what Chris has to say." It was the best I could do.

We left Daniel and Dean sleeping, not wanting them to share this new fear, needing for the moment to keep it to only us, the remainder of our original group and Chris, who from our arrival had almost been an honorary member. In only his underpants, John sat on the examination bed, the one in which not so long ago Dave had taken his own life, and swung his legs while Chris checked him over.

"It seems they're limited to his chest at the moment. Pretty much only in the upper abdomen and the sternum area. There's nothing on his legs or arms."

"Yes, but what the fuck is it?" The agitation was obvious in John's voice now, and I couldn't blame him for it. I guess by sharing it with us, he had to accept it was really happening, and that couldn't be a good feeling. Chris turned away, leaning against the counter behind him and sighed.

"You think I've got one of those fuckers growing inside me, don't you? Oh, Jesus. Shit." John stared down at himself in horror, and I could almost see the cold sweat breaking out on him in small drops.

George handed the young man a fresh cigarette and lit it for him. "We don't know what's happening, John, and that's the truth of it. It was you that said that all this was only just the beginning. It may be nothing. We're just going to have to wait and see." George's naturally gravelly, calm voice wasn't working for John and it wasn't working for me. What the fuck were we going to have to deal with now? Wasn't there enough shit going off out there? And now I had Rebecca and the baby to think of. After what happened with Chloe, I knew I would rather die than let anything bad happen to them, and that wasn't me being selfless but quite the opposite. I knew I couldn't survive that kind of loss twice. It would be better to give up and die.

"I think it was only a matter of time before this happened." Chris turned round and for the first time since I'd known him, I saw no hint of excitement in his face at the thought of a new scientific discovery, however gruesome.

"Before what fucking happened?" I don't think any of us wanted the answer to John's questions, but we all needed it. I sat on the examination bed next to John and between us we created a cloud of cancerous cigarette smoke. It seemed like as good a way as any to hear some bad news.

"Well, it's been bothering me for a while, but I haven't wanted to mention it. All these widows are everywhere and they all evolved from women, yes?"

I nodded, wondering what he was driving at. "And?"

"Logic would therefore dictate that they're female spiders. It may be guesswork, but it would make sense. We certainly think of them as female."

"I'm not following."

His own eyes were looking afraid, and I didn't like

323

that at all. "Well, if they're all female, how the hell are they going to breed?"

The words hung in the air in front of us all, so thick with meaning we could almost see them. The cigarette smoke burned my nose and eyes, but I didn't care, the weight of what he was saying blocking out everything else.

"So are you saying we're all going to turn into the widows? After all of this?" My own heart was suddenly racing. Not after everything we'd been through. Surely not. Not after all of this.

"Oh, fucking shit, you are saying I've got one of those inside me." John's breath was coming in fast pants. .

"No, no, no." Chris steadied him, lifting the boy's chin so he could meet his gaze. "What I'm saying is that we don't know. Something is growing inside you, yes, but maybe you'll just shit it out. Maybe what they need to reproduce isn't in the same form as them. Maybe it's something completely different."

John's hand was shaking so much he could barely get his cigarette to his lips. "Oh, fuck. Oh, holy fuck."

"And as for your comment," Chris turned his attention to me, "no, maybe it won't happen to all of us. I doubt it will. If I had to put a bet on it, I'd say it would depend on your hormonal levels. That's how all this started, wasn't that our conclusion? All the people like me messing around with the hormones and genes in things?"

George handed John his T-shirt, helping him pull it over his head, hiding the cause of his, and our, terror.

"But what about John? What can we do for him?"

Chris's scientist's curiosity wasn't entirely dead.

"Well, it might be best if we just wait and see what develops so we know what we're dealing with."

"Fuck off!" John was off the table and reaching for the twitchy doctor to wring his neck, George and I holding him back.

"But obviously, we won't be doing that." Chris had stepped as far back as the counter behind him would allow.

"No, we won't." I glared at him. For a moment it was almost like having Nigel back. It was disregard for human life that had got us all into this mess, and I was fucked if I was going to let us use John as an experiment, however wise it may have been.

"There is one thing we could try to kill whatever it is."

"What?" The anger was gone from John now, replaced with awful hope.

"Rebecca's blood." Whitehead looked at each of us. "He could drink some of Rebecca's blood. That might do it."

"Whatever we do, can we do it quickly?" John stood up from the table, his eyes cast downwards at the material of his T-shirt. "I think I can feel the lumps moving."

We took a precious pint of Rebecca's blood and that was all. Back in the old world there was no way she would have been allowed to donate it, but we were both banking on her being hardier than that, and that it wouldn't affect the baby. It was her that was adamant about giving it, anyway. She said she couldn't live with herself if anything happened to John and it turned out she could have prevented it.

I pushed to take the blood from Chester, but Chris

thought that human blood would be better. It would mix with John's system better. Not that he really knew what he was talking about any better than the rest of us. He was in unknown territory, as were we all.

It was still warm when we handed him the beaker, Rebecca laying and recovering on the table, George fetching her a strong cup of sweet tea, just like they would have done in the old world that existed only in our dreams, and John stared down at the thick liquid for a moment before raising it to his lips. He grinned and his teeth shone like a death mask, only gallows humour there. "Cheers!"

I watched as he drank from it greedily, some of the thick liquid dribbling down his chin until all that was left was a coating of red on the inside of the beaker, and the pungent sweet smell lingering in the air. Jesus. He'd swallowed it all as if it had been the clearest, coolest water taken straight from a spring and he was a wanderer lost in the desert.

Putting down the empty vessel, he reached for another cigarette and lit it. His eyes shook and he'd paled, but those were the only signs that he'd found anything disgusting in drinking hot human blood. I'd expected him to gag, to instinctively throw some of it back up, but he didn't even belch. How much would we accept in an effort to save ourselves? For the first time since the incident with Nigel, I worried for Rebecca's safety. If this worked, then her blood would become a precious commodity, even more valuable than it was now as a weapon against the widows. And what if it looked like it wasn't going to work—what would happen then? Would some crazy bastard try to cook and eat her or something equally crazy? Nothing seemed too far-fetched at that moment.

John sucked in a good lungful of smoke. "So, what now?" When he pulled the cigarette away from his mouth the tip was coated with red, as if there were lipstick on it, and as he spoke I could see the blood clinging to some of his teeth. My stomach churned slightly.

Chris was checking that Rebecca's dressing and plaster were holding up. He turned and shrugged. "We wait."

And so we waited there, watching the minutes ticking away on the white face of the clock, conversation dwindling down to nothing, in the main just trying to avoid each other's eyes, lost in our own worlds. We'd thought that the dangers we had to face in the new world would come only from the women. Now only God knew what our bodies might or might not be planning against us. My skin itched slightly, phantom bugs crawling on me.

Every half hour or so, we checked to see how he was doing, and for the first couple of hours he seemed sure that he felt a bit better and that the lumps were going down, but as far as I could see, that wasn't the case. And how could he be feeling better? He hadn't been feeling ill in the first place. Still, after seeing what Rebecca's blood could do to that widow outside, I could only hope that if it did get rid of whatever was inside him that it didn't kill him, too.

"I think we should go to the dorm and try and get some sleep." George stood up from where he'd been sitting in a hard upright chair in the corner, his old limbs almost visibly creaking as he stretched. "There's no change, and we could sit up all night, and all that will happen is that we'll be dog tired in the morning."

"I agree." Rebecca had gone to bed straight after giving blood, and I was eager to join her and take comfort in her warmth and our unborn child. There was no way we were going to get any real rest in the clinical confines of the medical room.

"I don't think there's any way I'm going to be able to fucking sleep." Despite his adamant insistence, John looked tired. His eyes had lost that wide manic expression and were now just bloodshot and drooping.

"Yes you will, mate." I took his arm and pulled him down off the trolley-style bed. "That blood's going to take some time to get into your system and get to work on those lumps. You might as well sleep while it does."

He stared down, but didn't lift his T-shirt. "You really think it's going to work?"

"Yeah, I think so. It worked on those ones outside. Think positive." I smiled at him, and he returned it tentatively.

"Maybe I am going to be fucking all right after all."

"That's the spirit."

My own legs feeling tight from the tension and uncomfortable surroundings, I was pleased to step outside into the humid air.

"At least it's not raining." Chris followed behind, locking up the room, probably out of habit rather than any need for security. I wondered if he'd really ever got a grip on what was happening in the world around us, if he'd really accepted how everything had changed. Sometimes I forgot he had been safe in the compound all the way through the times when everything was going crazy. Maybe that's why he kept up his routines of keys and locks and safety. Or maybe that was just part of who he was.

It had been a long time since we'd had a dry night and as we trotted silently up the stairs and into the dorm, I wondered if it had any significance. Was it a sign of things settling down? Was it a sign that the beginning at least was over? Watching John lay down on his bed, keeping his T-shirt on despite the heat, I pushed the thought out of my head. There was too much to worry about without trying to find significance in everything that seemed a little out of the ordinary. Whatever ordinary was these days.

"Good night, mate. Sleep well."

He grunted a response and I nodded at Chris and George through the gloom, their white skin brighter than their faces as they stripped, ready to try and sleep in the heat we'd slowly got accustomed to.

Creeping into the small single room I pulled off my own clothes and slipped under the sheet next to Rebecca. She smelled sweet and her olive skin was cool despite the warmth. Wrapping my arm around her curled-up body, I held her close and smiled to feel her responding, half-asleep, pulling my arm closer to her, resting my hand under her cheek. It was good, that's the only word I can think of to describe the feeling I had there next to her, and despite what was happening or not happening to John next door and how it could affect me, I had a smile on my face as I drifted into sleep.

"Matt! Matt!"

George was shouting my name and shaking me so hard that Rebecca was awake before I was, bleary and dazed. Pushing his hands away a little I sat up.

"What's the matter?" The light was on, but outside the small window the world was dark. "What the fuck is the matter?"

"Something's happening to John. It's not good."

"Oh shit." Grabbing my trousers I pulled them on,

throwing a top over my shoulder for Rebecca, not that from the panicked look on the old man's face anyone was too concerned about seeing a naked woman.

Still doing up my trousers, I followed him back into the dorm to John's bed. Everyone was awake now, staring with dread, Daniel sitting on the opposite bed, Chris and Dean hunched over the boy. All I could see at first were his feet hanging over the edge, shaking, hands drumming fast into the mattress beneath him, the toes stretched taut. Dean stepped back to let George and I through, his own face a mask of terror. John's eyes were wide with shock, staring up at the ceiling as his whole body convulsed angrily on the bed. Like his toes, his fingers were stretched tight, as if every sinew in his thin young body was straining to escape and his torso shook and shivered aggressively.

"John? John? Can you hear me?"

There was no response except a small trickle of drool escaping from the side of his open mouth.

"What is happening, Chris? What's happening to him?"

He stared at me. "How the hell am I supposed to know?"

Reaching forward, I grabbed the top of the grey T-shirt, which was now black with sweat, and ripped it down the middle, exposing John's chest.

"Oh, shit. Oh fucking shit." Involuntarily I stepped backwards, banging my calf into the bed behind me. John's chest was alive with movement, the bumps rippling under his skin, jerkily breaking free from wherever they had attached themselves inside and making their way upwards. One protrusion pushed up over his sternum and into his neck, stretching his Adam's apple, forcing his breath out in chokes and coughs as it wormed its way up into his throat. Whatever it was, I expected to see it emerge through his open mouth, but there was nothing. It seemed to have just disappeared.

"Where the fuck did it go?"

"Wherever the others are going." George's voice was shaking with his own terror as we stared at the disappearing lumps following that first into his neck. Once the final one had vanished, John's convulsions stopped instantly, leaving him panting for breath. He blinked for a moment, and then his eyes moved round the room, focussed again. None of us able to speak, we watched as he pulled himself up into a sitting position, his fingers running down his normal torso. He grinned.

"They're gone." Looking round at us in amazement, he laughed slightly. "They're fucking gone!"

My heart hammered in my chest. Yes, they were gone, but where? Had they just dissolved?

"What did you feel when you were convulsing?" Chris didn't look too convinced. "Could you feel them moving?"

"Convulsing?" Reaching for his cigarettes, John paused, his smile wavering a little with confusion. "I wasn't convulsing. I was asleep. You guys just woke me up."

"No, you were..."

"*Nggnnnnnnn...*"

Chris was cut off by the keening noise that suddenly came from John, his hand dropping his unlit cigarette and flying to his head. Wincing, his mouth opened wider, almost reluctantly, as if being forced apart, letting the sound build into a shaking scream, his eyes meeting each of our horrified gazes with too vivid a consciousness before he pushed past me and ran to the door, escaping into the night.

Following him, the scream becoming less human with each second, but oh so full of agony, we stepped back into the humid air, George holding us back on the stairs, not letting anyone run down to where John had fallen on his hands and knees, his fingers clawing into the earth, digging deep furrows in the grass as he raised his head to look at us, still letting out that awful shriek.

The skin on his face was bleeding, and I couldn't see where from, thinking he must have cut himself when he fell, but then I realised that his whole face was bleeding, bleeding through the pores, some dripping down from his hair. Grabbing Rebecca, I pushed her face into my chest, forcing her to stop looking, and smothering her own sobs into me.

He was shaking again now, his head distorting, and as the scream rose to almost a whistle the flesh of his cheeks and throat finally gave way, hard shiny black legs forcing their way through, ripping at him, tearing the life from him, aggressively bursting into the world.

Have you seen any black widows at your end? Smaller than the normal ones?

Oh God. That's what the man in London had asked. He'd heard a broadcast about black widows. That was what was coming out of John. It had to be. Rebecca's blood hadn't killed it. From here it just looked like we'd royally pissed it off.

With John still screeching, but thankfully losing any real grip on life, the body of the thing pushed it's way out through his extended mouth, all hard shiny shell, more like a beetle in a spider shape, its squat legs hairy and thicker than those of its giant mate, only two red angry pinprick eyes rather than a whole bank. Finally free, it twisted swiftly round and with a sharp hiss reached into the destroyed head and bit the tongue out, the two large mandibles sucking it in, chewing on it as it leapt away and disappeared across the grass into the dark half of the compound, where it could hide in the comfort of the night.

The silence was broken by the sound of Chris throwing up over the barrier, but no one moved. I could feel Rebecca's breath coming hard on my chest, creating a damp space there, but I still gripped her tight, not yet ready or able to let go. Oh fuck. Oh, holy fuck. Was that going to happen to me?

We must have stood there for at least ten minutes, too shocked to move, the only sounds being Chris's small moans as he finished being sick; then Dean spoke from the doorway, his tone monotonous with disbelief.

"I've got a lump on my chest. Oh God, I've got a lump on my chest."

CHAPTER TWENTY-THREE

It was two days after that that George and I found the black spider fried by the main gate. It had obviously tried to scale it, and come off worse against the electricity. At least we knew they could die, that was a slight upside, and it seemed that maybe they weren't party to that communal mind thing that the women had. That didn't surprise me. As a species we'd never really known what was going on in women's heads and I figured that Mother Nature wasn't going to change that now. Staring down at the obscene creature, it was hard to associate it with John, even though it had evolved from his flesh and blood.

Sniffing, the damp air giving us the constant feeling of a slight cold, I looked over my shoulder at where Rebecca was throwing a stick for Chester, the two of them bouncing with happiness.

"You got any lumps, George?"

After John, Dean had been the first to show signs of the growths on his chest, but Daniel and Chris had joined him late in the afternoon of the next day. So far they were all still alive, the lumps not yet moving, but the atmosphere in the hut was sombre with the weighty anticipation of death. Dean hadn't stopped crying yet, despite the sedatives Chris had issued him.

We'd decided it was giving John Rebecca's blood that had speeded up the process, making the body less inhabitable for the newly evolving male and forcing it to hurry its own birthing process up, and that maybe it would take longer with the rest. Chris still claimed to be searching for a cure, experimenting with drugs in the medical room, but the couple of times I'd been in to see him I'd found him staring at his newly ter-raformed skin under his shirt with abject horror. I didn't think he really had any hope of finding some-thing to provide him with a miracle cure.

George lifted his head. "No, no new lumps. Just an old man's body under this shirt. You?"

I shook my head. Despite finding myself checking every twenty minutes or so with a feeling of dread, I still had yet to find any evidence of anything growing inside me. My chest was smooth.

"The others are starting to give us funny looks. Like they hate us."

George shrugged, lighting his pipe. "It's only natural. They're terrified. At least John didn't know what was coming. They do. They've seen it firsthand. They're terrified and we're lump-free. Hell, I'd hate us."

I stared out at the fence. The widows had pretty much abandoned their vigil now. Maybe they could sense the change happening in the men, or maybe they were off mating with their newly found partners. It wasn't a pleasant thought. Once again the oppressive atmosphere in the compound pressed down on me.

"Rebecca and I are thinking of leaving. We can't

stay here. Not even if the others, you know…die or change or whatever. We'll stagnate. We want to find others out there. Especially now we've got the baby coming."

I'd taken George into our confidence the night John had died and Dean found the first signs of change in himself. I'd needed to talk about something good and talk we had, well into the morning.

"I was expecting you to say something like that." He peered at me from behind his smoke. "Where were you thinking of heading?"

"North. You know, we keep thinking about that broadcast about the colony of children? Maybe there's nothing in it, but maybe there is. It seems as good a place to head as any. See if we meet up with any other survivors on the way." I stared at him, waiting for him to say something, but he didn't, so I carried on.

"We wanted you to come with us."

It was George's turn to stare out at the fence, and watching him I realised just how fond I'd become of him during the time we'd known each other. He was a good man, and a pretty wise one. I hoped he didn't want to stay behind here and rot his remaining days away in this relic of a place.

"That's very kind of you. I've been thinking of moving on myself, but I don't think I'll be able to come with you. I'll head up to that colony if there is such a thing eventually, but there's somewhere I've got to go first."

"What do you mean?"

The air was quiet except for the lone sound of a bird calling out from one of the trees, its song muffled in the still of the morning.

"Do you remember asking where I'd learned to sign, and I told you that my grandson was deaf?

I nodded.

"Well, I've been thinking about him a lot recently. About how he'd be like Rebecca and Chester and that maybe there was a pretty good chance that he'd still be alive out there somewhere and needing me."

"But that's all the way down in Cornwall, George...."

He hushed me with a smile and a hand on my shoulder. "It's okay. I know you two have your priorities now. You've got that baby coming and you need to find some kind of community quickly. I'm just going to have to catch you up later, that's all."

Taking in a deep breath, he put one arm round my shoulder and steered me away from the rotting spider.

"I think we need to pack. Now that we've decided, I guess we need to be getting on our way, don't you?"

I nodded, but my heart was heavy with the idea of him going off on his own. His chances were slim at best, but I knew that we couldn't go with him. He was right. The baby was our priority.

We'd had to jumpstart the two Jeeps, but once they were purring they seemed happy enough to run. Dean and Daniel stayed in the hut, but Chris came out to see us off. He was pale and sweating, tears threatening his eyes.

"You lot take care now."

I nodded and shook his cold clammy hand, not knowing what to say. "What will you do?"

"Well, I'll let you out and then shut the gate...."

"No, Chris, what will you *do?*" I stared at him, my heart full of pity.

He shrugged. "If it comes to it, I'll just blow my

brains out." His smile was bitter at the edges. "But it's amazing how much hope you can cling on to when you have to. Who knows, I might find a cure."

"Well if you do, then get on the radios. Let the world know."

"I will. I will. Look, I'd better..."

He didn't finish his sentence, but instead scurried away towards the comms hut to get ready to open the gate.

We'd loaded up with plenty of food and equipment, no one having made any mention of us not taking anything, and we'd also packed up quite a lot of weaponry, as well as filling up some pressurised water sprayers, normally used for weedkillers, with blood solutions from Chester and Rebecca.

Rebecca and the dog were already in the passenger side when I wandered up to George to say farewell. He was standing tall and proud, but he still looked like a fragile old man. My heart aching, I looked at him, saving him to memory. There was little real hope of ever seeing him again and that must have shone out of my face, because I saw it reflected back in his.

"Don't worry, son. I'll be all right."

My throat was choking up with tears, and instead of speaking I embraced him in a hug until he pushed me away.

"We'd better be getting along now."

Nodding, I turned and headed back to the truck and climbed in alongside Rebecca and the dog, all of us watching as George made his lonely way to the vehicle ahead of us. Jesus, I hoped he'd make it.

Just as he was pulling open the door, Chester burst out barking and leapt out of the open window, running to catch the old man up. Without looking back, he jumped in. I called in vain after him, but he didn't reappear. I guessed he'd decided that if George was going to have a chance of making it up to Scotland to meet us, then he was going to ride along. When the old man looked up to give us his final wave good-bye, this time both our grins were genuine. Chester would look out for him as best he could, and I felt better knowing that his journey would no longer be taken alone.

Following them out of the compound, we waited until the gates had shut and George and Chester had disappeared into the distance before we turned to the left and started our own journey into whatever the future held, a small hope growing in our hearts and Rebecca's belly. A hope for mankind. A hope for us.

THE
RECKONING
SARAH PINBOROUGH

They were children then, in that magical summer so long ago when Robert, Carrie-Anne, and Jason first met Gina. It was a summer of fun, of friendship, and of discoveries—including the discovery of Gina's strange abilities. But it all ended in a moment of madness and blood.

Now, twenty years later, Robert is still haunted by nightmares of that time. He has returned to his small hometown to confront his past and reclaim his life, but his homecoming is far from happy. Gina moved away long ago. Jason is bitter and resentful. And Carrie-Anne is about to commit an act that will horrify them all. Something unexplainable has infected the town. Could the secret lie in the past, in Gina's old house, abandoned long ago but never quite empty?

GRAHAM MASTERTON

NIGHT WARS

They are five ordinary people, forced to do battle on the most terrifying field imaginable—the landscape of nightmares. They are the Night Warriors and only they can defeat the evil that has invaded our world through our dreams.

Two of the cruelest and most horrific apparitions ever seen are attempting to destroy our world by entering the dreams of expectant mothers. They bring with them armies of nightmare creatures, horrible beings that could only spring from someone's worst fear. It is against these demons, in an unreal world of terror, that the five Night Warriors must prepare to fight the...

NIGHT WARS

DEBORAH LEBLANC

A HOUSE DIVIDED

Keith Lafleur, Louisiana's largest and greediest building contractor, thinks he's cut the deal of a lifetime. The huge old two-story clapboard house is his for the taking as long as he can move it to a new location. It's too big to move as it is, but Lafleur's solution is simple: divide it in half. He has no idea, though, that by splitting the house he'll be dividing a family—a family long dead, a family that still exists in the house, including a mother who will destroy anyone who keeps her apart from her children.

Dorchester Publishing Co., Inc.
P.O. Box 6640   ___5730-1
Wayne, PA 19087-8640 $6.99 US/$8.99 CAN

RAPTURE

THOMAS TESSIER

Jeff has always loved Georgianne, ever since they were kids—with a love so strong, so obsessive, it sometimes drives him to do crazy things. Scary things. Like stalking Georgianne and everyone she loves, including her caring husband and her innocent teenage daughter. Jeff doesn't think there's room in Georgianne's life for anyone but him, and if he has to, he's ready to kill all the others... until he's the only one left.

"Ingenious. A nerve-paralyzing story."
—*Publishers Weekly*